THE
CORNISH KNOT

Books by Vicky Adin

The Cornish Knot
Portrait of a Man

Brigid The Girl from County Clare
Gwenna The Welsh Confectioner
The Costumier's Gift

The Disenchanted Soldier

The Art of Secrets

"An engaging tale of grief, loss, love and family intrigue
... wonderful story, and a real page-turner, which leads
the reader through all the twists and turns of a well-
constructed plot. I loved the insightful descriptions of
family relationships, the fully realised characters and the
various locations in which the action takes place. Seldom
have I read such a poignant and faithful account of the
effects of bereavement. I can't wait to read more."

**** 4-star Amazon review

THE
CORNISH KNOT

VICKY ADIN

THE CORNISH KNOT

ISBN 978-0-9922628-8-4

Also available as Kindle ISBN 978-0-9922628-6-0

A catalogue record for this book is available from the National Library of New Zealand.

First published in 2014 for Vicky Adin by
AM Publishing New Zealand   www.ampublishingnz.com

To order copies of Vicky Adin's print books:
www.vickyadin.co.nz, www.amazon.com

Ebooks available from www.amazon.com

DEDICATION

To family and their stories

With fond memories of Cornwall

CORNISH KNOT
a motif for the circle of life.

TREVALLYAN FAMILY TREE

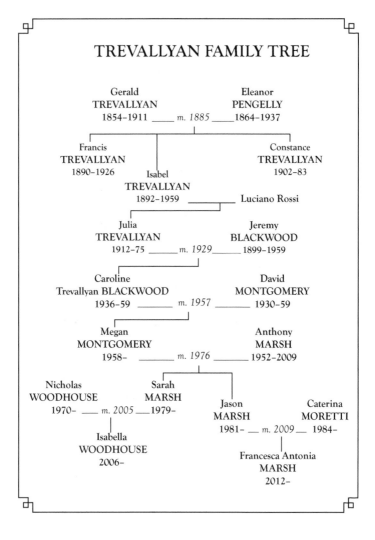

Gerald
TREVALLYAN
1854–1911 ____ m. 1885 ____ 1864–1937
Eleanor
PENGELLY

Francis
TREVALLYAN
1890–1926
Constance
TREVALLYAN
1902–83

Isabel
TREVALLYAN
1892–1959 _____ Luciano Rossi

Julia
TREVALLYAN
1912–75 _____ m. 1929 _____ 1899–1959
Jeremy
BLACKWOOD

Caroline
Trevallyan **BLACKWOOD**
1936–59 _____ m. 1957 _____ 1930–59
David
MONTGOMERY

Megan
MONTGOMERY
1958– _____ m. 1976 _____ 1952–2009
Anthony
MARSH

Nicholas
WOODHOUSE
1970– ____ m. 2005 ____ 1979–
Sarah
MARSH

Jason
MARSH
1981– __ m. 2009 __ 1984–
Caterina
MORETTI

Isabella
WOODHOUSE
2006–

Francesca Antonia
MARSH
2012–

CHAPTER 1

The doorbell rang, its strident call shattering her melancholic state. Megan didn't want visitors. Not today.

The bell rang again, more insistently. Still she sat, unable or unwilling to move. Once before, a year ago, on an early spring morning when the sun shone and life was good, she had answered the door … She couldn't bear to think about it.

A whole year had passed since that terrible day when she had lost her Tony, and the pain was still raw. Sleepless and disconsolate, Megan had risen before dawn to sit in her favourite armchair and stare out the window into the invisible garden. Night slowly turned into day. In her dressing gown, with a half-empty cup of cold tea on the table beside her, she sat motionless – remembering.

He had been a young fifty-seven with no hint of any heart problems. She saw him off to work, little realising she would never see him again. His sudden death heralded the end of life as she knew it. Spiralling deeper into the dark well of pointlessness as the months passed, she finally gave up the struggle and abruptly sold her vintage dress shop. She'd walked away without a backward glance to retreat into her private world where only emptiness lived.

Determined knocking pounded on the door. Her throat constricted.

Reluctantly, she rose and answered it.

"Mrs Marsh?" enquired the courier driver.

She nodded and her body drooped with relief. History was not repeating itself.

"Sign here."

She accepted the brown-paper package, turning it over to check the return address. It meant nothing.

Back in the family room, she dropped the parcel on the table and stared at it: plain, ordinary, book-like, tied with string.

Whatever it was, she didn't want it.

Her carefully constructed shield began to crack and tears ran down her face.

What in hell's name does a lawyer in Cornwall want with me?

CHAPTER 2

Megan had been too afraid to cry – too afraid to let go, in case she couldn't stop, in case the pain didn't go away. She buried her sorrow under a steaming shower, sliding down the wall to sit small, in a huddle, while the hot water rained down and washed away her torment.

Finally spent, her eyes now empty of tears, she dragged herself upright.

She chose a pair of well-cut dress jeans and a softly draped aqua tunic top that had been a favourite of Tony's. She wanted to look good today, for his sake. Tony often told her she looked beautiful and she missed his reassurances.

As she slipped a simple black pearl pendant around her neck and put on the matching earrings, Megan stared at herself in the mirror. As a teen, she'd felt average – average height, average weight, brown eyes, brown wavy hair – and ordinary. These days, with a few added highlights, she wore her hair cut softly around her ears with a flattering half fringe. For fifty-two, she thought she'd aged well and was more comfortable with her appearance.

She had barely finished dressing and was blow-drying her hair into shape when the phone rang. "Good morning, this is Megan." Well trained, she spoke automatically, listlessly.

"Hi, Mum." Her daughter sounded falsely cheerful on the other end.

Megan attempted a more upbeat tone. "Morning, Sarah. How are you?"

"I'm OK. More to the point, how are you today?"

Megan didn't need reminding, nor did she want to remember. She would not commemorate this day, not now, not ever. That would make it too real. "I'm fine, Sarah," she lied. "Just about to make myself some coffee and sit in the sunshine. Maybe I'll read for a while."

Megan had not been able to visit the cemetery nor would she today. She didn't want to remember Tony in a place like that. He belonged with her, here, in their home.

"I've got an hour spare before my next meeting. I could do with a coffee. Be round in a jiff."

Sarah hung up before Megan had a chance to respond.

Her spirits lifted slightly. Sarah had become Megan's rock and one of her great joys in the darkness. Her granddaughter Isabella was another. In contrast, her son Jason had shut himself off completely and disappeared overseas again the day after the funeral, leaving her feeling forsaken.

Jason was her baby, single, a pilot and living a life she couldn't imagine. She regretted losing some of the closeness they once shared since he had moved to London a couple of years earlier. But it was more than that – she couldn't quite communicate with him any more. Not like she did with Sarah. Jason was more – she couldn't put her finger on it – detached. *No, that's unfair. It's just ...* Something was missing.

Tony would have understood. Tony always understood.

Megan switched on the electric jug, put extra coffee into the plunger and reached for her daughter's favourite mug. Taller, slimmer and fairer than her mother, Sarah worked as a graphic artist and often amazed Megan with her creative instincts. Where had she come from? Thanks to her architect husband Nick, her bouncy personality and positive outlook, Sarah had rallied more quickly after her father's death, but Megan knew her daughter still grieved, deep down.

As if on cue, the young woman burst in through the unlocked front door, dressed in fashion statement clothes with high heels and chunky jewellery. "I'm here."

Megan applauded her daughter's style. Sometimes she wished she could be brave enough to emulate Sarah but had learnt to stick with what suited her best – well-cut clothes that flattered her trim figure, and understated jewellery, and she refused to wear black.

Megan filled the cups with the strong dark liquid. "And here's your coffee."

"Mum, you're a wonder. Thank you."

Sarah kissed Megan on the cheek, eyeing her thoughtfully. She shrugged off her jacket and threw it over the back of the chair in one elegant move. Taking her coffee, Sarah crossed the room to sit on the sofa under the window. The September sun streamed in, highlighting the unwrapped package on the table. "What's this, Mum?"

"Oh. That. I don't know. It came this morning."

"Don't you want to open it?" Sarah flicked her long, fair hair behind her ear as she picked it up and turned it over, reading the English return address.

"Not right now." Megan's voice sounded deflated, even to her.

A strange parcel arriving on the first anniversary of Tony's death struck her as cruel. They would have opened it together, sharing in the excitement of discovery, eager to know what it meant. But now its presence simply served to heighten his absence – and her loss. For the best part of thirty-five years they had been the ideal couple – like a pair of comfortable shoes, perfect together but useless and unbalanced one without the other. No one had known her as long; no one knew her as well.

Megan felt drained and exhausted after her outburst, yet the black cloud of emptiness that normally floated in the recesses of her mind had begun to fade. A sense of release hovered amid the hurt.

Sipping her coffee, she sat in the chair beside Sarah.

"You look very pale. And you've been crying." Sarah reached out and placed her hand over her mother's. "Did you get any sleep last night?"

Megan shook her head. "Not much."

"I'm worried about you. You've increasingly shut yourself off from everything you once enjoyed and spend far too much time on your own. It's not good for you."

"Don't lecture me, please, darling. I appreciate your concern. But right now, I like my own company. Not that I don't enjoy you coming round, of course," she rushed on, feeling the need to justify her comment. "And your brother when he's in town," hoping he would remember

6

to phone her today. "Really, I do, but mostly I like being alone with my memories."

The last year had been hard, and the impact had not yet worn off. Some days her spirits were so low she struggled to function. Much of the time she felt old, worthless. Days when her hair lay flat, dark circles marred her skin and the crow's feet around her eyes deepened.

"Sorry, Mum. I don't mean to lecture. I want to see you happy again." Sarah paused. "I miss him, too."

Megan saw tears fill her daughter's eyes and felt guilty for her self-absorption. "I know you do, sweetheart. You always were your dad's girl."

"Hey, I've got an idea." Suddenly Sarah stood up and busied herself washing the coffee mugs, forcing back tears. "I'll cancel my meeting and we'll go shopping. Come on, Mum. Please? Come with me. Anywhere. How about a walk? I've got a change of shoes. Or lunch? Anything, but let's get out of here."

Megan, hearing the desperation in her daughter's voice, conceded. "Okay, but let's go for a walk along the beach. I can't stand the noise of the mall."

Growing up as an only child, Megan had been a solitary person at the best of times, but in the last few months she'd become positively antisocial. "Sorry, love. I don't like being around other people these days."

As they wandered along Milford Beach, the sea alive with light where the sun shimmered on the ever-moving waves, Megan let her mind drift. Sarah chatted away about plans for her future.

"I'd love to get involved directly with clients rather than designing in the backroom, and Nick wants his own practice one day, too, but they're simply dreams at this stage."

Sarah's idea for a walk had been a good one. Megan was finding the beach, where she had spent so much time with Tony, soothing. Sometimes she sensed him still beside her.

Sarah's voice penetrated her thoughts. "Promise me, Mum?"

"Sorry, darling. Promise you what? I wasn't listening."

"I know!" Sarah laughed. "What I was saying, Mother dearest, is, I want to help. I want you to find some hope in the future. You are still young. You're smart and you look gorgeous, I'd like to see you young at heart again. I'd like you to do something special for your birthday. I'll organise it. A party maybe? Or a trip somewhere? You need to get out, make some new friends. You've got six months to decide. Just think about it. Promise me?"

"Oh. I don't ..."

"Stop. Don't say 'I don't want anything' yet. Think about it first, please. What would Dad have done?"

The spectre of Tony's smiling face suddenly filled the frame, and Megan knew Sarah was right – again – he would have done something special. He always did. He would want her to find new life and new hope.

"All right. I'll think about it."

"And one more thing. Let's open that parcel from England as soon as we get back. I'd like to find out what it's all about, even if you don't."

* * * * *

My dear girl,

I am not sure I remember your name, if I ever knew it. If you are reading this, then I have gone to my Maker and you have in your possession the indiscreet writings of someone who should have known better.

My elder sister had too many silly and romantic notions, which got her into more trouble than she knew how to handle. After she left our father's house in disgrace, never to return, I found this diary of hers and have kept it hidden for too many decades.

Nearly fifty years later, shortly before her death, she wrote to me telling me she had become a great-grandmother – you were that child. She was happy with the news but it was tinged with sadness: she knew she was dying. She asked me to take up her role, albeit from a distance. I agreed.

I am sorry to say I did not fulfil that promise. You don't need to know why, simply accept that as I prepare for my imminent demise I have regrets for many errors of judgement in my life.

I am now an old woman attempting to rectify some of those lapses. As you have now passed the age of majority, I believe you should have the diary.

I apologise for having withheld it for so long. I cannot undo the past, but these writings may help you to understand.

Your great aunt,
Constance Trevallyan
October 1983

CHAPTER 3

Hours after Sarah had left, Megan reflected on the contents of the package, struggling to comprehend.

The first envelope contained a letter from the lawyer asking Megan to verify her identity as he held pertinent information about the family. The second envelope contained a handwritten note from an unknown great aunt. Dated nearly thirty years earlier, the ink had faded and the paper discoloured with age, Megan and Sarah had taken quite some time to decipher the spidery script.

No matter how many times Megan read the letters, she couldn't quite fit everything together. Constance Trevallyan, a great aunt she never knew she had, or rather a great-great-aunt to be correct, had left her some papers. Megan could only describe her history as sketchy. Fleeting images flicked through her memory.

Megan was seventeen when her grandma Julia died. Her grandmother had raised her from a young age after her parents and grandfather perished in a car accident. She didn't recall ever knowing the details of the accident, Grandma Julia never spoke about it. There'd only ever been the two of them. But this letter from the lawyer had nothing to do with her paternal side. The letters from

Cornwall were about the maternal side of the family: the Trevallyans.

Shivering in the cool evening air, Megan put aside the papers, shut the curtains against the darkening skies and turned on the heat pump.

The whole day had gone without a word from Jason. *Maybe he's flying, or in the wrong time zone*, she thought, always willing to give him the benefit of the doubt. Her soft spot for Jason was no secret. He'd been an easy-going, lovable child, the living image of his father. Soft-hearted in many ways, he would do anything to please if asked, but he could be equally as thoughtless. In that, he was nothing like his father, who was the most caring person she had ever known.

Megan had a hunch something momentous lay concealed in the papers spread over the coffee table but wasn't sure she was ready to find out. To delay the inevitable, she poured herself a glass of wine and put some cheese and crackers on a plate before she rang Jason's cell phone. It went straight to voicemail. "Damn," she muttered, and put the phone down, not bothering to leave a message. How would they ever find a connection again if they didn't talk?

After spending the afternoon reading and rereading the two letters, she was no further ahead in her understanding. The formal letter said they believed Megan was the great-granddaughter of some mysterious older sister – the one who had written the diary referred to in this Great Aunt Constance's letter – but nowhere had she found a name for the young woman. The lawyer, in very formal tones, had said its omittance was deliberate. Legally, Megan was required to prove who she was before they 'could confirm if indeed she was whom they believed'. The official paperwork the lawyer wanted in return was too long-winded, monotonous and confusing, with far too many pages and attachments. She put it aside to action later.

Megan turned to the faded and battered box containing the diary mentioned in Great Aunt Constance's letter, but it was the letter that vexed her the most. Why had it taken so long to find her? And how could she begin to find out the sister's name?

She reached for the box.

Earlier, when Megan had untied the nearly threadbare ribbon and tentatively lifted the lid on the tatty old box, both she and Sarah had gasped, astonished by the journal lying within the folds of the fragile satin lining. Megan had a passion for beautiful old things, and this was one of the most beautiful compendiums she'd ever seen – and was obviously much loved.

Now, Megan gingerly picked up the diary, with its creamy leather cover overlaid with heavy gold embossing, and rested it on her knee. A gold clasp held the gilt-edged pages in place, and two flamboyant, intertwined and indecipherable initials decorated the centrepiece: IT or TT maybe. Some of the embossing around the clasp and close to the spine, where unknown hands had held it, was no longer visible.

Megan stared at the keepsake, gently rubbing the soft leather. *Why would someone leave something so exquisite lying around forgotten all these long years?* She flicked the clasp open and turned to the first page. Almost transparent with age, the paper was of fine quality. The initials on the front were repeated on the fly page. It was dedicated:

To my darling daughter, as she embarks
on her trip of a lifetime.
Father, 1910

Megan turned a few more pages, searching for a clue to the author's name, without luck. Whoever she was, this daughter, the planned journey would be a lengthy one. Going back to the beginning, Megan read through the enviable list of place names: a stopover in Bath, two weeks in London, a month in Paris, then train journeys throughout Europe and finally to Italy, to spend the summer in Florence – a journey of twelve months. If the mysterious daughter did indeed travel to all those sites, she most definitely had embarked on a trip of a lifetime.

With nothing consistent about the locations other than their European and romantic reputations, the list gave Megan little to go on. She couldn't say for certain where the journal had originated. Cornwall, presumably, since the lawyer's letter had come from there.

Megan read late into the night. Her wine glass sat empty alongside the plate, yet she couldn't recollect finishing their contents. The tension in her neck and shoulders eventually forced her to shut the journal. Using the letter from Great Aunt Constance as a bookmark, Megan carefully put it back in the box. She hadn't thought of Tony for hours and was grateful something new had occupied her time. Now other thoughts were flying around her head.

After making a hot chocolate she checked her emails one more time. *Thinking of you*, wrote Jason. Happy he'd remembered, she smiled; her day complete, it was time for bed.

As she finished her nightly routine, Megan stared at her reflection in the mirror. Questions raced through her mind. Did she look like any of the people she'd read about? Did her children?

Fair-haired Sarah didn't quite look like either of her dark-haired parents, but Jason looked too much like his father for comfort.

Megan changed into her fine cambric nightgown, relishing its softness and vintage design, and wondered if her ancestor had worn something similar.

With that in mind, she turned back the sheets, climbed into bed and settled comfortably on the pillows. She tried to read while she sipped her drink but couldn't concentrate on the words in front of her, while the words from another book floated in her mind.

Finally, turning out the light and snuggling down to sleep, her thoughts drifted to the mysterious woman in the diary and the woman known only as Great Aunt Constance.

She woke from a restless sleep in the middle of the night. Reaching for the set of Tony's pyjamas she secretly kept under the pillow – to remind her of his smell when sleep eluded her – she clutched them to her.

Tony's voice resounded in her head. *"Of course you should, sweetheart. There's nothing stopping you. Go on. Do it. Find your family."*

She turned to his side of the bed, pulled the duvet up and, still smiling, fell into a dreamless sleep.

Isabel's Journal
30 October 1910

I am so cross. Mother fussed over all the things we'd put away, refolding everything until all were packed properly and 'to my entire satisfaction', she had told the maid in that haughty voice of hers. She really was tiresome. I was fed up with her tut-tutting over things I had chosen and replacing them with her choices. And then giving me instructions on how I was to wear this gown or that, and which hat and gloves or parasol and shawl or brooch, until I could have screamed with it all. Really! As if I can't dress myself.

Finally, the driver brought the coach around to the front and the footmen loaded my trunks and hatboxes. I waited impatiently at the top of the stone steps leading to the driveway. The large, heavy wooden doors stood open behind me. It took all my willpower not to race down those few steps to escape as fast as I could, but that would have been most unladylike. I had to walk slowly as Mother liked and say goodbye to the staff lined up like statues along the way. Honestly, it's all so stuck-up and old-fashioned.

Not before time, my journey began and I took great enjoyment in the passing landscape. Although I'd known it all my life and ridden it many times, today everything seemed fresh and pleasing and encouraging. I was freer than I'd ever been before.

I didn't want to delay one moment more. Our destination was the Redruth train station where I was to meet my companion who would bring me the newest of experiences.

CHAPTER 4

Megan woke the next morning refreshed and far more cheerful than at any time during the past year. *Maybe the traditions of previous eras, with their strict observance of a mourning period, have some point after all*, she thought, noticing she had colour in her cheeks.

With a lighter heart, she hurried through her morning routine, singing softly as she hung out the washing and completed her chores in record time. She had things to do. The beautiful September day helped. The sun shone from a clear blue sky, as only a New Zealand sky could be, as she listened to the birds chirping their morning songs.

Having made her decision to do as the lawyer suggested and trace her family tree, Megan had no idea how to start. She opened up the computer and googled the Edwardian period, when the journal was written. The search brought up many websites on the fashion of the time, which held her attention as she scanned through the pages and lingered to admire this dress line or that hat. Once, in another lifetime, she had loved her little boutique full of vintage clothes, jewellery, laces and other trappings of eras past, but now that, too, was in the past and Megan wanted to look forward.

She changed the search request and found numerous sites about modes of transport, but they gave her far too many details to answer her questions. She bookmarked one or two and kept looking. Another search brought up pages of history – another fascinating topic. Tony had been an avid historian, and together they would read copious books, watch documentaries and talk endlessly about their current historical period of interest.

Thoughts of Tony brought a smile to her lips. British history was something he'd thought too mundane and too 'like ours'. Megan disagreed. The two of them had often indulged in a happy argument about whether Britain was 'home' to generations – him included, if he'd cared to admit it – or whether New Zealand had broken free to allow the people to become Kiwis and be proud of it. Tony was a first-generation while she ... well, that's what she was going to find out. She thought she was at least third-generation: herself, her mother and her grandmother.

"Yes, yes, you have the advantage there," Tony would argue, "but look at our laws – and our buildings. All based on British regulations and designs. And don't forget our armed forces – the army, in particular. Not that long ago, our ancestors fought for the British."

Megan would retaliate. Tony would smile that special smile of his, and she'd know he'd deliberately provoked her. He'd taught her to speak up rather than remain quiet to keep the peace. Something that went against everything Grandma Julia had taught her.

With his amazing memory, he could recite history as well as he could describe his own backyard, while she worried about making a fool of herself. She also trusted his judgement more than her own, except now she had to learn to trust her instincts. He would no longer act as her logical side while her emotional one ran riot. She could almost hear him telling her to calm down and think ... and face up to things she couldn't change.

Megan stopped to stretch, surprised to see the morning had disappeared. Her stomach rumbled. She was hungry. Her appetite had waned in the last year and she ate from habit more than desire. She smiled, life was returning. Her research had sparked a memory and given her some ideas. Megan made up her mind to go to the city library and see what they could offer.

A quick change into her dress jeans and a mesh top that fitted perfectly, a brush of her thick, wavy hair and some soft rose-coloured lipstick, and she was in the car and on her way. Halfway into the city she began to have doubts again. It had been a long time since she had driven over the harbour bridge, and the traffic was much heavier than she remembered. Her confidence started to evaporate, but by the time she had taken the exit onto the once-familiar streets and found the parking building easier than she'd expected, she felt better.

Then she discovered she'd forgotten to bring a pen and notebook, which simply epitomised her last year. Some days she could forget her name. Frustrated at her lack of thought, she joined the mass of people clustered at the lights, wondering if she could ask someone where to find a stationer's. She looked around at the people. Despite the mix of ages, genders and nationalities, most of them were not paying the slightest attention to their surroundings. Either engaged in animated conversation in languages she couldn't understand – sometimes with the person next to them, but more often into the phone clutched to their ear – or with their fingers and thumbs flying over the tiny keyboards, they seemed oblivious to anything else. Had she really got that much out of touch in such a short time?

The lights changed and the buzzer sounded, signalling the flock to move and be on their way. Megan crossed the road into the narrow lane that once served as an access way and was pleasantly surprised to discover it now housed specialty stores, cafés and bars. A few steps along the street, she found a card shop and stopped in to buy a simple notepad and cheap pen, but she couldn't help lingering. Filled with elegant notebooks and journals artistically displayed on shelves alongside boxed gift cards and stationery sets, the shop was lovely. It brought back memories of her boutique. As she thought about those days, it came as no surprise to find she didn't miss them. Tony was the one she missed. Maybe the time was right for her to tackle something new after all.

Eventually she chose an ornate notebook with an antique floral pattern for her research notes and an elegant – and expensive – gold and black pen with a fine point.

"Is there anything else you'd like today?" asked the shopkeeper.

Megan started to say no but then noticed a journal on the shelf behind the counter.

"Could I look at that, please?" she pointed.

The sales assistant took the journal from its resting place and handed it to Megan. "Beautiful, isn't it? I've only this minute put it out. I've never seen anything quite like this before. It's Italian-made, so I couldn't resist."

Megan could hardly believe what she saw. The cover of soft cream calfskin with a large gold Celtic knot design stamped into the oval centrepiece was uncannily like the century-old diary belonging to her mysterious ancestor. A brass clasp held the gold-edged pages together.

"Are you thinking of travelling?"

"Um. No." Megan stared briefly at the woman. The question triggered an unexpected thought. There was no reason why she shouldn't travel. "But then again, maybe, yes." Megan ignored the price tag. "I'll take it."

The woman laid it within folds of tissue in a protective box almost exactly like the original sitting on her table at home. To complete the symmetry, the sales lady placed Megan's purchases in a patterned carry bag evocative of times past. Some things were meant to be.

By the time Megan finally arrived at the library it was after three o'clock. She asked at the desk where to find the family history section.

"Can I help you with anything?" asked the librarian.

"Actually, yes. Please. I wish to trace an ancestor who travelled in Europe in the early part of last century. But I don't know where to start."

"Come with me."

Megan gathered her belongings and followed the woman.

"The family history section is open until eight o'clock tonight. I'll introduce you."

With the next librarian's help, Megan found a host of references to birth, death and marriage certificates. Getting out her new notebook and pen, she headed up the first page with a flourish and put the date on the second line. She was ready.

In a short while, she was perched on the edge of the seat. Her handwriting became a scrawl but she didn't care, she would worry about deciphering it all later. Right now, the answers she wanted poured from the pages in front of her. Absorbed, she lost track of time.

The librarian disturbed her. "We'll be closing soon. Would you like to take any of the material with you?"

Laden with books, printouts and photocopies, and a list of websites she could tap into from home, Megan's head buzzed with ideas. She crammed everything into her carry bag and made her way out of the library. Much to her surprise, it was dark.

After paying the exorbitant parking fee, Megan turned the car for home. Humming along with a tune on the radio, she thought about what to do next. With less traffic on the road, the return journey was much quicker, but it had given her enough time to reach a decision. She'd barely got inside and was still unloading when someone began hammering on the door. Startled, she rushed to unlock it when she heard her daughter's voice.

"Mum!" cried Sarah. "Are you all right? I phoned and phoned. Where've you been? I've been worried. I tried your cell phone and sent you a text. Why didn't you answer? Didn't you have it with you?"

For a minute, Megan couldn't get a word in edgeways until Sarah took a breath and wrapped her arms around her mother's neck.

"Sorry, darling. I forgot about it. It's in a drawer somewhere. I don't use it these days."

"Do you realise what time it is? Where *have* you been?" Sarah stepped back to study her mother.

"Yes, I know what time it is. I'm sorry if I worried you. I've been out."

"Out! Out, where? Mum, you don't go out."

"Well, I will be from now on." Megan readied herself for her big announcement. "I plan to travel."

The look on Sarah's face was priceless. "Pardon?"

Megan laughed, almost surprised she remembered how. "You offered to help me organise a trip or something for my birthday. Remember? I'm going to take you up on it."

Megan looked at her watch. "I haven't eaten for hours and I'm starved. There's still enough time. Do you want to join me? I think I'll go down to that little Italian place."

"Mum, what's got into you? This is not like you. You're making me nervous."

"Grab a bottle of red wine and come with me. I'll tell you all about it."

Megan's eyes sparkled and her face wore an enormous grin. Feeling young and silly, she would have kicked her heels together had she been able.

Sarah reached for the phone. "Let me call Nick and tell him I'll be late. There's no way I'm missing this."

CHAPTER 5

"Now tell me," urged Megan after they had settled at the table and placed their order, while the waiter poured their wine. "What's so important you needed to ring me several times and come knocking at my door?"

"I was worried about you. You seemed down yesterday and, I might add, not keen to go out." Sarah stared pointedly at her mother. "I thought I'd see if you were OK. When I couldn't get hold of you, I started to wonder why you weren't answering."

"Oh, sweetheart. That's kind of you, but what did you think I was doing? You don't normally check up on me every day."

"No. I know. But my imagination started running riot, and I had to find you. You could have had a heart attack or a fall. Or something ..." Sarah trailed off. "I know that sounds silly, but I was frightened I'd lose you, too."

"I'm sorry if I frightened you." Megan gently squeezed her daughter's hand across the table in apology.

"Doesn't matter now. You're safe. That's all that counts. But Mum, what've you been doing? The change in you in twenty-four hours is not only immense, it's alarming."

"Well, don't fret. I feel like a different person. My confidence is coming back, and I think I'm ready to tackle something fresh. You may not believe it, but I talked with your father in my dreams last night."

The waiter arrived with their bread and dips, temporarily distracting them.

"Back to the point," said Sarah, biting into a slice of ciabatta. "I'm glad to hear you're feeling more like your old self, but talking to Dad? That's weird."

"It's not weird. It makes sense to me. I've talked things through with your dad since I was eighteen years old. I'm not going to stop now. It helps clear things in my mind, even if I already know what he's going to say."

"You and Dad always did have the uncanny knack of finishing each other's sentences. Worse still, you understood half-finished sentences that made no sense to Jason and me when we were kids."

"Yes, well. Parents have to keep one step ahead somehow." Megan smiled. "But you know what? I don't think it's that I'm back to my old self as such, but as if I'm about to find a new self."

"Mum, now you're really not making sense. Enough wine for you if you keep talking like this. What are you on about?"

"Ever since I opened the package from the lawyer yesterday, something inside me has woken up. Last night, I started to read that gorgeous journal. I stayed up quite late and still haven't finished the whole thing, but I had a weird sense of belonging as I read it. The young girl writing the diary echoed my inner self. It could have been me - except it wasn't, of course. She wrote it a hundred years ago."

"And I thought the letter from the stuffy sounding Great Aunt Constance was interesting, but this sounds much better. Where did you disappear to today?"

"The central library."

"Wow. Why?"

Their meals arrived at that moment, and Megan's explanation had to wait.

"This is delicious. How's yours?" Megan asked.

"Yum, too," Sarah agreed, refilling their wine glasses. "But what were you hoping to find at the library?"

"The lawyer hinted there might be something of great importance and value, if I can prove who I am."

"Really? That's exciting."

"So, I'm on the hunt for my ancestors."

Megan explained how she'd found a range of birth, death and marriage records for the New Zealand part of the family. Some records were not old enough to be accessed through the digital records, and she would have to request the originals. She also found some wills, probates and court records, some of which were quite shocking.

"Poor Grandma Julia suffered a lot. She effectively lost her entire family in one swoop. I'm still trying to understand it all, but 1959 was a catastrophic year for her. It would have broken a lesser woman."

Megan listed what she had learnt. "It turns out Grandpa Jeremy was killed in the same car accident that killed my parents. I never knew. How tragic to lose husband and daughter at the same time. I've been a mess coping with one loss. I don't know how I would have coped if I'd lost you, too."

The significance of her words burned deep. Her

grandmother had put aside her grief to raise a child, while Megan had floundered, swallowed by her grief, without purpose or direction, until yesterday, when that purpose had been delivered to her door.

"To make matters worse, the driver was my other grandfather, my father's father, and he died, too. Imagine, her daughter, husband, son-in-law and his father all perished in one car accident."

Megan suspected that was why she knew nothing about her paternal side. She'd take a bet her respective grandmothers never spoke to each other again.

"That's the New Zealand part. For Grandma Julia's side, I need to go to Cornwall."

While they indulged in some dessert and emptied the bottle of wine, Megan told Sarah about all the certificates she'd found, and the dates, and promised she would draw up a chart to show her the details later.

She paused, trying to judge how Sarah would react to her next announcement.

"Never mind what I find about the family, here or in Cornwall, or anything about some vague inheritance, I want to find more about this young girl who wrote the journal. The thing is, I want to follow her footsteps as she travelled the world. I don't know her name. But the more I've thought about it, the more it seems right – which is the core of the conversation I had with your father. He assured me my impulse is timely and I can do it."

Megan couldn't explain why she wanted to embark on this journey. The young woman of the journal was barely more than a child. How could a mature woman conjure up similar feelings and possibilities? Nevertheless, she was determined to try. "What do you think?" Megan hoped her expression looked calm but suspected it portrayed her qualms. "I know my whole idea could fall down like a pack of cards. There is little to justify any of it, but my instinct says it's the right thing to do. I could be away for months, even a year."

Megan waited for her daughter's approval.

Sarah's face only occasionally betrayed her thoughts as she looked steadily at her mother, analysing what Megan had said. Several long seconds passed before she answered. "I can't decide if I'm excited for you or terrified at the thought of you traipsing around the world on your own."

A few more moments passed. Sarah took a deep breath. "Mum, I think your idea is wonderful. And yes, you should do it. Just promise me one thing? Well, several things really."

"Depends on what you want," Megan teased.

"Firstly, let me help you plan the trip. Jason could prove helpful here for a change." Sarah ticked the list off on her fingers. "Secondly, you must keep in touch by text or email and phone at least once a week. I want to know where you are and that you're safe at all times. And thirdly, please write it all down exactly as your ancestor did."

Megan could feel the tears prickling, but these were tears of joy not sadness. Relief flooded through her. "Now that I can do."

CHAPTER 6

A few days later, Megan heard what sounded like someone kicking the door. When she opened it, she was faced with a solid board.

"Give me a hand," said the muffled voice.

Megan dodged around the frame to see the bizarre sight of Sarah leaning on the doorpost, struggling with a box balanced on one arm. Her bag had slid off her shoulder to hang in the crook of her elbow; a folder was wedged between her teeth and an easel rested on her knee. Trying not to laugh, Megan took the box and folder, put them on the floor and helped Sarah carry the flip chart and easel through to the family room.

"What's going on? What's this for?" asked Megan, trotting behind with the rest of the materials.

"I borrowed this stuff to help with the planning."

"But Sarah, what's it all for?" Megan repeated. "Where did this stuff come from?"

"The office. They're obsolete after the refit. It's OK, Mum. I checked with my boss," she assured her. "I've picked up some brochures and maps and suchlike. I thought it'd help if we wrote up some of this stuff as a chart. I've also got some Blu-Tack and map pins. We can sketch out what we know and then pin the maps and pages to the wall so we can track it better."

Sarah was in her organising element. She loved it. Whether it was for people, events or houses, Sarah always liked to be involved.

"That's a good idea. We could pin them up in the garage, I suppose."

"No, Mum, not there. You don't want to work in the garage. It's too cold anyway. Let's see." Sarah headed off down the hall. "Let's take these photos down and put them in the spare room for now, and we can line the walls in sequence."

Sarah talked as she took the photos off the wall and handed them to her mother. "You can check it when you go past and add things as you think of them. Oh, and by the way, I spoke to Jason. He's told me what he needs to know so he can start to make enquiries as to what flights are available. Now, what's our deadline?"

"Deadline? What deadline? What are you talking about?"

"What's the date on the first page of the journal? If you are going to start this journey you need to start on the same day, don't you? How much time have we got?"

Megan looked blank for a moment, but Sarah was right. She knew without looking. "Thirtieth of October." A little over six weeks.

For the next hour, as they talked about what needed to be done and in what order, Sarah drew up a dateline, attaching each chart to the wall as it was finished. Some things were obvious: check the expiry date on her passport, work out the itinerary and book flights and accommodation.

Megan admitted Sarah was thinking well ahead of her. She bullet-pointed the things for Megan to do: buy a new easy-to-manage set of luggage with wheels and a detachable carry bag; get a new vanity bag with the right size bottles for going through customs; update to a smartphone and get roaming for each country; invest in the latest laptop; organise foreign money; and set up a way to transfer funds when she needed to.

"Okay, Mum, that'll do for now. I'd better go. Nick will have picked Bella up from day care and he'll be wondering where I am. Have you got enough to go on with?"

"More than enough. Thanks, honey," laughed Megan, looking at the notes.

"What you need to do now is draw up the family tree as you know it, highlight the missing bits and make a list of what you want to find out. Don't know if I can do much of that, but it might help sort out what order you want to do things in."

Sarah picked up her bag, gave her mother a kiss and with a cheery 'bye' vanished through the door. Megan went back to the spare room to sort the photos haphazardly spread on the bed. She wrapped and stacked them in the empty drawers of the unit, thinking about what she needed to do first. With some ideas in mind, she went back to the flip chart to write them all down while they were still fresh. To her surprise, Sarah had left her a message: *What do you want to do about the house?*

Megan sat down, letting her breath go in one whoosh. She'd avoided the topic for a year. She loved her sunny, light-filled home, where everything had a place and everything was in its place. It was all she and Tony wanted, but now she didn't quite fill the space. It wasn't hard to look after, but the logic of keeping a family home going for one person didn't add up. But she felt safe here with her memories.

All of a sudden her wish to travel appeared fraught. Sarah's message had forced her to confront her future head-on. Within a few minutes, Megan knew the answer. In her heart, she'd known for some time, but making the break had been too much to face on her own. Now it made sense. She would sell the house, packing away only the things she wanted to keep. When she came back, she could buy her dream cottage, or maybe an apartment, somewhere overlooking a beach.

A weight lifted off her shoulders and, filled with energy, Megan started to make a new list. There was no time to waste. The next six weeks would be busy. Grabbing the old suitcases she was going to replace and a couple of large rubbish bags, Megan started to fill them. She went through her wardrobe first and ruthlessly threw out clothes she'd kept for years. They could go to the charity shop. Then she tackled the hard part.

Although Tony's clothes had already been sorted and given away – most of them anyway – there were things she'd kept that were quintessentially Tony: his books, DVDs and CDs – not always to her taste – his favourite pen, cufflinks and his Irish tweed jacket. She rubbed her hand over the rough cloth, remembering the strength of his arm beneath her hand as they walked arm in arm. Memories washed over her as she buried her head in the fabric, still able to discern his unique smell.

She and Tony met at an office ball, clichéd as it sounded, but they were the rage in the seventies. Arriving at the Peter Pan Ballroom in Upper Queen Street, Megan found they were seated at tables in groups of ten. Before long, this generous, fun-filled, intelligent man had her laughing for the first time since Grandma Julia had died the previous year. They fell in love that night, and he had been her anchor ever since.

With the sound of his laugh ringing in her head, she decided to keep the jacket, and his pen and cufflinks; the rest could go. With a pounding heart, she stuffed what she could into the black bags and tied the books into bundles before she could change her mind.

The evening wore on until her aching back forced her to admit she was too tired to do any more. She made a cup of tea and sat down to check her lists before calling it a night. Happy she could cross off several items and pleased some decisions had been easier than she thought, she wrote another list: things to sell, things to store and the odds and ends to give away. Sarah would be proud of her.

For the next two days Megan worked non-stop, even while doubts niggled. On one hand she argued she shouldn't be doing this, that she owed it to Tony's memory to leave everything as it was. Then she'd have another of the many imaginary discussions with Tony, who said she must move on and make a new life for herself. Megan knew she was wasting her energy with these useless and repetitive arguments. She was committed to her decision, but realising it had been hers and hers alone was frightening.

One of the hardest jobs was sorting the ornaments and treasured knick-knacks filling the china cabinet. She knelt on the floor and weighed up the value and importance of each item: those once belonging to her grandmother, those Tony had given her and those she had collected on their travels. Some were easy to dispose of, knowing neither Sarah nor Jason would be the slightest bit interested; others, not so. Some would have to stay.

The photos meant the most, but the frames she wouldn't need. She removed the pictures and set them aside to be placed into albums and stored, while the frames went into the suitcases alongside the knick-knacks.

When she boiled it all down, the essential things were those she couldn't replace. China and glassware didn't matter. The only items she kept were the photos and the keepsakes Tony had given her – the ones that brought back memories of happy times.

With the difficult tasks completed and her unwanted possessions disposed of, Megan put the house in the hands of a real estate agent.

* * * * *

Before she knew it, auction day was upon her. Fresh flowers arrived, courtesy of Sarah, who had stylishly arranged the house like a showpiece for prospective buyers. Megan nervously paced the house letting her agitation get the better of her. She opened windows, fluffed the perfectly aligned cushions and fussed with the also perfect flower arrangements. If the house sold, it wouldn't take long to clear the last of her belongings, and the final remnants of her life with Tony would be gone.

Megan didn't think she'd ever felt quite so nervous and excited at the same time – well, maybe once, on her wedding day all those decades ago. This journey was similar to that one – a step into the unknown, and one that presented both opportunities and pitfalls. Developing a life with Tony as a wife, a mother, and later a businesswoman had been a journey. Building on each experience that led to another and another had given Megan confidence and the freedom to reach for higher goals. Now she was on the verge of yet *another* journey, down paths she barely knew or understood, but where the unexpected could happen.

Did she have the confidence and strength to do this without Tony? Only time would tell, but she felt intoxicated, with a fizzing in the pit of her stomach like champagne bubbles ready to burst.

Barbara, the agent, arrived first to throw the house open for inspection, followed shortly after by Sarah, Nick and little Isabella, who proved a wonderful distraction. They opted to stay for the auction and walked around the garden during inspection time and hid in the kitchen where they could hear the auctioneer.

"Going once ... Going twice ..."

The tension amongst the bidders, the onlookers and the sellers was palpable. No one could tell who was the most excited but finally came those magic words.

"Sold!" Down came the hammer. "To the lady in blue."

Applause broke out in the garden, and behind her Megan heard the pop of champagne corks. Something inside burst. Elation? Euphoria? She didn't know what to call it; it sounded so OTT she couldn't put it into words but a huge sense of release. Gone was the black despair that had dogged her. Congratulations were offered to all. Papers signed, hands shaken and hugs given.

Her new life was about to begin.

Megan's Diary
Day One – 1 November 2010, London

I am here! And beginning to believe in my new adventure. But, unlike my young counterpart, whose life I'm following and who couldn't wait to get away, I am beset with doubts. There are so many firsts for me. The first time I've travelled without Tony – alone. I'm terrified. The first time I have only myself to rely on and I worry whether I am up to the task. The first time I've abandoned my family. Is abandoned too strong a word? Possibly, but I have left them behind, for who knows how long, and now this – my first entry in my journal. Where will I start? My young ancestor began with her packing and the coach journey to an unknown future. I will follow her lead.

The farewells at the airport were more of a wrench than I'd have imagined. But finally, with all the words said and the last-minute checks done, there were no more excuses, I had to go through the gates.

Whatever excitement I might have felt about what lay ahead was instantly curtailed by process and protocols. I hadn't realised before how bereft of atmosphere and how soul-destroying airport departure halls are. People move anxiously here and there, trusting no one, following endless lines. Tears flow, bags are rigorously guarded and the need to get going is tempered by the long queues and relentless wait. One can only watch one's fellow travellers and wonder what their stories might be – and whom they will tell.

Once on the plane and settled into my seat, I investigated the options available to keep me entertained. Hoping against hope that I might see it all through new eyes, but I'm too old for that and know long flights are an endurance test. There are always the physical discomforts giving travellers something to complain about, but it was the loneliness that tormented me. With no one to talk to, the hours were interminable. The couple beside me sat turned slightly towards each other, and while they didn't talk much, occasionally sharing a comment about something in the movie or book each of them was engrossed in, they shared that silent and sympathetic communication between couples I once had. I felt trapped in my seat, hardly able to move and restless to the point of screaming, yet perversely unwilling to disturb my neighbours. And the only person to notice or care was me! I resented them, an emotion I don't usually have to cope with.

The seemingly never-ending flight finally ended. I dragged myself off the plane, feeling thick and heavy in mind and body, made it through customs at the same slow pace one expects but hates, and lugged my suitcase onto the train, trying to adjust to the crowds of people everywhere.

I am here. Exhausted, drained and desperate for sleep, yet pent-up and edgy. My young relative was full of enthusiasm for what lay ahead. Can I admit to an underlying sense of anticipation, too? The war of emotions churning inside me is too hard to put into words. I must not allow this journal to become a junkyard for my thoughts. This is a story of life: her life, my life.

But right now, I have to sleep. Tomorrow is a new day.

CHAPTER 7

Megan awoke feeling surprisingly alert and ready to get moving. After luxuriating in a hot shower, she dressed simply in trousers and merino top, and bounced down the stairs to the dining room for breakfast. She was starving and looked forward to a traditional English breakfast to make up for what the airlines called food. Excitement coursed through her as she watched the countless people passing by the window. She was itching to join them.

Warmly wrapped in a coat and scarf, she headed out into a cold grey November day to join the throngs and soon located the office she was looking for. Like many London buildings, this one was old and steeped in history, with long corridors, wood-lined walls, imposing doorways and a hushed expectation. It was home to many records, far too numerous to consider searching unless one knew where and how to look. Which was why Megan had engaged advisors, researchers and record keepers to help her wade through the myriad of details to find what she was looking for. She hoped her contact, Mr Gordon McKenzie, would prove a worthy starting point.

"Good morning. My name is Megan Marsh. I have an appointment."

The girl smiled. "Please take a seat while I tell Mr McKenzie you are here."

Moments later, a man's rich voice greeted her from behind. "Good morning. Mrs Marsh?"

Megan's researcher came as quite a surprise. For a start, he was younger than she expected, somewhere in his late twenties or early thirties, and on the surface, far too young to be the owner of such a fine baritone voice. Perfectly groomed in a dark pinstripe suit, white shirt and subdued tie, knotted in an accomplished Windsor, he wore glasses that magnified his unusual green eyes. He appeared a young man any mother could be proud of. Megan immediately thought of Jason – her well-groomed and successful son and, unexpectedly, wondered how well she still knew him.

The man extended his hand. "I'm Gordon McKenzie. I believe I have some interesting papers for you to see. Please follow me."

They walked down a passageway, passing a row of doors, until he stepped aside and ushered her in front of him through an open doorway. The room was elegant with its high ceiling, ornate decorations and classical windows. It took her breath away. In the centre sat a highly polished, antique boardroom table.

"Please take a seat," Gordon invited.

On the table were several large books and two pairs of white gloves.

"Thank you for seeing me, Mr McKenzie."

She removed her coat and scarf, and the young man hung them on the coat stand out of the way.

"I've taken the liberty of drawing up a chart using some of the information you gave me, to make it easier to follow," he said returning to the table. "I've also located several certificates and records that will back up your initial research. I trust you will be satisfied."

His formal, well-modulated English sounded a bit too pompous, and his unobtrusive manner was a curious contrast to the more casual Kiwi manners she was used to, nevertheless, she warmed to him. She had learnt a similar if lesser degree of formality from her grandmother.

Grandma Julia, whose own upbringing was steeped in late-nineteenth-century mores, had insisted on clear speech, correct grammar and polite manners at all times. She said correctness was the mark of a lady. Words like restrained, obedient, polite and respectful were the core principles. Even all these years later, Megan found it hard to be the free spirit many Kiwis adopted naturally.

Mr McKenzie rolled out a long sheet of paper and anchored the corners with paperweights. He stood beside the chair, leaning slightly towards her with one hand on the table as he pointed to the bottom of the chart. She caught the aroma of his expensive aftershave and noted his well-kept fingernails. This Keeper of the Records was a meticulous man.

"Let me explain." His mellow voice resonated in her ear. "I'll start with you – what you already know and what you were able to tell me from your New Zealand discoveries. Here you are at the bottom in Generation Five. Megan Montgomery, born 1958, in Auckland."

"Yes, that's me." Smiling up at him, she hoped he would become a little friendlier.

"You married Anthony Michael Marsh in 1976."

"Right again."

A flicker of a smile almost creased the side of his mouth.

"Your husband was born in 1952 and died last year, in 2009." With hardly a break, he added, "My condolences on your loss."

"Thank you. That's why I'm here, trying to move on."

Megan sensed his hesitation and wondered if he would say something but he was too polite.

"Moving back one generation to Generation Four, we have your mother. Caroline Blackwood, born 1936 in Auckland, married in 1957 to your father, David Montgomery. I note they both died at a very young age in 1959 – as a result of a car crash, I believe you said – when you were a few months old. Your grandmother raised you. Is that correct?"

"Yes," answered Megan. "You're getting good at this," she teased.

This time he did smile. "I sincerely hope so," he replied, straightening his already straight tie. "It seems 1959 was a momentous year for your family. Do you know anything about your father's side of the family?"

"No. I don't think I ever heard my grandmother speak of them. After the accident, I think Grandma Julia shut herself off from everyone else."

"If my memory serves me, you said your paternal grandfather, Malcolm Montgomery, was the driver and was also killed in the accident. From my experience, that could well be the reason your grandmother never spoke of it."

"I thought that, too," she agreed.

"Do you wish to find the paternal side of the family as well?" he enquired further, looking more interested.

"Not at this stage, thanks. I really want to find the author of the diary I've inherited. I understand it came from my grandmother's side, but I don't know her name."

Mr McKenzie nodded. "Very well. We then come to Generation Three, your grandparents. "Your grandmother, Julia Trevallyan, 1912–1975, married at the age of seventeen to Jeremy Blackwood, thirteen years her senior. As you know, he also died in the car accident of 1959."

She nodded, so far nothing new – except ... "Tell me, why was my grandmother's name Trevallyan?"

Megan was confused by this discrepancy. She had never given her grandmother's maiden name any thought, but if Great Aunt Constance was a Trevallyan, how could Julia, a niece and a generation further on, also be a Trevallyan?

"That is part of the mystery you are trying to resolve. These are the facts at this stage. I do have other documents and certificates to show you ... There is something extra. Details you do not seem to have discovered in your searches. Your grandmother Julia gave birth to two earlier children. A stillborn boy in 1931 and another son, Carl, in 1933. He lived a few days only."

Megan stared at him in horror with a gut-wrenching feeling that only a mother could understand. "She lost two other children? Heaven help her. No wonder she never spoke of her past." Losing a child at birth, or near enough to it, would be terrible, but to lose two – and then to lose your precious daughter to a car accident would have been devastating. Enough to damage the

43

strongest woman. The distress on Megan's face must have registered with Gordon.

Softly he said, "I believe we should continue ... to Generation Two, your great-grandparents. I can find no record of your great-grandfather. Your great-grandmother has shown up one Isabel Trevallyan."

"Isabel?" Megan interrupted. "Spelt with an 'a'? What a coincidence. My granddaughter is named Isabella."

"That's a nice happenstance. It's much easier to trace families who carry on a name, either as a middle name or as a derivative, but to do so without knowing is a delightful story."

Now he was being rather too correct in his speech. 'Happenstance'! Who uses words like that these days? But there was something more curious in what he'd said.

"How odd, her name is also Trevallyan. Was that her married name – did she marry another Trevallyan – or her maiden name? Wouldn't it have been unusual for a woman to keep her maiden name in those times?"

"Yes, it would. Please let me continue. I have more information."

He obviously doesn't like being interrupted, thought Megan. Questions would have to come later.

"Isabel Trevallyan was born in 1892. She had an elder brother, Francis, two years her senior, and a younger sister Constance."

"Great Aunt Constance of the letter!" exclaimed Megan. "I'm here because of her."

"She would, in fact, have been your great-great aunt and ten years the junior."

"Do you know what happened to my great-grandmother?"

44

"I'm sorry, no. I can find no further records for Isabel, including her death certificate."

"Oh, is that because she died in New Zealand?"

"No, not at all. I've checked the New Zealand end, and there is no evidence of an Isabel Trevallyan in New Zealand at all. Nothing."

Megan blanched, staring at him in disbelief. If she had understood him correctly, there were no records for Grandma Julia's mother, Isabel Trevallyan, or her father, whoever he was.

Megan threw question after question at her informant trying to find some answers but he couldn't tell her anything more. Isabel had disappeared.

Noticing her pallor, Gordon hesitated. "Are you all right? Shall I continue?"

Megan nodded. Bad news doesn't get any better by avoiding it.

He returned their attention to the chart. "Lastly, we have Generation One – which is as far back as I have delved – your maternal great-great-grandparents, Gerald Trevallyan and Eleanor Pengelly. Gerald was born in 1854 and died of heart failure at the age of fifty-seven in 1911. Eleanor was made of sterner stuff, living to the age of seventy-three and departing this world in 1937. The death certificate stated senile decay as the cause of death, although it was common practice to use that explanation for many things, including dementia. I believe this information will give you something to work from."

"Thank you, Mr McKenzie. I appreciate your efforts. You've done an amazing job," she concluded, waving her hand expansively over the chart.

"It's been no trouble at all, Mrs Marsh. No trouble at all."

"You must spend an awful lot of time looking for other people's families. I hope everyone appreciates you. But tell me, do you enjoy what you do?" With her love of the past, Megan was inordinately interested in other people's reasons for wandering down memory lane into bygone days.

She had fanned a flame. His passion for the subject flared and his formality fell away like a sheet falling off the line. "Oh yes, I do, very much. Family history is like a mysterious, twisted knot with no beginning and no end. I find it a fascinating subject and am always excited to unearth a new link in the chain," he said ardently. "Unravelling secrets, revealing truths and making connections is a just reward." Slightly embarrassed by his unexpected torrent of enthusiasm, he coughed and busied himself tidying up some papers.

"And can you prove all this through certificates and other documents?" Megan reverted to business, giving him time to resume his customary demeanour.

"Yes, most certainly, there is attested proof to back up everything on this chart," he confirmed, back to his normal self. He paused. "However, there is one more item."

Putting on a pair of white gloves, he moved to the other side of the table and picked up one of the books. Carefully setting it down on a stand, he turned to a previously marked page. "Gerald Trevallyan was a wealthy mine owner and farmer in Cornwall. His estate was quite substantial in those days, and they kept meticulous records, which we have here." Gordon pointed to the largest tome. "I believe your great-grandmother Isabel was the author of your diary. I have found something that could be of great interest. In 1910, at the age of eighteen,

Isabel's father gave her a generous allowance and sent her away to act as companion to a Mrs Baragwanath."

At last! She had a name.

The mysterious author of the journal was Isabel Trevallyan, her great-grandmother!

* * * * *

A week later, armed with all the information Gordon McKenzie had provided and additional notes she'd taken, Megan packed up her suitcase, collected her hire car and headed south-west to Cornwall. Since the lawyer representing Constance was based in Truro, it made sense to start there. Isabel had been born in the coastal village of Portreath, not far from Redruth. Cornwall had to be the first link in the chain.

Megan tried to capture the excitement of London that Isabel wrote about during her time there. She, too, went sightseeing, visited galleries and saw a show, and had enjoyed every moment, but the time had come to move on.

After an hour or so on the motorway, Megan found she was gripping the steering wheel tighter and tighter as the minutes ticked by. She was not used to driving long distances. Tony had always driven when they were together, and these busy English motorways unnerved her. She pulled off to rest. Maybe it would be better to follow the minor roads and take her time. There was no rush to find this lawyer in Truro. She checked the map and found her way to the slower paced roads.

At a small English pub dating back to the 18th century, festooned with drinking mugs hanging from the rafters, Megan pulled out Isabel's journal. Even though she was doing this part of the journey the opposite way to Isabel – on her way *to* Cornwall, rather than from there – she reread the early pages where the girl described her journey: First to Redruth by coach, because her father's prized possession, the new automobile, was only used on rare occasions. There, she met Mrs Baragwanath and caught the train to Truro, changing lines to take the London train as far as Salisbury where they stayed the night. After viewing the cathedral the next day, they took another coach to Bath since the rail line was too inconvenient. The pair went to a lot of trouble to get there.

Megan assumed Bath in 1910 was still 'the' place to be seen, and decided to visit. This trip was as much about the journey as the destination and she wanted to stop along the way, as Isabel had done. When travelling with Tony, Megan had enjoyed their stopovers in pretty English villages with ancient market places, and where she could go shopping in quaint stores that offered customers a taste of years gone by. Hoping Tony's absence wouldn't be too noticeable, she replicated her earlier experiences, studiously avoiding the tacky souvenir shops, and found shops with quality linens and cottons, or china, ceramics and glassware. Antique shops became her favourite haunts.

By evening, she had travelled as far as Bath where she would stay for a couple of days. The city was more famous for its Roman and Georgian history, which lovers of Jane Austen knew about, but it was still fashionable during the late-Victorian era and into the

Edwardian. Megan found a guesthouse in an elegant Victorian villa and with a visitor guide in hand dutifully toured the historic sites in the town, concentrating on those listed in Isabel's journal.

Within a short time, she realised how lucky she'd been that Great Aunt Constance had kept it protected for so many decades. For such an old diary, it was in great condition with only a few stains here and there, and the paper had deepened in colour to a rich buff, but otherwise it was relatively undamaged.

At the end of her second day in Bath, she rang Sarah.

"Hello?" Sarah's voice at the end of the line sounded hurried.

"Hello, sweetheart." Megan belatedly checked her watch, realising it would be the morning rush hour over there. "Have I caught you at a bad time?"

"No. No. It's fine. Just hang on a sec."

Precious seconds ticked by, as Megan hung on the end of the phone not sure what the noises meant.

"Hello, Mum. Sorry about that. That was another mother from day care calling to pick up Bella. You talk and I'll listen, but bear with me while I make some coffee. Where are you?"

"That's fine, honey. I'm in Bath. Just thought I'd like to talk to someone for a change. Emails and texts are great, but ..." Megan trailed off.

"Keep talking, Mum. I've put you on speakerphone."

"I suppose I'm feeling a bit lonely. Apart from the brief discussions with people to get food and accommodation, I haven't talked with anyone in days. It's nice to hear your voice."

"Tell me what you've been doing."

Megan launched into her discoveries at the London Public Record Office, trying to simplify it as best she could. "It appears definite. I am a descendant of the Trevallyan family and my great-grandmother Isabel was the author of the journal. Reading it through again as I get to each place is helping me know a lot more about her and understand why she did what she did. The things I found out about Grandma Julia still really upset me, though. I can't get them out of my head. The things she had to cope with! Losing all her children like that. Makes *me* look weak. And we have no idea what happened to her mother."

"Don't fret, Mum. And don't think you're weak. It sounds to me like you come from a long line of strong women. What have you been doing in Bath?"

"I've been on a history trail. I followed the list in Isabel's journal and visited the Assembly Rooms, the cathedral and Pulteney Bridge. I had the most delicious afternoon tea in traditional Georgian style at the Pump Room. It's a real pleasure being here."

"Sounds lovely, Mum."

"It's the history of the place that gets me. It's hard to believe I am literally walking on the same stones in the same places Isabel walked."

Sarah and Megan laughed over other pieces of trivia about life at home and her plans for the next few days before saying goodbye. Megan felt better for having talked with Sarah.

Maybe she could keep the loneliness at bay after all.

Isabel's Journal
2 November 1910 — Bath

The Royal Crescent here in Bath is very elegant and obviously for the wealthy. The area is open and airy with a park across the road. I love the way the sun, when it shines, glints off the light coloured stones, although even this early in November it's colder here than at home. Mrs Baragwanath certainly knows a lot of people, and the Georgian manor we are staying in is the epitome of style. I've never seen such fine furniture. I thought Father and Mother had good taste but I can see their belongings are very rustic in comparison to this household.

Today we explored some of the town. It has some very old buildings and the architecture is quite grand, but the shopping here is delightful. They cater for a much more discerning set than at home. The quality of the cloth is exquisite. I bought a new pair of gloves and a fan, both of which are very fine.

We visit the Assembly Rooms every day, to see who else is there. It seems the tradition has been handed down for generations, and the elite are not prepared to give up a tradition. I'm not sure I understand the need to wander around nodding at people or have a gentleman tip his hat at us. Why can't we talk to one another? Just when I think Mrs B is modern and prepared to bend convention, she slips back into olden days!

We also visit the Roman Bath House to take the waters, much as they have done for many years. It tastes awful, but one is not allowed to show distaste – that, in itself, is distasteful.

I found Pulteney Bridge quite interesting, lined as it is with quaint shops. I enjoyed shopping for knick-knacks and some surprisingly fine fabric. Mrs B says I will see a similar bridge, although much older, lined with shops in Florence, when we get there.

We walked past the abbey where we will go on Sunday for church.

Mother will be pleased Mrs Baragwanath is seeing to my spiritual education as well as my social. Personally, I prefer socialising more.

CHAPTER 8

The next morning dawned grey and overcast, threatening rain. After her decision not to rush, Megan enjoyed the feeling of freedom as she travelled south-west through Somerset. With time on her hands, she found reasons to stop along the way, aware she was deliberately living in the detail and avoiding the larger picture – as if afraid of what would she find once she reached her destination.

She drove into Midsomer Norton, Wells and Glastonbury. There she visited the cathedral, the ruins of the ancient abbey and climbed the Tor for the best view she could get. The rain had held off, but the biting wind made sure Megan didn't linger. She went in search of somewhere warm.

Back in the town centre she was grateful to find a small tearoom that smelt of delicious food and good coffee. Since it was the off season for tourists and there were only a few locals in, the woman behind the counter was soon happy to chat to a newcomer. Megan let her rattle on about the history of the town, its myths and legends, and gossip about the townsfolk. Eventually, during a break in the conversation, Megan grasped the opportunity she had been looking for.

53

"I'm on my way to Redruth," she began. "Looking at the map, I seem to have two choices: the main route south through Bodmin or the more westerly route through Barnstaple. Which way would you recommend? How long would it take?"

"Luvvy, it be neither here nor there time-wise. Only take you a couple o' hour or so, no more'n three on the worst day down them motorways like, to go through Taunton, but 'ee don't want to go that way. Not unless 'ee be in a hurry, like. Are 'ee?" Megan shook her head. "Well then, avoid Bodmin and the moors, they be real grey at this time o' the year. It be fifty mile at most to Barnstaple. Lovely place, Barnstaple. Lots to do and see, ev'n at this time o' the year. Then it's maybe seventy or eighty more to where 'ee going. It's not as quick maybe but better, I reckon. Yeah, better b' far. Go through the national park. It's really pretty and a good road an' all."

Megan thanked the lady for the advice, paid for her meal and collected her coat. As she was leaving, the woman called out, "If'n 'ee not in a hurry, and you ain't been there afore, then Clovelly is a fine place to stay. Can't miss it."

Since neither road Megan was considering went near the route Isabel's train took, it mattered little which way she drove. She unfolded the map to check the road number and direction and set off towards Minehead and through the northern section of the Exmoor National Park.

It wasn't long before Megan knew she had made the right decision. Once she got past Bridgwater and onto a lesser main road, the countryside was indeed as pretty as the woman had said, especially during the odd break in the cloud cover. She caught glimpses of wild ponies and a lone mountain goat and loved to see the sheep wandering wherever they chose through the villages.

A few miles further, the grey skies darkened and Megan began to feel anxious. The smell of misty ocean spray drifted up from cliffs that plunged to villages at their base, where the waves crashed onto the shore, but she could see nothing. On a clear day, she imagined, they would have been spectacular, but now it felt eerie and lonely travelling through the deepening mist.

She didn't want to drive at night and decided to stop in Barnstaple after all. It was coming up to four o'clock when she pulled into the town and found the information office.

"Excuse me," she said to the man taking in the sign. "Can you help me please? I was thinking of going further, but the weather seems to be closing in. I thought I should stay somewhere nearby."

"Wise choice. Yes, very wise indeed. Weather round 'ere has the 'abit of closing in quick, like. Not pleasant. Not pleasant at all. Now what did 'ee have in mind? I were about to shut up shop, but I can spare a few minutes."

"How far is it to Clovelly? Someone recommended it as a good place to stay."

"Well, if'n you likes that sort of thing. 'Tis a bit commercial for my tastes."

Megan wondered why his taste should come into the discussion, but he hadn't finished.

"They charge 'ee to enter these days, 'ee know. It's all private land. Been owned by the same family for centuries, but now they charge. Not right, to my mind. Not right at all. So, what 'en? You want to go there?"

"Well, yes. I think so. Can you make a room booking for me please?"

"'Ee sure you don't want to stay around these parts, 'en?" the man countered.

"No. Thanks." Megan decided she needed to be firm if she was going to get anywhere. "Clovelly. Please."

"Righto, then. How long? Dinner? B&B? In the village or outside? Price range?" He fired questions and Megan made her choices, eventually settling on The Red Lion Hotel on the quay. At length, ignoring the man's continued negative discourse on the area, she came away with a handful of pamphlets, the booking vouchers and some maps, and left the man to close up. Megan had shaken her head in bewilderment at his manner, but in the end, he'd been helpful, giving her directions and making some suggestions.

As the woman in the tearooms back in Glastonbury had said, it wasn't far between Barnstaple and Clovelly, but before long she had to turn the headlights on. She was more than relieved to get there and wanted to get settled quickly. Tiredness washed over her like the misty fog rolling in from the sea. She would have to wait until tomorrow to see the village.

Parking at the top, as she was told to do, she was grateful the man in Barnstaple had arranged for the Land Rover service. She hadn't realised there was only a private road access to take her and her luggage down to the quay. Her room at the front of the hotel had a balcony and views of both the harbour and the sea, they assured her, but this evening there was nothing visible but shadowy shapes under dark grey clouds meeting a darker grey sea.

"Welcome." Her hostess greeted Megan as she entered the dining room. "Come in to the warmth, dear. Come on in. There's a right ol' storm brewing, I can tell ye."

Taking her seat, Megan asked, "What would you recommend?"

"The house specialty is my famous fish pie," answered the woman proudly. "Made the traditional way with whiting, smoked haddock and salmon, and topped with mashed potato."

"Sounds delicious."

When she'd finished, Megan moved to the guest lounge where the waiter brought her some of the equally famous Exmoor Blue cheese, which she washed down with a glass of scrumpy, the local cider. She relaxed for the first time in hours. As the tension drained away, and thinking her day could not have ended better, she randomly opened Isabel's diary.

Isabel's Journal
15 November 1910 – London

I find Mrs Baragwanath an amusing travelling companion. She knows so many people where we are invited to stay. She must be ancient though with all her baggy chins and heavy wrinkles, but she wears the most beautiful jewellery. Her demands on me are light. She has a maid to help with her hair and dressing and all those personal needs. I, on the other hand, get to read to her, take a walk, when she feels inclined for some fresh air, which is not often, and play the odd hand of whist in the afternoon.

We are currently reading E. M. Forster's book, Howards End. She says the author has captured the classes capably. Mrs B prefers poetry before retiring, especially the poetry of Elizabeth Barratt Browning, mostly, she says, because EBB defied her father, rather than the fact she married for love. She has an ear for Kipling and an appreciation of Wordsworth, whom she says is a 'good sort' since he cares for his sister. Her latest interest is a new poet, the New Englander, Amy Lowell. I struggle sometimes to grasp the full meaning behind some of their words, but Mrs B assures me I will learn to appreciate it more when I grow up. I do wish she wouldn't treat me quite like an uneducated child sometimes.

We attend many house parties and soirées, which I am thoroughly enjoying, with hardly an evening to ourselves. I take great pleasure in dressing up and seeing some of the most modern fashions imaginable, especially during our lengthy stay in London. I can't wait until we get to Paris. A whole month in Paris!

Mother would be horrified if she could hear some of Mrs B's opinions, especially when speaking of the fight for women's rights, suffragettes she calls them. Mrs Baragwanath appears to be all smiles and good manners but has a cutting wit she uses against those who pretend to be other than what they are or are too overly ingratiating.

Young men who try to flatter her are the main targets. She says they know she has money and they think they can win her favour by their adulation. She enjoys leading them on and then cutting them down. Silly them, I say. If only they could hear what she says about them behind their backs. She doesn't have much time for silly girls who blush and giggle either. Women, she says, have to be in control of their lives and lead them to the best of their ability. That is what is best for their family and their country.

I am learning a lot from her. She is refreshingly different to Mother and her circle. It is pleasing to know my own primitive thoughts are not so avant-garde after all.

*   *   *   *   *

The storm broke during the night. Megan woke from her restless dreams to torrential rain beating against her window. The wind howled and whistled, and the relentless pounding of the waves sent shivers through her. Although she'd read the sea wall had been there since the thirteenth century and had withstood many storms, she got out of bed and drew back the curtains to see for herself.

It was pitch black, except for the white tips of the waves as they surged up the granite wall to crash over the top. From where Megan stood, they appeared to be dancing, reaching and stretching. A graceful spray arched over the wall to fall away before extending its arms again in an elaborate ballet. She stood mesmerised watching their play, no longer alarmed and surprisingly comforted, as though the storm had cleansed something deep within her.

Instinctively, Megan knew this place was special. It would give her a chance to think and come to terms with what she had been avoiding. She decided to stay an extra day. The lawyer in Truro could wait. She sat at the table by the window and began to write in her diary.

The day dawned calm but still grey after the onslaught of the storm. Megan stepped outside to the tang of seaweed and salt-laden air. Fishermen were out looking for any damage to their boats or gear, heartened the lifeboat had not been needed. Women busily swept the paths clearing away any detritus that had landed where it shouldn't, but no one appeared unduly alarmed. Positioned in a sheltered bay and protected from the westerlies by the sea wall, the harbour had long since been a safe haven.

Megan hadn't realised the village was, basically, one very steep cobblestone lane running straight up the hill. It came as quite a shock as she looked upwards at how sheer it was, but she smiled when she learnt those at its base called the lane 'Up-a-long' and the ones at the top called it 'Down-a-long'. The logic of it all amused her, but the village donkeys charmed her most. They once carried everything up and down that lane, either in panniers on their backs or dragging sleds – people, luggage, food, fuel, but especially the famous herring catch. After taxing herself with the climb to the top and back, and delighting in the ancient buildings, the quaint shops and unique character of the place, she wandered along the beach, attracted by the sound of a waterfall.

Stories of smuggling, shipwrecks and piracy abounded in these ancient fishing villages scattered along the coast of Devon and Cornwall. Local legend held that Merlin the Magician was born in the cave hidden by the waterfall for those still gullible enough to believe in fairy tales. She turned and headed back along the beach to visit Crazy Kate's Cottage, the oldest in the village dating from the fifteenth century. Its story was far more credible and very sad.

Kate had been watching a storm – as Megan had done last night – waiting for her husband's fishing boat to return from its regular trip. She stayed at the window throughout the night, watching as the boat foundered and her husband drowned in front of her eyes. The villagers said she went crazy that night and a few days later put on her wedding dress and walked out into the sea to join him in eternity. Megan felt a kinship with this Kate, perfectly understanding the woman's pain.

In the late afternoon, Megan walked along the lower part of the sea wall. The clouds were still leaden, but a lighter sky to the west with a touch of blue promised a better day tomorrow. She climbed the steps to stand at the furthest point of the wall. Exposed to the elements, Megan was glad of her winter coat. She pulled the woollen scarf closer and thrust her cold hands into her pockets. Many metres below, the waves lapped gently at its base, calmer now after the storm, like her. For several moments she stood, head bent looking down beyond her feet to another time and place. Looking up again, she stared at the expanse of sea, feeling more alone than ever, but no longer could she hide. Move on she must – and would.

Her thoughts kept drifting back to her diary and the words she had written during the night.

Megan's Diary
14 November 2010 – Clovelly

My stomach is churning and my nerves are on edge. I'm frightened. I hate to admit it, but I am. Oh, Tony, I came here to say goodbye. I thought I'd reached the point where I could carry on without thinking of you every moment, without wanting to talk to you about every decision and action, but … I can't.

I've read my great-grandmother's journal over and over again. I think I know it, and her as a young woman, as well as anyone can from such a distance of time, but the twists and turns I keep coming across are confusing me. The lawyers in Truro are waiting for me to call as soon as I arrive, and I expect they will have new information, with more surprises for me to digest.

I thought, maybe, if I could get you out of my head, if I could stop relying on you, I could cope with this better. But now I'm here, I know I'm wrong. It's not your memory that's clouding my thinking. It's what I've discovered. What I've learnt from the records office, and what the lawyer said, that is breaking my heart anew. I think the lawyers are about to tell me things I'm not sure I want to know and I'm scared. I'm really scared everything is about to change. So, guess what, my darling? You get to stay. You get to help me through this. But you already knew that, didn't you?

When I started on this journey, I never for one moment thought I'd get so caught up in the past. I was going on a journey of renewal, but it seems there are people from the past who want their story told first.

CHAPTER 9

"Welcome, Mrs Marsh." James Boscowan the Third extended his hand in greeting.

Megan shook hands with the lawyer who had written to her two months ago and instigated her journey. A man, she estimated, in his early sixties with English public school and wealth written all over him.

"Where are you staying? At the Hall? Are you comfortable?"

"I'm at a B&B in Redruth until I get my bearings," Megan told him, misunderstanding his reference to the Hall.

"Oh!" He looked momentarily startled. "Righto. Good. Good. Now to business. Where shall we start?"

Megan surveyed the room while the lawyer fussed around re-sorting papers clearly already sorted. She felt sure he knew exactly where to start. Expecting a typical Victorian set of offices for a law practice purported to have been established one hundred and fifty years ago, and in the same family ever since, these rooms came as a total surprise. Boscowan and Sons were doing very well. The ultramodern office building, and in particular his office on the third floor, boasting floor-to-ceiling glass walls overlooking the cathedral and river, was quite stunning. She could tell no expense had been spared on the furniture, although it wasn't to her taste. He was obviously a man with a vision for the future. "Mr Boscowan, if it's all the same to you, I think we'd better start with why I'm here."

"Yes, yes, of course. Why you're here? Yes, a good place to start."

Megan refrained from rolling her eyes, thinking this was going to be a difficult interview. Maybe she was wrong; maybe he was stuck in the past after all.

"I think you will recall, when I wrote to you, that I needed you to confirm your identity to establish whether you had any connection to my client and her family."

Megan nodded, but she needn't have bothered – he was talking to the papers with his head down.

"And I can see, from the notarised documents you provided, you have successfully done that."

"Yes," confirmed Megan again, wondering where he was going.

Raising his head, he took off his glasses and leaned into the high-backed executive chair as if summing her up. Megan met his gaze without flinching or fidgeting.

"I'm pleased to meet you at last." He paused again. "Before I tell you the final part to the story, I think you need to have some background to put things in context. You have certificates giving evidence of your maternal line, but there are many nuances you have yet to understand."

Wondering when, or if, he was ever going to get to the point, Megan tried not to show her impatience as he waffled on about the history of mining in the area.

How the family fitted into the scene as mine owners and employers. He then explained how his father, and his father before him, had handled all the affairs of the estate belonging to her great-great-grandfather, Gerald Trevallyan, and how large the estate had been with its tenant farms.

"And so, we come to the specifics. I presume you have read the journal I sent you?"

"Yes, many times. Thank you."

"Good. Good. I am only vaguely aware of its contents. Our client gave strict instructions it was only for your eyes. She left a brief outline and directions that once I was satisfied with your validity, I was to advise you it belonged to your great-grandmother, Isabel, who had travelled extensively."

"Yes, I eventually found out her name when I was in London. But please, why the scepticism? If you already knew I existed and where to find me, why do I need to be so thorough in proving who I am? Why send me the journal at all, if it might not be mine? If, as you earlier intimated, I might not be who I say I am?" Megan hadn't meant to be quite as confrontational, but all the secrecy was putting her on edge.

However, this man could not be hurried.

"I'll come to that." His tone was markedly cooler and condescending. He obviously didn't like her.

He looked intently at her again and then, as if accepting the inevitable, suddenly announced, "You are about to become a very wealthy woman, Mrs Marsh. However, there are conditions."

Her frustration vanished and shock began to set in as the tragedies and successes of the Trevallyan story slowly unfolded. How could she possibly believe what he was telling her?

After several more minutes of one-way conversation, she cut short his narrative. "Could I have a glass of water, please?"

He shot her a blank look – as if he'd forgotten she was there and was seemingly disconcerted at being prevented from continuing his chronicle uninterrupted – but good manners demanded he meet her request. "Are you all right?"

She nodded as she gulped down the water, feeling rather bewildered.

"I'll continue then, shall I?"

Again, Megan nodded, not trusting herself to speak.

"... And that sums up the contents of the will," he finally concluded, another ten minutes later.

Taking a deep breath, she let a few moments of silence settle on them as she assembled her thoughts. "Before I ask any questions, can you please explain why it has taken the best part of thirty years to reach me?"

"Ah, yes. Well, yes. I really must apologise. It was an error for which Boscowan and Sons must take full responsibility. I offer no excuses, only the facts."

James explained how his grandfather – the first James Boscowan, grandson of the founder of the firm – had lived a very long and active life keeping a few private clients well after his retirement, including the Trevallyans. He died sitting at his desk at the age of eighty-three, only a matter of weeks after his client, Constance Trevallyan. Only he knew all the details, but when his office was being cleared out, the closed files were sent to storage, the Trevallyan file among them, even though its business was not quite finalised.

"The files were left undisturbed until three years ago when I moved to new premises. Once I discovered the error, I immediately undertook the task myself. It's taken me until recently to sort out the details and to trace you. Again, I offer my sincere apologies."

"I see. Thank you for your honesty. As a matter of interest, is there a James Boscowan the Fourth?"

For the first time, a small smile creased his face. "No, there isn't. But there is a Jessica Boscowan, who is urging me to change the name to Boscowan and Daughter. I am certain some of our older clients would not approve, but this is the twenty-first century, and I will concede." The thin smile deepened. "In my own good time."

"I'm pleased to hear it." Megan rose to take her leave. "I need to think about this information you have given me before I comment further. Thank you." She extended her hand.

"Before you go, Mrs Marsh, there is one other thing. Miss Trevallyan's ashes have been kept in the vault since her death. Could you please advise me what you would like done with them?"

Megan withdrew her hand and sank back into her chair. She needed a few more minutes to gather her wits.

* * * * *

Several hours later, having pulled herself together, Megan recalled one of the things Mr Boscowan told her: the original Trevallyan Manor was now called Trevennick Hall, hence his reference to the Hall. It and the surrounding estate had been put into a perpetual trust to come into effect after Constance's death. Today it operated as a thriving farm and hotel. *No wonder he looked surprised to find me at a B&B.*

She had a lot to learn about this unusual Great Aunt Constance – a tough businesswoman, a loyal master and a capricious young woman all rolled into one.

Megan had smothered her laughter as best she could when James Boscowan explained Constance had changed the name of the manor house, shortly after her mother's death in 1937, to Trevennick Hall because she'd liked the character in Edith Wharton's novel, *The Buccaneers.*

It seemed almost farcical, but Megan had far more important mysteries to unravel.

Grateful Sarah had insisted she buy a new laptop, Megan quickly found the renamed Trevennick Hall on the Internet and made a booking. Saying thank you to the B&B and getting directions, she headed off to Portreath.

The view, as she approached down the winding driveway, took her breath away. The long, whitewashed, two-storeyed stone house facing her gleamed, in spite of the November cloud. A set of gracious double doors sat at the top of a short flight of curved stone steps, exactly as Isabel had described in her journal. With five bays and a wing on either side, the house was simple and elegant. Megan loved it at first sight.

The turning circle in front of the house led her through the walled archway into a parking area that once would have been the stables. Following the sign, she entered the door from the courtyard and, weaving her way along a wood-panelled corridor, wound up in the spacious reception area. A round, Chippendale-style table adorned with an impressive vase of flowers with trailing greenery dominated the central area.

Megan approached the reception desk as the grandfather clock standing between two gracious doorways tolled the hour. Introducing herself to the woman behind the counter, she signed the visitors' book and received an old-fashioned door key in return.

"I haven't seen one of these for years," said Megan. "How delightful. I love it. Sorry, I didn't catch your name?"

"I'm Jenna. Jenna Pawley. Pleased to meet you, Mrs Marsh." The woman smiled. Megan estimated she would be in her early forties. Elegantly but severely dressed in black, with dark hair pulled back into a tight chignon and impeccable make up, she looked the essence of an old-style housekeeper.

"Thank you, Jenna. I might end up staying a while, if that is all right."

"Certainly. Stay as long as you like. It's off season, and quiet at present. Let me know if you need anything. Your room is up the stairs to the right at the front. I've given you one of the best rooms with great views across the park. Are you wanting to eat in tonight?"

"Yes, please. If it's no trouble."

"No trouble at all. The restaurant operates all year since it brings in the locals. I'll call Kitto to help you with your bags. No lifts around here, I'm afraid." Jenna smiled again, belying her appearance.

Expecting a man of similar age to her hostess, Megan was somewhat surprised to see a very elderly, slightly bent man waddle in from an entrance near the staircase. Smiling inwardly, she could put no other word to it – he definitely waddled from side to side.

"Thanks, Kitto. Could you take Mrs Marsh's bags up to the Isabel Room please?"

Megan heeded the name, but bit her tongue and didn't ask any questions. There would be a better time later.

Jenna turned her attention back to Megan. "When you are settled and want to come downstairs again, the library is there to your right and the lounge and dining room over here through those doors. Make yourself at home."

Megan thanked Jenna before leading Kitto to her car to gather her belongings. Feeling somewhat uncomfortable as she followed him upstairs to her room, she said, "I'm quite sure I can manage these myself."

Kitto thought otherwise. "I've been gardener, handyman, porter and general factotum around 'ere since I were a boy, like me father afore me, and a little bag like this ain't goin' to stop us now. Takes pride in what I do. Miss Constance, God rest her soul, wouldn't have it any other way."

"Miss Constance? Constance Trevallyan?" queried Megan.

"Yep. Who else?" He eyed her up and down, but whatever more he was going to say never left his lips. He tipped his hat and was gone, leaving Megan to appraise the room.

It looked as she imagined it would have a hundred years ago. Decorated in cream regency wallpaper, the heavy matching drapes framing the two sash windows were held by tasselled tie-backs and topped with frilled pelmets. The bedstead was made of ivory and brass, and two pale-green velvet high-back armchairs sat either side of the second window. An occasional table set with some magazines and a small sign saying 'free Wi-Fi available' made her feel very much at home – except modern broadband seemed incongruous in such an old building.

Megan started to unpack. She put some of her things into the Edwardian mahogany dressing table and hung her jackets and trousers in the matching wardrobe. Setting her books on the bedside table, she stopped to admire the vintage white embroidered bed linen and cover.

A small painting hanging above the bed caught her eye – an Edwardian girl in a garden, wearing a large hat, with a younger child in the background. Immediately, she thought of something she'd read in Isabel's journal. *Could it be?* Picking it up she flicked through some of the early entries until she found the page she sought.

Mama was mean not letting me take my painting to show off to people in Florence. It is mine, not hers. It was so much fun that summer with Wil and Jane. How Papa persuaded them to stay I have no idea, but Wil always had a paintbrush in his hand and Jane was so fashionable I envied her clothes. Jane liked to paint too and she did some wonderful work, but Wil chose to paint <u>me</u> – in the garden under the shade of the tree. Constance wouldn't sit still so she looks like a blob of white playing on the lawn, but there is no mistaking me in my favourite hat. But would Mama let me have the painting?

No, she would not. She wanted it to remind her of me, she said. Remind her, what tosh! She couldn't wait to be rid of me. She hates me. I know it.

△ △ △

Megan hardly believed it possible, but she'd had every other sense of the ridiculous and impossible presented to her, so why not? If her instinct was right, then here in front of her eyes was the image of Isabel and her younger sister Constance. The soft palette and shady positioning screamed Edwardian.

Small though it was, the older girl's face was quite detailed, with the flush of youth and clear warm eyes with similar colouring as herself. Her face was fine-boned with a soft prettiness Megan found appealing. The set of her shoulders showed poise and calm. The younger girl dressed in white was less distinct, playing in the background exactly as described.

Megan was disturbed that a girl could think her mother hated her, but if she felt that strongly about it, the mother must have done something to make her feel unloved.

With a quick check of her watch, Megan decided it was too early to phone home and talk to Sarah. She changed into a skirt and top with low heels, suitable for dinner. There was time for some exploring first.

The uneven and sloping polished wooden floors of the wide corridor were partly covered by an ancient carpet runner and smelt faintly of furniture polish and musty carpets. Paintings hung on the walls and an antique chest, table or chair sat beside each door. Megan wandered along the creaking floorboards to look more closely at the names on the doors. She briefly wondered if she would find a Constance Room somewhere. All the other rooms were named after a family member, a colour or an era, so the possibility remained high. Retracing her footsteps, she made her way down the staircase.

Following Jenna's instructions, she looked into the library. Megan thought she'd walked into another era. Dark wood shelves lined the room almost floor to ceiling, bulging with books seemingly untouched for generations. A strip of highly polished, rich-chestnut panelling ran around the room at waist height, where, hidden in the decoration, Megan discovered two wide drawers, with elaborate handles and three pull-out shelves where books could rest.

She studied the portrait hanging above the magnificent fireplace of a young woman dressed in an elaborately beaded 1920s outfit. The shape of the girl's face and her fair colouring reminded her distinctly of Sarah. The small brass plaque read:

MISS CONSTANCE TREVALLYAN AGED 21 (1923)

CONSTANCE TREVALLYAN WAS THE
YOUNGEST DAUGHTER OF GERALD AND ELEANOR TREVALLYAN
WHO OWNED THIS HOUSE WHEN TIN MINING IN CORNWALL
WAS AT ITS HEIGHT IN THE MID-19TH CENTURY.
THROUGH A SERIES OF TRAGEDIES,
CONSTANCE TREVALLYAN INHERITED THE ESTATE IN 1926
ON THE DEATH OF HER BROTHER,
FRANCIS TREVALLYAN.

Megan knew this already from what Mr Boscowan had told her earlier in the day. Even so, she hadn't imagined the house would have remained almost untouched, except for some period updates, given it was a thriving commercial venture these days. The history buff in her was excited by this find. The more she looked around, the more she realised many of the furnishings were original and were now valuable antiques. There was much more to Constance Trevallyan than she'd thought.

Megan closed the library door behind her and crossed the tiled reception area towards the lounge, her heels echoing through the empty space. A welcoming fire had been lit, giving the lounge a warming glow. Megan sat in one of the button-backed armchairs near the window looking up the driveway. As if on cue, a waiter appeared and asked if she would care for anything.

Ordering a glass of red wine and some cashew nuts, she relaxed in the warmth of the room and admired the last of the light casting shadows across the garden. For the first time since meeting Mr Boscowan, Megan let herself think about all he had told her. She could barely conceive it, despite the paperwork confirming the details – Constance Trevallyan really had left her personal fortune to 'the great-granddaughter of my sister Isabel, whom I forgive'.

In short, to her – but with strings attached.

How on earth am I going to meet the conditions in Constance's will?

Isabel's Journal
25 November 1910 — London

Really! This is just too much. Mrs Baragwanath has only now told me off for being petulant. Just because I was bemoaning my situation and telling her my mother's latest list of complaints. She said that now I had turned 18 it was time I behaved as 'becoming of a lady' and being ill-humoured was not attractive.

Fortunately, there was no one to witness my humiliation or, I regret to admit, see my face redden in a most unflattering way. But I'm bored, bored, bored. I'm tired of reading and playing whist with Mrs B and her acquaintances. I want something to happen to me for a change!

With the death of the King in May, everything is so quiet. Many people are in mourning and wearing black, even at Ascot. It's dull. The London season was virtually cancelled. It was only slightly possible I could have attended this year but it was something to look forward to. I will never be presented at court now.

Paris had better be more fun or I will start to wish I'd stayed at home! Well, maybe not, now I think of it. That would have been truly boring.

CHAPTER 10

"Mrs Marsh?" Jenna's voice made her jump, halting any further consideration of her momentous news. "Sorry to startle you, but I was wondering if you would like to join us in the bar. We have a few locals in tonight."

"Thank you, Jenna, yes. How thoughtful of you." Megan followed Jenna through the dining room to the replica Edwardian bar. The dining room had obviously been the ballroom at one time, with its intricately decorated ceiling and two sets of original French doors leading to the patio.

Jenna introduced the couple sitting beside her, Tristan and Lowenna, and Jack, the middle-aged man from the far end of the bar, came along to say hello. An older couple walked in and sat at the round table by the corner settle on her left. Once the introductions were complete and drinks ordered, Jenna left them to talk.

"Where you from then, girlie?' asked the older man who'd been introduced as Hugh, with his wife Mabel.

"New Zealand," she told them and was immediately plied with questions. Proudly, she told them about her country – the space, the bright colours of greens and blues, of the forests and farmland and the oceans and the skies. She tried to explain about the Kiwi outdoor lifestyle, barbecues, Māori culture and rugby, a popular subject with the well-informed Tristan.

After a while Jack announced, "I'm away home for my dinner. I'll see you tomorrow, Jenna."

Taking his departure as a cue, Tristan suggested they should eat too. "We could share a table. If you don't mind, that is, Megan. I'm rather interested in hearing more."

"Thank you, Tristan. I'd be glad of the company."

Over dinner, the lively conversation continued with her telling them more about New Zealand, and they explained about village life.

Hugh suddenly said, "Every now and then you remind me of someone. I can't put my finger on it yet, but there's something. Do you have family from around these parts?"

Megan stopped short, frantically searching for an answer that wouldn't give the whole story away – not yet. Many other questions needed answers first. "I'd like to try and trace my great-grandmother while I'm here, if I can. I believe she may have come from Cornwall. But someone else intrigues me more right now. Can any of you tell me about Constance Trevallyan? I found her portrait hanging in the library. I got the impression from Kitto she was an important figure round here."

It was as though Megan had released a helium balloon. Hugh and Mabel, who had said very little up until now, were almost tripping over one other, each trying to give Megan every possible detail before the other.

"It was after her sister, Miss Isabel, ran away," said

Mabel, "when it all started. She couldn't have been more than a wee mite. Maybe nine or ten if she were a day."

Hugh interrupted. "Isabel were her father's favourite, see. But Francis, the boy, he were the mother's – by far. But he were nothing but a wastrel. I tell ye. If it weren't for Constance Trevallyan, this place would'a be done for."

As they both continued their story, Megan tried to work out the time frames. Hugh and Mabel would have known Constance in her later years, but not at the time they were talking about. Their tale must have been handed down – several times, Megan suspected.

"Isabel was sent off to be companion to old Mrs Baragwanath," continued Mabel. "Young Mrs Baragwanath that followed told me all about it many a time. It seems the old lady came back alone having left Miss Isabel in Florence. That's in Italy, you know."

Megan nodded and smiled, thinking she knew a lot more about Florence than her entertaining storyteller ever would.

"Well, as the story goes. Mrs Baragwanath was home only a few days before the squire bade her to call. 'Where's my daughter, madam?' he asked. 'And why are you here without her?' Very haughty he could be when he wanted. But Mrs Baragwanath weren't bothered by him at all. No, not at all. She told him in no uncertain words, so it be told. Isabel was very happy and settled in Florence, teaching music to the English children, and he should leave her alone."

"The squire was having none of that, no matter what anyone said," Hugh butted in again. "As any father would."

Megan recognised parts of this story from Isabel's writings, although her version was somewhat different.

Mabel continued as if Hugh had not spoken. "And then the poor girl's mother went off in a swoon, going on about how her daughter was ruined. Totally ruined, she said. What with her living in Italy unchaperoned 'n all. And how she'd brought shame on the family and saying she would never welcome 'that chit of a girl' back into the house ever again."

Isabel was right, thought Megan. *Her mother didn't want her.*

Tristan refilled the glasses, and he and Lowenna sat back in their chairs, clearly happy to listen to the story as it unfolded. The glance Megan intercepted between them told her they'd heard the story before.

"Anyway, the squire he sent for Miss Isabel and ordered her home. The postmistress at the time told all, she did. Isabel refused. Shortly after that, the old squire took ill. He was so bad he were laid up for many a week. Finally, the mother sent another missive to Isabel."

"That brought Miss Isabel home quick as a flash. She only just made it in time. The old squire passed away not long after. Miss Isabel, she were that heartbroken by all accounts, but that's when all the troubles started. She were pregnant you see, with no husband in sight and hadn't told no one. Well, once the funeral was over, Mrs Trevallyan lost all sense and banished her daughter like she said she would and ..."

Hugh finished her sentence, "... and that Francis never said a word, despite him being the new squire 'n all, but then nobody 'ad any respect for him much anyways."

Lowenna added softly, "From what my mother and grandmother told me, I believe Isabel returned to Italy. No one knows what happened to her after that."

Except Constance, thought Megan, *who definitely knew what happened to her sister. At least Isabel's visit home could explain how the precious journal came to be left at Trevallyan House rather than remaining with her. Poor girl – young, pregnant, and alone.*

"Fascinating story, but it doesn't tell me how Constance became the person she obviously was," prompted Megan.

"I think we're confusing Megan. Let's fast-forward a bit, shall we?"

Tristan's modulated and modern manner of speaking was a pleasant contrast to the increasingly Cornish inflections of Hugh and Mabel. He continued telling the story while Megan listened carefully, matching what she had been told by James Boscowan with what Tristan was saying.

"Over time Francis lost the family fortune through his dissolute and self-indulgent ways. Always up and down to London and living the high life. Gambling was his final downfall. Francis was killed in 1926 while riding to hounds somewhere with some of the rich set. 'Accidental death' said the official report, but everyone knew he'd been too drunk to hold his seat. Meanwhile, Constance set about creating her own fortune."

Gerald Trevallyan had bestowed a small annual sum on both his daughters in their own names for their sole use. After his death, no one had thought to stop those payments. They continued, providing the girls with a private income until Francis's death when Constance took over the estate. By that time, Constance had become a shareholder in many of the new growth industries, investing in a variety of companies while sitting on governing boards and accumulating her own wealth.

"No one really understood how she did it," said Hugh. "My father, God rest his soul, often wondered how a slip of a girl like that knew anything about money."

"Don't be old-fashioned, Hugh." Mabel patted his arm. "Women today are very capable. She being university educated 'n all."

Megan looked at her watch, surprised at the late hour. She decided to wind the conversation up; she wanted to email Sarah and write up her diary. There was much to put down. "It's been a pleasure. Thank you for your company and interesting conversation. I really mustn't keep you talking all night, but I'm curious. How do you know so much about the Trevallyan family?"

They looked at each other first and then at her before Hugh, somewhat bewildered, said, "Everyone knows everyone here. Why wouldn't we? It's our village."

Tristan, again, came to her rescue. "We were all born here and descend from the original families at the time the squire died. Family, in the broader sense, you understand. At the time Constance took over, Hugh's ancestor was the farm factor; Mabel's family were housekeepers; Jenna's great-grandfather was the mine manager; and Lowenna is related to the nurse hired to care for Eleanor. Jack's relative was the governess. And you've already met my father, the one and only Christopher Pendarvis." Megan looked confused. "Kitto," he laughed. "We all go back a very long way. Loyalty was important to Constance."

Megan's Diary
25 November 2010

I haven't done very well keeping up with my diary even after Sarah's prodding. Time has utterly disappeared in the whirl of surprises and new discoveries I can hardly comprehend. My original plans have disappeared out the door, and I'm left trying to work out some realities. For a start, I didn't intend to stay in Cornwall as long. In my mind, I was coming here to sign some papers with the lawyers and be on my way. I didn't expect to be caught up in Constance's wishes the way I have. My goodness, she was, and still is, a control freak.

The people here are very nice, but I wonder what their reaction will be when they find out my connection. Isabel is hardly remembered and never talked about. It's all about Constance.

If I'd been true to Isabel's journal, I should be heading towards the south of France by now, having already visited Paris and a few other places along the way. Instead, it looks like I'll be here for some weeks to come, although I didn't come prepared for it. I'll need more clothes, but if I must spend winter in England, Cornwall is the best part to be, I suppose.

I've engaged Jessica Boscowan to act for me and help me sort out all the legalities and finalise all the paperwork. She and I seem to get on well and I think she could prove invaluable. It's all much bigger than I thought. I feel quite bewildered. My next task is to confirm a few details and follow up on my search into Isabel's life. I need to work out how I'm going to meet Constance's demands. Maybe after that I'll be able to start following Isabel.

I've talked to Jenna about staying longer. That will get me through to late December. I've got some ideas for what I'd like to do over Christmas and the New Year since I obviously won't be where Isabel spent her Christmas. Hopefully, they will work. I'll talk to Sarah soon.

CHAPTER 11

"Hello. Gordon." Megan had eventually reached a first name relationship with her Keeper of the Records from London, as she had nicknamed him. "I need you to do me another favour, please." Reading from her notebook, Megan reeled off a list of records she wanted.

True to his word, within a few days Gordon posted what he'd found to Trevennick Hall.

At the lawyers' office, she'd begged a few minutes with Mr Boscowan. "I need confirmation on some information I've been given. Can you find these details for me, please?" she asked, handing him another list of questions.

Megan quickly said her goodbyes and headed off in search of some general history about the area – the mines, farms, fishing fleets and the growth industries of the time. Industries that had attracted Constance and from which she'd made her fortune.

Likewise, James Boscowan answered her questions within a few days. Somewhat taken aback, she learnt there were two camps in the village: those who loved Constance and those who didn't.

The next two weeks passed quickly as she occupied herself with seeking more facts, and she still hadn't found the right moment to tell anyone her place in their story. Somehow, she didn't feel comfortable about it all. She was a little surprised no hints had come from Mr Boscowan's office, knowing everything would have to come out soon anyway. Her estimation of him and Jessica had gone up.

After a couple of false starts, she managed to get Sarah on Skype by resorting to email to set up a time and day. Megan began the conversation with general chitchat about life at home, until Sarah finally interrupted.

"What's the matter, Mum? What's wrong?"

"Nothing, honey. Nothing at all."

"Okay, if nothing's wrong, what's bothering you? You were determined to call, so you must want to talk about more than the weather at home and what Bella did at day care."

Megan sighed, wondering how to approach what she wanted to say. Deciding to take the bull by the horns she announced, "I couldn't stand the thought of spending Christmas with strangers. I want my family around me, and I need to talk to you and Jason about what I've found here."

"Are you coming home?" Sarah sounded excited about the prospect.

"No. I'm not. I want you to book flights to Honolulu for all of you. I've already booked the accommodation."

After discussing the details, Megan won the argument over who should pay, with an intimation of a small bequest, without letting on about the full inheritance.

Sarah responded instantly. "We'll be there. I'll change whatever plans I have to and reorganise things. Nothing will stop me."

Megan ended the call, satisfied. A warm feeling spread over her and she couldn't stop laughing, cheered by the girl's exuberance. The phone call with Jason was not nearly as rewarding. Jason, full of ums and ahs and constantly giving excuses about how difficult it would be, simply made her cross. "Jason." Megan was firm when interrupting his flow of words. "It's less than a month away, are your shifts for those dates confirmed?"

As he started jabbering on again, Megan forced an answer. "Yes or no?" she demanded.

"Yes," he agreed, reluctantly.

"If I heard you correctly you have four free days over that time. I'll settle for that, if you really can't stay any longer, but I will not accept anything less." Megan softened her tone. "We'd like to see more of you. Sarah, Nick and Bella are coming for ten days – do try."

Hearing another 'but' she jumped in. "No, Jason. No more buts. For once, you will do as I ask."

She disconnected without waiting for his response and wished she had been using an old-style cradle phone so she could physically slam the receiver down. Instead, she threw her cell phone onto the bed.

The feeling of euphoria disappeared faster than water down a plughole. With a deep sigh, her anger dissolved to be replaced by despondency. She was disappointed in her son's reaction. What was wrong with Jason? Since Tony had gone, she'd hardly seen anything of him. Now he obviously didn't want to share family time either.

Megan's Diary
10 December 2010 – Portreath

I'm a bit in limbo while I wait for legal papers to be finalised. I think I will have to wait until next year now before I can tell anyone anything formally. I'm spending more and more time with Jessica while we sort everything out. She's a nice girl, and I like her. I enjoy talking with her about life in Cornwall in general. Meanwhile, I'm filling in time sightseeing.

Cornwall has such a fascinating history and is famous for its shipwrecks, smuggling and pirates. Mining was the source of the family's wealth, until it slipped into serious decline and ceased any significant dealings by the early twentieth century. That forced the Trevallyans to find other sources of income, even before Constance took control.

I've driven around much of the southern part and visited many of the places I've read about. I enjoyed exploring in and out of little coves and hamlets because they are there. I could write a book about my travels, but I won't – not here anyway. Photos will tell their own story when I get back.

I love visiting these quaint villages steeped in history. I went to Cadgwith – the tiniest of villages with claims to being the second home of some artist and his artist wife. At the opposite end of the scale, I managed to squeak in a trip to the Eden Project. What an amazing place. Nothing historic about their look or approach, the place is all about the future.

Winter in Cornwall is not as good as I'd hoped. Whether it's the lowering cloud, sea mist or fog, which cloaks the entire peninsula making visibility almost nil, or the famous gale winds that pound the sea against the cliffs, I find the whole area very desolate.

I feel lonely and miss Tony so much. I'm trying not to wish he was with me all the time, but travelling on my own is not fun.

CHAPTER 12

Their Hawaiian resort on one of the outer islands – hidden well away from the hustle and bustle of Waikiki – was close to paradise. The three side-by-side bungalows, with a large private swimming pool and garden, led directly onto the almost-white sand beach and blue ocean beyond.

"Mum, what a fabulous place," said Sarah gushing. "Much more than I expected. This is pure luxury."

Megan was stretched out on the sunlounger under the shade of a large canopy when her daughter joined her later in the day. Sarah threw her towel on the adjacent lounger and looked across at Bella who was playing happily close by – she'd quickly worked out she could wander between Nana's room and her own without Mummy calling her.

Megan wondered how to approach things. She was nervous about all the news she had to tell them and wondered how they would react. In her disquiet, she overcompensated by over organising. "I've ordered a barbecue pack delivery around five o'clock. Everything comes prepared, other than cooking the fish and meats, that is. I thought it easier for us to have a dinner 'at home', so to speak, on your first night. I checked out one of the restaurants last night, too, and have some ideas for the next few days and nights, but right now you probably need a restful evening more than anything else. Jet lag will catch up sooner or later." Megan finished rattling off her speech.

"Stop fussing, Mum. It sounds ideal. Just like this place … but, um, you will get around to telling us what all this is about soon, won't you?" Sarah hid her eyes behind sunglasses, clearly not expecting Megan to answer immediately.

Her mother didn't disappoint and changed the topic. "Jason's plane lands late tomorrow afternoon, and I've booked for Christmas Eve dinner. And before you ask, I've also booked a babysitter for Bella."

"That's going a bit overboard, isn't it?"

"Not really. Then after dinner I'll come back here and stay with her. You young ones can go party somewhere to your hearts' content."

"Nice idea, Mum, but you've forgotten one thing."

"What's that?"

"Bella knows Christmas means presents. She'll be up with the sun – if not before. I can't afford to party all night."

"That's OK, I've thought of that, too. She can sleep in my unit, and I'll see to the early morning and the Christmas stocking. I can take her to see the super-large Christmas tree displays around the complex until you're all up, and then we can meet up for breakfast. And I've taken care of Christmas dinner."

Sarah sat up, whipped off her sunglasses and glared at Megan. "Mum! Stop this. Stop gabbling and stop organising. You don't have to take care of Bella, or us, for that matter," she snapped, vaguely waving her hand. "Or all this."

"I wanted to spoil you a little." Surprised by Sarah's reaction, Megan put her hand on the girl's arm. "Please. Let me do this. After what I've found out in the last couple of months, I've realised how important family is. And what *not* having a family to care about can do to a person."

* * * * *

Megan checked Jason's flight schedules twice during the afternoon, wishing the hours would pass more quickly. Even though he would think her gestures unnecessary, she booked a car to collect him and ordered a welcome basket, and asked Sarah and Nick to let her see Jason alone. If only she could see his face before the shutters came down again, it might help her read his thoughts and understand what was going on.

With nothing more to do except wait, Megan tried reading. Idly flicking through a magazine, she hoped something would distract her, to no avail. Feeling unsettled, she threw the magazine on the couch and began pacing again, constantly looking at her watch as the minutes slowly ticked by. Finally, she grabbed her hat and sunglasses and strode out the door towards the beach. Maybe a walk would fill in enough time and give her something else to focus on.

She arrived back at the bungalows feeling more relaxed and surprisingly refreshed, despite the heat. Thinking to do a last-minute check on everything in

Jason's suite, she slid open the ranch slider in time to overhear Jason speaking to someone she couldn't see; his voice seemed to come from the bedroom.

"I'm sorry. I don't mean to shut you out. I really don't. But, please, please, let me see Mum first and try to explain to her."

Megan didn't hear the response but distinctly got the impression this conversation was ongoing and unresolved.

Jason appeared as she was on the point of deciding whether to sneak out, pretending she hadn't heard anything, or to announce herself. His face fell. Looking ·uncomfortable and flushed, he dashed forward and wrapped her in a brief hug. "Mum! How wonderful to see you. How long have you been standing there? Sorry, I didn't hear you knock." His tone indicated rebuke, yet the words were said at such a pace they simply confirmed his agitation. He rushed on, while opening the fridge to investigate its contents before Megan could speak. "I could do with a drink. It's so hot here. Do you want anything?"

"Thank you, yes. You can pour me a white wine." By biting her tongue, she stopped herself saying anything further until he'd had a chance to explain. She threw her hat and sunglasses on the nearby chair and crossed the room to sit on the couch. Jason made small talk about the flight, its early arrival and getting through customs, as he opened and shut cupboards looking for glasses and pouring drinks. At last he sat at the other end of the L-shaped couch and almost drained his beer in one go.

"What's all this about, Mum? Why the secrecy and your insistence we 'be here together'? It really has been a hassle."

"Hassle? You think spending Christmas with your mother and sister and her family is a hassle?" Her voice rose uncontrollably as she struggled to contain the hurt.

"Well, no. Not exactly, I didn't quite mean it that way. I meant the hassle of having to make bookings and change plans, and stuff. And for what reason? Other than Christmas, I fail to understand."

Tempted to tell him to go to hell, she swallowed the rising bitterness. "You shouldn't need to understand, Jason. You're here because I asked you, and I'd hoped you'd be pleased to see me. However, I won't detain or bother you more than I have to."

A few moments' silence followed. She tried to get hold of her emotions and not explode with anger or say things she couldn't take back. "Who have you got hiding in the bedroom?"

The look on his face confirmed he was indeed hiding something – and someone. Resentment flared between them.

"Don't try lying, Jason. I didn't mean to invade your privacy. I didn't know you were here. You arrived early, as you pointed out. I opened the door and heard you speaking and, as there doesn't appear to be anyone else in the room at the moment ..."

She looked around the room to make her point. "Were you talking to yourself? Or is there someone else here?"

Her polite sarcasm was not lost on him.

Jason ran his hand through his hair and, turning his face away from his mother, looked out the window to the view beyond. Megan studied her boy carefully. Her heart skipped a beat. He looked so much like a younger version of his father. His hair, dark and wavy like hers, gleamed, and his skin was clear. Although his eyes were turned away, she remembered their deep brown depths and the extra-long lashes that used to make his sister jealous. Long-limbed, slim and graceful – a rather unusual way of describing a man maybe, but the image popped into her head. He looked a picture of health and, she suddenly realised, happiness. In contrast, his pose was tense and his movements jerky.

Abruptly, he stood and headed into the bedroom. Minutes passed. Megan sat as quietly as she could and tried to control the fear growing inside. Fear of what, she wasn't sure, but something odd was going on here. More minutes passed. She sipped her wine slowly.

Finally, she heard the door behind her open.

"Mum." He sounded more strained than earlier. "I'd like you to meet someone."

Megan rose and turned towards him.

"What's the matter, Jason? You know your friends are always welcome."

Jason didn't answer. He simply stepped aside so Megan could see a petite girl with dark hair cascading over her shoulders. She looked beautiful.

"This is Caterina. Trina, my wife."

Megan gasped and shot him a look of total confusion. "Your wife?"

She turned to look at the girl again – she was obviously nervous and biting her lip. In a matter of seconds, Megan's thoughts covered a lot of ground. She resorted to formality as the only way to stay in control. She would talk to Jason in private later. Now was not the time to subject the girl to a family fight.

"I'm sorry Jason didn't see fit to introduce us sooner. I'm very pleased to meet you and look forward to knowing more about you."

Megan took a few steps towards the girl and extended her hand, which Trina shook. At least the girl was smiling now, shyly.

"I'm sure you have your reasons for not telling me, Jason, and I can't deny I'm hurt by your decision. I would like an explanation but not now. It's Christmas Eve. Let's enjoy the evening and get to know one another better over dinner. Your sister will be back shortly. I'll tell her you're here. I'm sure she will be thrilled with your news. You won't recognise Bella. She's grown so much. Dinner is at seven."

Her rapid staccato sentences blocked any response. Collecting her hat and sunglasses, Megan made her escape. If she stayed any longer, she would not be able to contain her anger nor the tears threatening to overflow.

* * * * *

Before she had a chance to tell Sarah about Jason and Caterina, Megan knew the girl was out of sorts and not her usual cheerful self. Now Sarah exploded. She was furious at what he'd done and wanted to rush straight in and confront him, but Megan begged her not to cause a scene.

"For Trina's sake."

Caterina deserved to be made welcome. It was not her fault. The time to talk to Jason alone would come later.

"Don't let him off the hook like that. He's been abominably selfish!"

For the first hour, an uncomfortable tension settled around the dinner table. The process of ordering drinks and food gave them time to sort their thoughts into what could and could not be said.

Trina unwittingly saved the evening and quickly became the focus of their attention. "My family came from Tuscany originally, from a village not far from Florence. The family is large with numerous branches," she explained. "Sometimes the eldest cousin of one branch is old enough to be the parent of cousins in another branch. It's all far too complicated to explain unless you've grown up with it."

Happy to share her story, her new family gratefully plied Trina with questions, which solved two problems. First, it avoided the necessity of having to talk to each other, bypassing topics that could erupt into accusations and arguments, and second, it gave them all a chance to learn a bit about her.

"Does anyone else in your family work in the creative arts?" asked Sarah, interested to learn Trina had an arts degree.

"Long time ago my great-grandfather was an artist – although not a very famous one. He earned his money painting frescoes and ceilings in some of the wealthy homes and a few of the smaller churches. Being an artist was different, better than being a peasant. My grandmother talked about him a lot. She was proud of him."

"What did your grandmother and mother do?" asked Megan.

"Nonna was a great cook and ran her own *ristorante*, becoming famous locally for her pasta sauces, but not my mama. She rebelled, escaping the kitchen as soon as she could. She loved fashion and was drawn to America, to what New York could offer."

"Is that why your English is so good?" asked Sarah.

"No, not exactly. I learnt English at university. She met my father in America, but I grew up in Italy. Unfortunately, her dreams didn't work out."

"What a pity. What happened?" queried Megan.

"She wanted to be a *stilista di moda* – a fashion designer, you know. She was full of hopes but she ended up working long hours in one of the rag trade factories as a machinist. My father soon lost interest and one day never came home again."

"I'm sorry to hear that. A child needs a family. It must have been difficult for you and your mum."

"On the contrary. That is not what I meant at all. Mama returned to Italy. I had family; I was raised by everyone – my mother, my grandparents, uncles, aunts and cousins. Mine was a good childhood, just no father. My mother's dreams eventually did come true in a different way."

Trina's story enthralled them, and some of the tension eased. "My uncle was, by then, in the leather trade, so the family established a shop selling shoes and handbags. Mama was in her element and proved a natural retailer. She began telling the designers what women wanted from their handbags and shoes. She was the one who introduced colour and styles no one had considered before. The shop quickly became very popular, growing into the upmarket and exclusive boutique it is today."

"Does your mother still run the store?" asked Megan, interested in the story of a like-minded woman.

"Sadly, no. She died of cancer ... September last year."

Megan considered the coincidence with Tony's date too frightening for words. She smothered the gasp seeking to escape but Sarah saw the fleeting expression on her mother's face and quickly stepped in.

"How awful for you. And our condolences, of course, but how odd. Our Dad died last September, too."

"Yes, I know. Jason told me. I'm sorry." Trina's voice dropped to a whisper.

Sarah threw an angry look at her brother. "Yes. I suppose he would have. But then, you would know a lot more about us than we know about you. Wouldn't she, Jason?"

Sarah paused to check her temper before turning back to Trina. "It seems we share more than we realised. Hard as these things are. But to better news ... tell me – when did you and Jason meet?"

Trina looked askance at Jason. He had remained unusually silent during the conversation. Now he shifted uncomfortably in his chair and refilled his wine. Everyone waited.

Clearing his throat, he muttered, "December. Two years ago."

Even Nick was astounded. "And you never told anyone? Why man, for goodness' sake, why? After all your mother and sister have been through. You should be ashamed of yourself." He got up and left the table.

"That was the Christmas you didn't come home, I remember now." Sarah's voice sounded flat and barely above a whisper. "The last one Dad had."

Megan sensed Sarah was extremely angry. Nick, too, she thought, since his reaction was out of character. He didn't often express an opinion on matters between siblings – especially not in public.

"How could you?" Sarah hissed between gritted teeth.

Jason jerked his head towards Sarah, his face reddening with rage. "Now, listen here ..."

Megan, worried harsh words would be said that could not be retracted, quickly spoke over him. "Stop it, you two. Now is not the time. We are supposed to be celebrating. And welcoming Caterina to the family. Jason, go dance with your wife."

CHAPTER 13

Oh, Tony, where did I go wrong? A small tear escaped the corner of her eye as Megan lay in bed after a restless night. Her earlier suggestion the young ones go partying together didn't eventuate. Jason, eagerly taking his mother's advice, disappeared onto the dance floor with Trina and never returned. Sarah went in search of Nick, saying she would have an early night, leaving Megan at the table on her own.

So here she lay, at dawn on Christmas morning, alone and agitated – although Tony had, again, been annoyingly logical during their midnight discussions. *"Trust him, darling. I'm sure he had his reasons,"* but she needed to hear them.

Megan had left Jason a note asking him to join her for a walk this morning. With an hour to fill before she expected him, she rose, dressed in off-white linen trousers and tunic, threw back the curtain on a perfect scene and made some tea. About the time she started fretting whether Jason would turn up, he appeared at the door.

"Good morning. I was hoping you'd join me. Tea? Coffee?"

He shook his head.

"Let's walk then."

Linking her arm in his, she guided him down to the beach chatting idly. They were forced to separate as they made their way across the soft sand. Jason took the chance to put distance between them as he splashed through the waves ebbing and flowing on the shore.

Megan broke the silence. "I know your father's heart attack came as a shock. It was a shock to all of us – there'd been no hint. There was no time to prepare or say our goodbyes." She paused briefly. How would she say what needed to be said? By keeping a rigid control on her temper, she hoped to sound calm and rational. "His death deeply affected us all – separately and collectively – and we're still coming to terms with our loss, in our own way. I understand that. I tried to explain that to myself as months went by and I barely heard from you."

Megan paused again to give Jason time to say something, but he remained silent.

"Now I find out you and Trina have been together for over two years. Two years! You knew each other for months before your father died but didn't think to tell us you had someone important in your life! Not once! Why, Jason, why?"

Still Jason said nothing.

Megan could feel her control slipping as her anger bubbled closer to the surface. "I have no idea what is going on with you, or why you wanted to exclude your family from your life, but I think I deserve an explanation. Don't you?"

A few moments of awkward silence followed before

Jason hesitantly answered. "I'm sorry. I didn't mean to exclude you or hurt you."

"Well, you managed both," her bitter tone not helping him one little bit.

"It was a kind of a long-distance relationship to start with, and I didn't think there was much to tell. But the months went by and then her mum got really sick."

Now Megan remained silent. They walked on side by side while Megan waited for him to speak again.

"Trina was upset. We talked every day and met up as often as we could. Sometimes we'd meet halfway between Milan and wherever my flight landed, or at the airport, depending on the schedule." He obviously didn't spend a lot of time in London where he supposedly lived. "Or I'd go to her. And you heard how large her family is and everything. They welcomed me and ..."

"And, what, Jason? It's not as if you don't have a family of your own who welcome you – and your friends."

"Well, yes, I know, but this was different, Mum. New. Exciting. They were fun times. Lots of food and laughter ... and Trina and I ... we were happy together."

Megan stole a sideways glance at his face as he looked out to sea. She could read the torn emotions of this happy–sad story in his expression. Still shocked and bewildered by his secrecy, she'd started to grasp how important this girl was to him. His voice was different when he talked about Trina, almost impassioned. But Megan wasn't going to let him see that yet.

"Her mum wanted to see Trina married before she died. The only thing she talked about – the only thing that kept her going was the thought there would be a wedding."

"So?"

Clearly disconcerted by her terse response, Jason tried again to explain it better. "Trina broke down one night, sobbing her heart out. I didn't know how to deal with her grief and thinking it would help, sort of suggested we do it. Get married, I mean. I ... um, you know me, impulsive at the best of times. But then I didn't know how to tell you and Dad."

Not telling them was the part that really hurt. Not that he'd found a girl or fallen in love or hadn't got around to telling them, but getting married without them cut her deeply. Trina's mother got her wish. Why not them?

Megan stopped walking to look at Jason. "A simple phone call to say, 'hey, I'm getting married, do you want to come?' would've done. Explanations could've come later." With mounting despair, she failed to keep her anger under control and out of her voice. "Why was it so hard to tell us, Jason? Why couldn't your dad and I have been given the same respect as Trina's mother? Why!"

Jason stepped back from the force of her fury. "I don't know," he said honestly. "I don't know why I didn't. It all happened so fast. I could hardly believe it myself."

He told her how it had only taken a couple of days to organise. He'd been caught up in the commotion and any opportunity he might have had got lost.

Megan watched her son's face. She couldn't help wondering whether he'd made the right decision. What sort of marriage would they have given the circumstances? He looked bewildered and distressed, which was unlike Jason. Against her will, her heart went out to him. They started walking again. "I'm not sure I want to hear the answers, but I need to know two things. Firstly, when was your wedding?" Megan held her breath.

"The twenty-eighth of August."

A gasp escaped before she regained control. "Only days before your father died! Oh, Jason. I'm not sure why, but that makes it worse." She took another deep breath. "When did Trina's mother die?"

"Two weeks after Dad."

Megan's eyes widened with shock. "But ... I don't understand. That doesn't explain why you took off the day after your father's funeral with barely a word of goodbye, leaving me ..."

She broke off, quickening her pace to put space between them while she fought back tears. Straining through the soft sand, she headed towards the palm trees edging the beach. She didn't expect to be so upset by the news and struggled to accept he deliberately denied his father the chance to see him settled and happy. Regardless of the circumstances. They would have been happy for him. Instantly, she appreciated why Constance had put such store on loyalty.

Jason caught up with her. "I'm sorry, Mum. I really am." He reached out to catch her arm. "What can I say to make it up to you?"

Stopping again, she turned to look at him. "Actually, Jason. I don't think there is anything you can say. What's done is done. I'm going to have to figure out a way to forgive you, but don't think for one moment I will ever forget."

Jason looked suitably embarrassed and kicked at the sand with his bare feet. "She needed me, Mum." His eyes pleaded for forgiveness. "We were planning to go to New Zealand, as soon as her mother ... um ... when it was ... over – to tell you together. We thought we'd have a proper ceremony and party at home. But when Dad went like that, it didn't feel right any more. You had your own pain to deal with. I didn't want to make it worse." He ran his fingers through his hair and paced a circle, trying to find the words. "Telling you without Trina with me didn't seem right either – and she couldn't leave her mother. The three events were so close together I was reeling. The more time passed, the more difficult it got until I couldn't figure out how to tell you at all. I know I was wrong. I'm sorry."

Megan listened to his explanation all the while trying to reconcile her bitter, angry thoughts with the overwhelming love she held for her son. She hated seeing him torn apart, but she was hurting, too. "So you hid yourself away and said nothing? Hoping it would somehow solve itself?"

Jason nodded in agreement. "I'm sorry, Mum. Honestly, I am. But I had to be with her. We needed to be together to get through it all." He paused again, his voice breaking with emotion. "She's my best mate. I think ... I hope we will share something like you and Dad ..." And in a voice barely audible, "Please understand."

Despite her distress, Megan understood perfectly. It was everything she had ever wished for her baby – to be happy, to find a soul mate. She knew she would give in and forgive him yet again, as she had many times in the past. He had never learnt his easy-going manner was, at times, careless of other people's feelings. Maybe his wife could teach him something she hadn't been able to. She let out a deep sigh. "Oh, Jason. What am I going to do with you?" Her rhetorical question hung unanswered between them. Taking a step towards him, she wrapped her arms around his neck. "I am happy you've found someone special, my boy."

Within seconds, he hugged her back, tightly, relief emptying from every pore.

Pulling out of the embrace, Megan pointed along the beach. "You should get back, but I need to keep walking. I'm still far too upset. I need time to think this through and calm down."

She started to move away, then turned and, walking backwards, called out, "Merry Christmas!"

Isabel's Journal
22 December 1910 – Nice

Our hostess in Nice is a very flamboyant Frenchwoman whom Mrs B met some years ago. I forget the story she told me, it was too complicated and involved, far too many people. It seems Mrs B likes to catch up with Madame Veronique Le Beau when she can, especially the times when lots of food is involved. A week or two at Christmas proves an opportunity too good to miss. At least the weather is fine and sunny. The rains have passed, and while it isn't hot, it is mild enough to walk along the promenade.

Mme Le Beau is an odd mix. In the evenings she wears the most fashionable of gowns: sleek, floating silks and voiles sometimes heavily embroidered or beaded (although I suspect she still wears her old-fashioned corsets underneath), but her morning gowns are outdated: full, flared, frilled and lacy with huge petticoats, under which, I suspect, she doesn't wear corsets at all. How odd! She loves to smoke those new Gauloises. She constantly carries an excessively long cigarette holder, which can become quite dangerous if you are too close; such is her habit of waving her arms about when speaking. However, she is welcoming, and her villa is comfortable with wonderful views of the bay.

It's strange being here in a foreign place with strangers at Christmastime. I wonder what is happening at home. Not that Christmas at home was much fun anyway. Mama was a tyrant when organising the traditional social events. Francis could do no wrong, and Constance was allowed to do almost anything she wanted, as long as she wasn't underfoot. I was just someone to parade about at parties with her hinting all the time what a great prize I would be for someone. It was a meat market, and I was the meat – a nuisance with too many ideas. I enjoyed the music, the lights and the boring old neighbours who sometimes brought new visitors. I can't help but miss them, especially Papa.

CHAPTER 14

By the time Megan returned from her walk everyone was up and sharing in Bella's joy over the goodies from her Christmas stocking. Bella rushed up and jumped into her arms.

"Nana, Nana. See what I got."

For a couple of minutes Megan concentrated all her attention on her granddaughter. The day had not started out quite as she had imagined, and she was sad she'd missed an important part of the morning with Bella, but talking to Jason was more important.

He wasn't forgiven, not yet, not by a long way, and it would take more time before she could begin to forget. Megan hoped the rest of the day would prove festive, even if Jason and Sarah avoided one another. At least he seemed to have recovered some of his natural exuberance.

A knock on the door announced the arrival of room service brunch. Putting on their best behaviour, the family trooped out on the terrace to drink bubbles and orange juice and wear silly Christmas hats. They soon slipped into the spirit of the day with carefully chosen words and shared laughter over presents exchanged.

Bella eased any remaining disquiet. Squealing and laughing, she helped everyone rip the paper from their gifts before running around putting the fancy hats on every head and then taking them off again. Before long, with paper strewn from one end of the terrace to the other and everyone having received and given something, they looked expectantly at Megan.

Sarah spoke first. "Thanks for everything, Mum. You've spoilt us rotten, and I love this bracelet." She stretched her arm out to show off her gift. "It's been fantastic, but I think it's time you told us why you brought us all here."

Megan lifted Bella onto her knee, to help push buttons on some new electronic toy Jason had bought.

"You have a choice," said Megan, somewhat tongue-in-cheek. "A long, lazy afternoon swimming, walking, talking, or sleeping and getting ready for dinner. Or I can completely upset the applecart and bore your socks off with tales of my journey so far."

"I think Bella, Trina and I should take the first choice and make ourselves scarce," said Nick with an exaggerated yawn. "Sarah and Jason can stay and listen to your so-called boring tales." They knew he was teasing, while at the same time offering to give them space if they wanted it.

"No way," said Sarah, before anyone else had a chance. "If I have to listen to Mum's tales then so do you. However, I suspect what she's about to tell us will be anything but boring."

"I agree, Nick. Sorry. If we talk now, I think you and Trina should listen. It'll concern you all sooner or later." Hesitating briefly and trying not to sound harsh, Megan quizzed her son. "Jason? What about you? Where do you stand?"

"Fine by me," he answered with an eloquent shrug. "After all, you went out of your way to make this happen. Let's hear it."

"Good choice. You're not off the hook yet, by any means, but you're making progress." She sent him a glance she imagined he would remember from his childhood.

It worked.

"Truce, Mum." He raised his hands in supplication. "I'll make it up to you, I promise."

A look of renewed understanding passed between them.

"And I'll keep you to that promise."

Megan saw Sarah's enquiring look and nodded to confirm things were on the mend. There was no point in making matters worse between him and Sarah. His sister needed to work out how she felt about Jason's behaviour by herself.

"Righto, Mum. Let's get on with it, shall we?"

"All right. I'm as ready as I ever will be. But listen, there's a lot to take in, and it could take a while. Let me tell you what I know first – without interruptions, please. You can ask questions later."

As briefly as possible, she outlined how she fitted into the family tree, the people she'd met, about the loss of the family fortune and, especially, what she'd discovered about Constance and why her history was important.

The family had been unable to resist butting in with the odd question, but Megan managed to keep them more or less on track.

"And you should see the library. The panelling is superb," she finished, with a detailed description of the house. "Constance and someone before her were avid book collectors."

"How fascinating," said Sarah, although Megan could tell the boys were not interested in the manor house.

"Can you tell us more about Isabel?"

"Not yet, sweetheart. Great-grandmother Isabel's story is yet to come. She's hardly remembered in Cornwall and wasn't there for the time period I'm talking about."

It had taken Megan quite some time to get that far with her story, and she'd still kept back the bit about her inheritance and its wrinkles. She wasn't sure why she was withholding the most important part of the story, but it seemed right that Constance's story be told first.

"Enough for the time being, I think. I need a drink."

Given how quickly the men took off, heading straight for the pool, Megan figured they weren't all that interested in her family history. From their point of view, it wasn't all that meaningful so far – that part would come – but Megan wanted them to know the background to it first.

Sarah went to get the drinks with Bella. Trina remained, tentatively asking questions about the décor and the paintings. Encouraged by Trina's interest, Megan chatted on, pleased to discover they shared a similar love of antiquity.

She had been tempted to blame Trina for much of Jason's behaviour but knew that would be unfair on the girl. It wasn't her fault. Jason was responsible for his own actions. More importantly, she was beginning to like her new daughter-in-law and could see why Jason had been smitten. The girl was quiet but strong-willed and would anchor Jason to the real world.

"I'm sorry, Trina. With everything that's happened, I don't think we've done a good job of welcoming you to the family, nor found the time to get to know you better. I will, I promise. I'm so happy we have some interests in common."

"That's all right, Mrs Marsh," began Trina.

"Call me Megan, please. Mrs Marsh is far too formal, and I would like us to be friends."

"Megan, then. Thank you and yes, I would like to be friends, too. Jason talks about you all the time."

"He does?" Megan's eyebrows shot up.

"Yes, especially about what you and his dad shared." Trina reinforced Jason's words.

Megan was glad to know Jason valued his parents' relationship, despite his silences over the last couple of years. Whilst she would always be disappointed, for Tony's sake, she must learn not to dwell on it. "Tell me, Trina. Where do you work?"

"I work for a fine art dealer in Milan."

"How amazing. What a wonderful thing to do. But how did you and Jason meet? I don't think I've ever seen him in an art gallery in his life."

Trina laughed. "No, and you still won't, not willingly anyway. He looks like a fish out of water. He came to my rescue." Her eyes turned lovingly in his direction. "I slipped on some cobblestones on my way home after working late at an art auction. I fell, twisting my ankle, and broke the heel off my shoe. He picked me up and carried me home. The rest is history, as they say."

"Are you two still gossiping over there?" called Jason, coming back inside.

"We're not gossiping. We're sharing stories." She winked at Megan.

"Well, whatever you want to call it, sweetheart," Jason said, putting his arm around her, "enough of the tête-à-tête. We'd better hear the rest of Mum's story before dinner."

"Yes, Mum. Let's make the most of it while Bella has a nap, before we have to get ready," echoed Sarah.

"What, now? Can't it wait till tomorrow or the next day?" Megan was worried she was overloading them.

"No," came the chorus.

"Oh dear," she said, sitting down again. "Well, all right. This next piece is about Constance and the family business. It's also long and complicated, I'm afraid."

Once everyone was settled comfortably, Megan began.

"It seems our Constance Trevallyan had two sides to her, depending on who you talk to. The compassionate side, shown only to the people who had cared for her when she was young, and the ruthless businesswoman side."

"Business first," interrupted Jason. "I want to know what it means for us."

Megan related how, after her brother's death, Constance uncovered the extent of his recklessness and financial losses, by which time the family fortune had all gone.

"She had no option but to find ways to rebuild. By callously buying and selling failing businesses at rock-bottom prices, she ended up owning shares in most of the growth industries of the time – railways, refrigeration, fishing fleets and farms. Constance was a seriously wealthy woman, hated by some and beloved by others." This time she'd grabbed the boys' attention.

"Do we get anything?" asked Jason.

"I'm getting to that. Just wait."

Like her when she'd first heard the details, Megan's audience struggled to comprehend half of what she told them. She sympathised. The weight of her words would take time to sink in.

Nick, whose business brain was working overtime, couldn't resist asking questions.

"Yes, that's right," she answered. "Even today Constance controls what happens; it was all in her will. She bought loyalty. Everyone in the corporation gets a bonus based on how much profit goes to charity. The bigger the one, the better the other."

With its many twists and turns, Megan found it difficult to clearly outline the whole situation but persevered nevertheless. "The trust running the hotel and estate has to keep it more or less as it was. The descendants of the original families benefit hugely if they remain working on the estate. If not, they get nothing."

Megan reached for a glass of water, watching the four faces staring at her. The silence lengthened.

Jason asked the obvious question. "What's all this to do with us?"

"This part? Nothing, directly."

"Damn. And I thought you were going to tell us there was money in it," Jason laughed, dismissing the whole idea. "Oh, well. Too bad. Let's go to dinner. I'm starved."

Already a little uncomfortable knowing she hadn't told them everything, Megan quickly agreed. She hadn't yet mentioned dear old Constance's ashes or the conditions attached to her personal fortune, despite the opening Jason had given her. She wanted to pick the right time for that little bombshell.

The menu for Christmas luncheon is being discussed at length with heated disagreements between Cook, Mme Le Beau and Mrs B as to whether it should be goose or turkey as the main course. The argument against goose is that the foie gras will be served earlier. Whatever the outcome of their decision – although I would prefer turkey – there will be no moving Madame on the dessert menu. There will be what she calls 'Bûche de Noël', a yule log, which sounds to me like a rolled sponge cake filled with jam and cream covered in chocolate. She assures me I will love it, as I will the nougat made with candied nuts and fruit.

"Tu vas l'adorer, ma chère fille," she keeps telling me, "ça adorez." Time will tell how many of these so-called delicacies I will love. Some of them sound totally unpalatable.

One tradition I do like the sound of is what Mme Veronique calls 'Les Treize Desserts'. She says they symbolise the twelve apostles and Jesus and are often accompanied by thirteen different wines.

In Provence, apparently, the final dessert consisting of crushed almonds candied with melons and fruit syrup, dating back to the 15th century, is called 'Calisson d'Aix'. Now, that does sound delicious. She also informs me, if Cook has anything to say, they will serve sweet pastries, biscuits, dried fruit and nuts, tarts and quince jellies as well.

These desserts are to be set out tonight, Christmas Eve, where they remain for three days. Apparently, we will set it up before we go to midnight Mass. I do not particularly like the Catholic Mass, but as her guest I cannot decline, much as I would like to. Mother would have a fit if she knew. Church of England has always been good enough for Mother.

I think Mrs B and Mme Veronique will probably drink all of those thirteen wines if their practice so far is anything to go by. The climate here is such that a wine in the afternoons on the verandah is very pleasant, and we often linger into the evening before dining quite late.

CHAPTER 15

The days, filled with previously planned outdoor activities, were ticking by far too quickly. Unwilling to spoil their holiday fun, Megan hadn't found the right time to tell them the rest of her news. Much to her delight, Jason asked if he and Trina could stay on for one more day, giving her more time to think.

On their last night together, Megan decided to come clean. So far, the story of a small endowment from Isabel's dowry had explained how she could afford this holiday for them all. Now she'd run out of excuses.

Curled up on the couch with a hot chocolate, Sarah said, "It seems sad to me. Constance had all this money but no family to share in her success. I wonder why she never married."

"I suppose we'll never know, but I think she was an unhappy young woman who felt betrayed and abandoned by her entire family."

"What do you mean by that?" asked Nick. "She had an empire and a fortune in the end."

"Maybe, but look at her life. At age ten, her world turned upside down within a short space of time. Her

118

father died and her mother Eleanor was effectively lost to her not long after."

"What happened to her mother was very sad," said Trina, having learnt Eleanor's minor stroke most likely started her long decline into dementia. Left in the care of a nurse, she'd lived out her life in one wing of the house.

"She's not the only person to have lost a parent," muttered Jason ungraciously.

"No, she wasn't." Megan cast a sympathetic look his way. "But she lost her sister Isabel, too, when she disappeared overseas in disgrace, and soon after Constance found herself packed off to boarding school.

"To top it off, her brother Francis never cared for anyone but himself. The thought of losing her home – the one tangible thing she knew and treasured – must have been terrible. She was determined to keep it, and through it all she became a tough woman to be reckoned with."

Silence settled on the group as they digested Megan's compact version of events.

"Is that why she deliberately cut the family off from sharing any part of her estate?" asked Trina, innocently presenting Megan the opportunity she'd been waiting for.

Megan sighed, exhausted by the emotional topsy-turvy of the last months and the intense outpouring of the last two days, but it was now or never. "I don't know to be honest. But there's more to this story."

"Well, it's been a good story so far, Mum," said Sarah. "I know it's been a lot to take in and hard to believe. For all of us," Sarah included the others with a wave of her hand, "but what an amazing adventure. Something worthy of those TV programmes, *Heir hunters* or *Who do you think you are?*"

Megan laughed. "How true! I do feel like that sometimes."

"Come on then, out with it," encouraged Sarah.

Megan sat forward to the edge of the sofa, hands clasped on her knees, wondering why every nerve in her body was on edge. "Um. The fact is ... I'm about to come into a lot of money, more than I hinted at."

After a brief hesitation as the news sunk in, Jason burst out, "I knew it! I knew there was something more to it. Come on, cough up. How much?"

Everyone began talking at once. Megan didn't know whom to answer first. "Several million pounds!"

"Wow!" Nick whistled.

"How amazing," said Trina.

"Sorry I didn't say anything before. I'm still getting used to the idea. I don't know how to handle that much money."

"Oh, Mum. Don't worry. It's wonderful news," said Sarah, her face beaming.

"Yes, Mum. Great news. We'll help you spend it."

Megan smiled at Jason's smart comment.

"It doesn't matter how you got it or what you do with it," said Nick, "it's none of our business, but I'm pleased for you. But make sure you invest it wisely and are set up for the rest of your life."

Trust Nick to be practical about it all, thought Megan gratefully, visibly relaxing now her secret was out. "Thanks. Some secrets are harder to share than others. Aren't they, Jason?"

This time laughter filled the room.

"Are we even now?" he asked, giving her a bear hug. He lifted her up and swung her around.

"Put me down," Megan squealed, smiling up at him to soften her words. "Closer, but not quite up to your standard yet."

"That pretty much winds up Constance's story, but there's Isabel's story to come. I don't know much. I don't know which name she lived under in New Zealand. From what little I do know, it seems Grandma Julia was born in Italy, not New Zealand, and was illegitimate. Isabel never married her daughter's father – and I'm not sure who he was. There's no name on the birth certificate."

"What?" exclaimed Sarah. "Are you sure?"

Megan told them about Gordon at the records office and how he was working on finding something to disprove his assumptions, but he was fairly certain. The point of her announcement had legal connotations. She waited for Nick to pick it up and wasn't disappointed.

"So, if I've got this right, you are the direct descendant of Isabel's illegitimate child?"

Megan nodded.

"And Constance disinherited all misbegotten children?"

"Right again."

"In which case, how did you receive any inheritance?"

Megan shrugged. "Guilt, maybe, over time. Who knows. But Constance made it hard. There are three strict provisos to be met. And she left me her ashes!"

"Her ashes?" Sarah interrupted.

"Yep. She asked that her ashes be stored until someone cared enough to bury them."

"Boy, was she a control freak or what?" said Jason.

Trina thought otherwise. "Oh, that's sad."

Megan agreed. "Towards the end of her life, I'm sure Constance questioned some of her decisions. The letter she wrote to her lawyer, the older Boscowan, undoubtedly showed a change of heart. I believe Constance eventually realised there was no one to care what happened to her, or take over from her, or inherit her money. I think it's why she tied the business up as she did – tying people to her memory. What she privately owned she left to the only family she had."

"Put that way, Mum, it sounds awful," said Sarah.

"It does rather, doesn't it? She spent some money on things she loved and decorated the house with glorious furnishings and paintings. And she must have spent a fortune building up her library collection, but it was a drop in the ocean."

"What's happened with the money since she died?" asked Jason.

"It's been sitting in the bank collecting interest since 1983. Her letter said she forgave her sister and wanted to leave her personal capital to 'the female matriline of my sister, Isabel' which, according to James, means her daughter Julia, and Julia's daughter Caroline, and so on. The males of the line were specifically excluded – no way would she let another man like Francis anywhere near her money. Since everyone has gone, that only left me."

"So, what *are* these provisions?" asked Nick, cutting back to the chase.

"The first is the easiest: Lay Constance's ghost to rest. Number two is to find Isabel, and three is to honour Isabel's name."

Chapter 16

Returning from her walk the next morning, Megan found them all talking over breakfast.

"I'm sure my mum would be willing to help out for a while," said Nick.

"What are you lot plotting?" asked Megan, giving them all a surprise.

The look of guilt on Sarah's face confirmed Megan's suspicions. "Oh. Hi, Mum, you're back ... Um. We're not plotting. Just worried."

"Worried about what, sweetheart?" Megan pulled up a chair and chose some fruit and cereal from the selection on the table, while Nick made her a fresh pot of tea.

"You," said Sarah. "When you started all this, I thought a holiday would be great for you, but it's not been a restful holiday, more like an ordeal."

Megan looked at her daughter's face and understood her concern, but surprisingly, after all she'd been through, she was more determined than ever to find Isabel. There were more secrets waiting to be discovered. Isabel had hinted at something significant happening before she returned to England, leaving her precious journal behind with much unsaid.

And Constance's wishes were yet to be fulfilled.

Megan tried to keep her voice light and teasing. "Hardly an ordeal, but I admit things turned out quite differently from what I expected. What were you talking about when I came in, if you weren't plotting?"

After a moment's hesitation, Jason answered. "The girls are worried about you. They thought you might need company, in case there are any more shocks." A glint of humour shone in his eyes as he smiled at his mother.

"Hey, don't land me with it," said Trina. "You were the one who said Sarah should go with Megan. I simply pointed out she had Bella to think of, and it wasn't as simple as you made it sound."

"Which is where I came in, I gather, with Nick suggesting his mum could help look after Bella. Am I right?"

"More or less," agreed Nick. "You've had a lot to contend with, and maybe you should accept their support."

"I agree with Nick, Mum. You're not the same person. There was you before Dad died, then there was reclusive you for the whole year after, and now, only four months later, there's this new you."

"And we don't know what to do, except keep an eye on you," explained Jason, doing his best to appear the supportive son.

Megan put her hand over Sarah's and looked around the table at the others. "I'm grateful for your concern, but please, this is my journey. It was my decision to trace my family tree, and I'm enjoying learning about the women in my past. Even with the shocks."

She turned towards Jason. "Don't take it away from me. Please, let me do it my way."

"Where to next?" asked Nick.

"Back to Cornwall to start with – there's the unfinished business with Constance's ashes and some farewells – then Paris and probably Nice. I'll make up my mind after that exactly which route to take."

"Sounds OK," said Sarah.

Megan thought the look on her face wasn't as convincing as her words. "How about meeting me in Florence?" she said, offering a compromise. "Sarah, can you find a way of getting time off? Trina, would you like to join me there and show me something of your city? Boys?"

The girls looked at each other, then at Megan. This time their faces matched their words.

"Yes."

"*Fantastico.*"

The boys shook their heads. "No thanks," said Jason. "Sounds like a girls' thing to me."

"I can't be in two places at once," seconded Nick. "You need me at home if Sarah's going."

Megan put her hand on Nick's arm. "Thank you for offering to share the load. And thanks to your mum as well. I'm sure she'll be delighted to spend some time with Bella."

As if on cue, the child came skipping in from playing outside. "Come play with me, Nana. Mummy and Daddy talk too much."

The adults laughed. Megan happily went to play with her granddaughter, but she wondered if she had done the right thing inviting Trina to Florence.

CHAPTER 17

Megan returned to Portreath and Trevennick Hall to finalise the last details with the Boscowans. Of the three tasks she had to do, the simplest was laying Constance's ghost to rest. She hoped James approved of her idea.

By chance, she had already started Task Two. After some discussion with James, they agreed that 'find Isabel' meant discover the sort of person she turned into and what she did with her life. In short, get to know her, something Megan had planned to do all along.

'Honour her name' would be more difficult. James believed that would come from finding out what Isabel did and what she was passionate about. Clearly, Constance believed it was something significant. Once Megan learnt what the 'it' was, she could honour it in some way.

After each task was completed, Megan would receive another portion of the inheritance.

Before going away for Christmas, she had James arrange for her to attend the next combined meeting of the Board of Governors and Trevennick Hall Trust Board in the middle of January. On the day, she dressed carefully in a smart suit, ready for whatever happened.

"Good morning, Mrs Marsh. Welcome." James Boscowan addressed her formally once they had completed the initial greetings and she sat at the table. "I have apprised everyone here of your attendance this morning, if not the exact reason. You are free to speak openly."

Megan looked around the room, pleased to see two familiar faces in Jenna and Tristan, and that of her new friend and lawyer, Jessica Boscowan. James, who had lost some of his stuffy demeanour the more she got to know him, was being particularly circumspect. The remaining members were a balanced mix of gender and age – as Constance had insisted in her will. Some of the older members looked exceedingly displeased. Megan's presence clearly offended some of them.

"Thank you," she said, matching their solemn manner. "To begin, I think it only fair you should officially know I am the great-grandniece of Constance Trevallyan. Her sister Isabel was my great-grandmother."

Immediately she sensed their antagonism. There were intakes of breath, shifting of positions and turning of heads, and too many faces wore vexed expressions for her comfort. Obviously, her revelation came as an unpleasant surprise to some, while others already knew or had guessed.

"Mr Boscowan can confirm I am able to prove my connection."

Whispered conversations between neighbours filled the awkward silence. Megan waited for the mutterings to quieten down.

"What does this mean for the board, and us as governors?" demanded Mr Chegwin, the chair, in a haughty tone.

"I understand – and accept – I do not have any control or influence over the Trevallyan Corporation or the Trevennick Hall Trust. Constance's will was specific, as I'm sure you all know, so I can put your minds to rest on that score. I will not contest her estate in any way. But can I say how pleased I am to see her wishes are being followed, even this far removed in time."

The board chair remained silent and glared at her icily. A few nodded, some wrote on their notepads, others questioned James. Megan sat quietly, but she sensed relief in some quarters at her saying she would not challenge the status quo.

"Is there anything you wish to add?" asked Mr Chegwin.

"I do have two requests, if I may. Firstly, in her last letter to Mr Boscowan Senior, Constance requested her ashes be stored in his vault and, I quote, 'until someone cares what happens to me'. I would like to lay Constance to rest and inter her ashes."

This statement brought another series of angry snorts, confused looks and shifting positions. The board were definitely put out and clearly hadn't known about the ashes either.

Undeterred, Megan continued. "I think the time has come to give something back and show our appreciation for her generous gifts. Do you agree?"

They had politely listened while she spoke, but now the chair and a few of the members were openly hostile. James fielded the sharp questions fired at him, and quietly confirmed her account, temporarily silencing them.

Now Megan had come this far, she'd decided to put all her cards on the table at once. She outlined her plan hoping they would consent. The fixed expressions remained on the faces of some of the older members, but she could also read agreement in the body language of others. Relieved that at least some of the board were on her side, she felt more comfortable about her second request.

"Secondly, I would like to purchase the small painting in the Isabel Room. In her journal Isabel described a painting of her and Constance when they were young and I believe it is the same one."

Megan heard a disconcerted harrumph, and a 'we'll see' comment muttered under someone's breath, but waited for Mr Chegwin to speak.

"Unfortunate as it seems," continued the chair in his same haughty tone, "since only you and James have knowledge of this letter, I believe the board is not in a position to deny you the right to do with Constance's ashes as you choose. However, I for one wish to make further enquiries before any action takes place. In regard to your question about the painting, that will require deeper consideration."

Megan considered his tone pompous and condescending but held her tongue.

"Thank you for coming in, Mrs Marsh. We will discuss your request more fully and advise you accordingly in due course."

She was dismissed.

Jessica rose to escort Megan from the room. "I'll be able to get away from here in half an hour or so," she whispered. "Can you meet me for coffee? Usual place?"

"Thanks, Jessica. Yes. See you there."

Wrapping her scarf around her shoulders on top

of her warm coat, Megan made her way into the slushy streets of Truro. The wind chill factor that bit through to the bone was a huge contrast to a few weeks earlier in Hawaii. Megan wondered why she'd chosen to come back here so soon. She could have gone to the south of France or Italy – just about any of the places Isabel and her Mrs B had gone chasing a milder winter – but she knew the answer. She had wanted to put on a celebration for all the staff at Trevennick Hall and tell them who she was. She wouldn't return once she left Cornwall to follow Isabel's travels. There would be no need. She had no responsibilities here – Constance had seen to that. Her task was to find and honour Isabel.

With her errands soon completed, Megan hurried down the narrow, historic street, happy to get out of the cold to wait for Jessica. The ancient pub where they liked to meet had a snug with lounge chairs and the best barista in town – a smart trader who knew she would entice the ladies into the snug on a regular basis if she offered good coffee.

"Hi, Eileen," called Megan as she went in. "Jessica's on the way. Our usual coffees, please."

"Righto. My, don't you look smart today. Get yourself warm by the fire, and I'll bring them through as soon as she comes in."

Megan had barely removed her gloves and coat when Jessica arrived. "That was quick. I've ordered coffee. Do you want anything to eat?"

"No, thanks."

"How did things go?" Megan was surprised by her jitters. The hostility and formality of the whole thing had been quite daunting.

"The place erupted after you left. Poor Dad. He really got it in the neck for not telling them. Mr Chegwin was awfully angry. But I agree with Dad. Her personal assets were hers to dispose of as she saw fit – including her ashes – and nothing to do with the corporation or the trust. Legally, he had no alternative. Dad could not reveal client confidentiality. Only you could do that."

"What's happening now?"

"The meeting split up. The Board of Governors is going to lunch and will reconvene to discuss the normal business of the day. One or two, led by Mr Chegwin, are asking for a second legal opinion, but Dad will sort that out. There's nothing to worry about. You're safe. Constance's will was bombproof. They might not like it, but they have no option. Dad will win them over now he's free to talk about you. The trust members are going back to Trevennick Hall."

Eileen arrived with the coffee at that moment, so they changed the subject as they briefly chatted with her about the weather and other bits of gossip.

"Constance was an odd one," said Jessica, sipping her coffee. "I can never figure her out." ·

"She said in one letter that she regretted some of her actions," said Megan. "Do you know what she meant by that?"

"The name Constance Trevallyan can conjure up stories of good deeds and bad. Families of the businesses she bought out cheaply loathe her, saying she destroyed their lives. The ones who worked for her and benefit from her largesse think she's a paragon. People are very traditional around here and have long memories. If your grandfather was one of 'her' people, then so are you. The

131

opposite also applies. She made sure people stuck by her by what she offered them. If not, different rules applied. Maybe she wished she hadn't wrecked so many small family businesses."

"Could be. She certainly tied people up in knots. She still has everyone jumping to her command," laughed Megan, knowing she was one of them.

"Does she ever! She still controls how the Hall is run through rules in the deeds. Modern bathrooms and kitchens, yes. Changes to the library, furniture or artwork, no. But I think she was a lonely soul."

"Hmm. I thought that, too," agreed Megan.

"By the way, Jenna asked if you would talk to her and Tristan when you get back."

"Of course. I was going to anyway, but what about? Did she say?"

"No. But I suspect it's about how they tell the whole extended trust family."

"I've got ideas about that."

* * * * *

By the time Megan returned to Trevennick Hall, the afternoon light was fading and her mind was in yet another whirl. Her path was laid out before her and required little or no input from her, whether she liked it or not.

Jenna and Tristan almost ambushed her the moment she stepped into the foyer. They ushered her into the library and closed the door behind them. Tristan didn't waste any time coming to the point.

"Firstly, let me say Jenna and I are on your side."

After all this time, they were pleased to know Constance had family, even if well removed and far away, and were genuinely upset they hadn't known about Constance's ashes.

"We think your idea a fitting outcome. You needn't have any doubts or worries on that score. Some of the older board members will need further persuasion, but that is our problem not yours. I have to admit I did wonder why you were here. There had to be more to it than just visiting."

"Thanks, Tristan, Jenna. I really appreciate your support. I kept thinking it could go horribly wrong today in the meeting. Some of them weren't all that friendly."

"But now the whole board knows," said Jenna, "it would be better to tell everyone else who might be involved who you are before the rumour mill gets out of hand and stories start spreading. If some of that crowd get a whiff of an outsider, resentment will set in before they know the full story. Then there'll be no shifting them."

"Sorry I didn't tell you earlier, but I needed to get used to my new status and tell my family in New Zealand before I could face telling anyone here."

"That's all right, we understand, but I think it would be better coming from us to start with."

They agreed Jenna would send a quick email around to the key people inviting them to a Cornish Cream Tea on the following Saturday afternoon where Megan could be introduced.

"You won't stop them, nosy to the last, every one of them. They'll all be here. After that, the news will soon get around. Mark my words."

"Wonderful. Thank you. Now, I'd like to talk about how to deal with these ashes."

Sitting in the wing-back chair under the image of Constance on the wall, Megan outlined her thoughts. It quickly became evident they really were on her side. They applauded her ideas and were prepared to persuade the rest of the community round to their way of thinking. But first they needed a detailed plan.

"Let's make it the tenth of February, Constance's birthday. That'll give us a little over three weeks to make the arrangements," suggested Jenna. "Tristan can organise the gardeners and landscaping with Kitto. He'll be absolutely delighted that we should ask him, won't he, Tristan?"

"Totally. He'll be over the moon, and nothing will stop him."

Megan's Diary
25 January 2011 – Portreath

I think my journey here is coming to an end and my time to move on is near. Nearly all the people I've met have been kind and helpful, but I'm a bit concerned about the reception I'll get on Saturday. I'm not sure who these people are that Jenna wants me to meet. I'm glad she and Tristan are taking charge. I suppose I should expect some resentment and dark mutterings from those who don't know me, but it's nothing to do with them.

I'm going way beyond Constance's demand that I 'lay her ghost to rest'. I only need to inter her ashes and not do any of the extras, but I feel I should. That way I will be more comfortable accepting Constance's bequest. I will have left something behind for them to remember me – and remind them of everything Constance gave them. I'm sure the next three weeks will be a flurry of activity and excitement, but after 'The Event', I am determined to be on my way.

Constance's story has overshadowed my purpose in being here. It's <u>her</u> character that is strong and lives in the hearts and minds of the locals. Isabel is but a faint memory.

Maybe I'll find more of Isabel when I get to Italy.

I do hope so.

.

CHAPTER 18

Megan awoke the morning of Constance's birthday, glad the day had finally arrived. This day was for the 'People of the Trust' as she came to call them. She rushed downstairs to help Jenna since they were expecting a large crowd for the unveiling and dedication at the interment. Jenna was right – word did get around and quickly. A smaller, select group had been invited to attend the evening event.

"Mornin', Miss Megan," said Kitto, entering from the garden.

"Good morning, Kitto. I'm glad I've seen you. I wanted to thank you for all the hard work you've put in to make this happen. And some of your ideas were brilliant. Thank you."

"Nothin' to it, Miss. Glad to help, just like I always 'ave. Any friend of Miss Constance is a friend o' mine. I came to check what time everythin' needed to be laid out."

As Megan and Kitto finished discussing the timetable, she expressed her concerns about the weather.

"Won't rain today," he reassured her. "With the fog this low this morning it'll take a while to clear, but it won't rain." Kitto put his cap back on. "The sun'll shine this afternoon, mark my words," he muttered over his shoulder as he waddled back to his domain.

Relieved by that piece of news, Megan went in search of Jenna. Over coffee they compared notes, ticked off what they could from the To Do List and double-checked every last detail.

By lunchtime, everything was in place. The chef, happy to experiment with new flavours and steadfastly refusing to let anyone else in his kitchen, had excelled himself.

"How you bulldozed so many people into helping today is beyond me, Jenna, but I'm grateful. I really wanted to make sure the key people and the families would be able to take part in the celebrations without having to do all the work. You've performed miracles."

Jenna smiled. "It's definitely who you know," she said with a laugh. "But thanks for agreeing to hire the extra people we needed. It's made all the difference. I've done my dash now, for today at least, as I want to be one of those people celebrating. It's time we got changed."

Linking her arm in Megan's, she guided them through the ballroom, which was beautifully decorated with drapery and Lowenna's amazing cream-and-white floral displays perched on stands, like in Edwardian times. They stepped into the reception area where there were more flowers, colourful and natural, collected from various local gardens. They took a quick peek in the library where the photographer was set up and checked the front lounge was ready to receive guests, before escaping to their rooms to get ready.

Dressed for the outdoors, Megan joined those representing the original families one hundred years ago on the front steps at two-thirty on the dot. As Kitto had predicted, the grey skies had lifted shortly after lunch, and the occasional glimpse of blue could now be seen.

It looked as if the whole village had turned out. As Jenna had said they would, everyone who had heard of this long-lost relative from Down Under wanted to see what she was like. The large crowd stood in a semicircle on the far side of the circular driveway. Positioned between them in place of an old garden sat the new addition to Trevennick Hall hidden by a tarpaulin. Kitto and his helpers stood ready.

"Ladies and gentlemen," began James. "It is my pleasure to welcome you here today for the unveiling of a very important bequest to commemorate the life of Constance Trevallyan. I would like to introduce you all to Mrs Megan Marsh from New Zealand, who has a few words to say."

Megan stepped up to the microphone. "Thank you, Mr Boscowan. And thank you all for coming, despite the cold. I believe it is important to hold this ceremony today since it is Constance Trevallyan's birthday. We are here to pay our respects and lay her ashes to rest ..."

"Bitch," a voice called out.

An egg flew through the air and landed on the shoulder of James Boscowan who was standing beside Megan. Murmurs of consternation rippled through the crowd.

"I hope she burns in hell," yelled the man wearing a tweed long coat and houndstooth cap. "She were no friend of ours."

"Leave it out, John," shouted another voice.

James Boscowan removed his egg-covered coat and quickly took the microphone as Tristan and a couple of the groundsmen moved towards the man who threw the egg.

"This is not the time or place to air your grievances, Nankivill. Please leave if you can't be respectful."

"Like as hell, I will. I've as much right to be 'ere as the next. She ruined us, she did. My Granda and Da died 'cos of 'er."

The increasingly agitated crowd had turned to watch what would happen next.

"We know your story, and you've had your say more than once. Stay and be quiet, or go. The choice is yours."

Shaken by the turn of events, Megan stood to one side and watched as the two groundsmen tried to push the heckler away, but he was having none of it. She couldn't hear what Tristan said, but the man attempted to punch one of them. Luckily, his arm swung wide. By this time, some of the other village men had joined the group, and whatever they said must have made the difference, because the man started to walk away.

Waving his cap in the air, he shouted, "Don't believe 'em. All brainwashed, they is. They're just as bad as she were. You've not heard the last of me, I tell ye. Not by a long way." He carried on down the driveway, occasionally slapping his cap against his leg as he went, as if talking to himself.

Tristan returned to the steps and apologised to Megan for the disturbance.

"Who was that man?" she asked, feeling distinctly unsettled. "Why was he so upset?"

"His grandfather was one of the small business holders Constance bought out. According to the family, they lost everything, including their cottage. He's carried on the long-running feud ever since his father died a few years back."

"Shouldn't someone do something for him?"

"We've tried. Their cottage was on estate land and the rules forbid anyone who doesn't work for the trust to live in one. But Nankivill won't accept any of the compromises we've offered. The village is split over who is in the right. Don't worry. We're all friends here."

Megan was thankful they had tried to help the man, but for the first time she fully understood the impact Constance truly had on people in this small village.

James finished apologising to the crowd and had restored some equilibrium before he invited Megan back to the microphone. Her hands shook, but she hoped her nervousness would not sound in her voice. She cleared her throat.

"Thank you for your patience. As I started to say, it has been my great honour to be part of your community for nearly three months, and I have learnt much about your benefactor – both good and bad, it seems." A chuckle from the crowd gave her encouragement. "Constance's older sister Isabel was my great-grandmother. She has left me her own legacy in the form of a journal about her life, which I will treasure always."

A ripple of conversation ran through the crowd as everyone took in her words.

"But today is about Constance. In her memory, I would like to gift this garden to the people of the trust so those to come in the future will also remember Constance and the Trevallyan family."

Polite applause followed, and another murmur spread through the crowd.

On Megan's nod, Kitto and his team lifted back the covering to reveal a Cornish knot garden. The idea had come to her during a trip to the Torpoint area bordering Devon when she visited Antony House. The knot garden had been magnificent and reminded her of the one she had seen gracing the area in front of the stately railway station in Dunedin a long time ago. To her, it seemed a fitting link between the two countries.

The applause escalated.

Stepping back to allow Tristan to take the microphone, Megan was quickly surrounded by those on the steps who all began talking at once. Jessica pushed her way through to join them, while the photographer pranced around the crowd clicking from every angle.

Tristan put his hand up for quiet. "As chair of the Trevennick Hall Trust, I thank Megan for her generous gift and for making today special. Constance could not have wished for anything better – a symbol of life with no beginning and no end – like her legacy. Her ashes have been placed within the garden alongside a suitably engraved plaque.

"I'll now ask Megan to lay her wreath and Father Andrew to bless the site. You are invited to pay your respects. There are camellia flowers to throw if you wish."

After laying the wreath, Megan stood to one side to let others pass and acknowledged as many people as possible. Many said thanks or sorry, some nodded. Once most of the group had finished paying homage, Tristan addressed them again.

"There is one more part to Megan's bequest. You may have noticed, on your way here, some realignment of the driveway and new markers down either side. Each marker has a family name on it. These markers represent where a new tree will be planted to form an avenue of flowering shrubs all the way from the top of the drive to this garden. Camellias have been chosen. In time, we hope there will be a continuous showing of red blooms throughout the year."

More applause followed while people commented on the news, forcing Tristan to interrupt again. "I would now ask a representative of each of the families to join me, along with Kitto and his team, to officially plant the first of these trees. Afternoon tea will now be served in the reception rooms, and the gardeners will plant the remaining trees later."

A weak ray of sunshine broke through the clouds the moment he finished speaking. "Looks like there's a touch of spring in the air. Let's celebrate."

While Tristan, the delegated family members, the workers and the photographer went to do the ceremonial planting, the remaining crowd swarmed into the reception area, spreading through to the lounges. They were met with a large team of wait staff carrying refreshments and finger foods. For those who normally did the serving, this was indeed a treat.

By four o'clock, as per the invitation, the crowd were bidding their farewells.

"Phew," said Jenna. "Well, that part's over. I thought it went well, didn't you?"

"Brilliantly," agreed Tristan. "And you played your part very well, Mrs Marsh," giving her a mock bow.

"Why, thank you, kind sir. I'm honoured." Megan curtsied, making them all laugh. "Except, I can't help feeling sorry for Mr Nankivill. Isn't there something we can do?"

"There are some people you can't help, Megan." Tristan's tone changed. "And I'd appreciate it if you didn't interfere." He was polite but emphatic. "You're a visitor here, and we don't expect you to understand village politics, but it's not your problem. Nor is it your responsibility."

Left in no doubt where she stood, Megan didn't quite know what to say next.

Jenna broke the silence. "Time to get changed, I think. See you back here at seven."

* * * * *

In honour of the evening, Megan had had a replica made of the gown which Constance was wearing in the painting in the library. Now dressed in this 1920s glamour, she wondered if she was doing the right thing. They would all recognise the gown, but would they think it an insult or a compliment? It was meant as a tribute; she hoped everyone would appreciate her intention.

As she descended the stairs, she could hear the string quartet tuning up in the ballroom. The floral displays left a heady fragrance as she moved through each room trying to memorise every piece of furniture and every painting. On entering the ballroom, she was met by Jenna, Tristan and Lowenna.

"Wow, don't you look stunning!" said Jenna.

"I love it," echoed Lowenna. "It's the same as the one in the painting, isn't it?"

Tristan kissed her hand, his demeanour restored. Megan felt privileged to know these warm, generous people who had willingly accepted her – up to a point. Everything could have turned out very differently.

"Thank you. And you all look very glamorous, too."

Lowenna poured champagne for each of them. Raising her own glass, she offered a toast. "To Constance Trevallyan and the people of Trevennick Hall."

All too soon Tristan reminded them their guests would be arriving any minute so they had better form the welcoming committee.

Whilst the idea of an evening soirée was Megan's idea, Jenna and Tristan had insisted on it being a formal affair, with formal invitations and attire. The option of wearing period costume from an era of choice had worked in Megan's favour.

The Hall was set up similar to the Edwardian house parties of old where music, charades, bridge, and baccarat would be played during the evening. Every light was on, numerous candles decorated the tables, mantelpieces and window nooks, and the woodwork gleamed in their golden glow. The place looked impressive yet welcoming.

Right on time, the guests started appearing. James and Jessica were among the first group, along with Mabel and Hugh.

"You look lovely, Megan," flattered James.

"Wouldn't 'ave missed it for the world, lovey," said Mabel, tugging at Hugh's arm as she pushed past them and happily took a glass of refreshment from the trays held by the staff.

Groups soon formed, and Megan was introduced to many people she didn't know as she welcomed others she'd already met. The string quartet played in the background, setting the mood, and everyone was most complimentary.

When the last of the guests had arrived and the doors shut, Megan and the others mingled while the canapés and drinks were discreetly offered. The atmosphere was buoyant, and laughter often rang out from one group or another. Some of the older people had taken seats at the card tables. Megan could see several hands of whist and a rubber of bridge. Two men were in the midst of a game of chess, but mostly people were happy to gossip, admire the decor and listen to the music.

At nine o'clock, Tristan called everyone into the ballroom where seats had been set out. After a few short introductions and words of thanks to everyone for attending, he invited James Boscowan to take the podium.

"There is one last thing we would like to do," he announced. "Megan has informed us she will be leaving here in a couple of days. She plans to follow the quest that brought her to us in the first place – that of pursuing Isabel throughout her journey to New Zealand. We wish her well in her venture and hope she finds what she seeks."

Soft murmurs followed his announcement, whether in surprise or relief at her leaving, Megan wasn't sure. Some people were still antagonistic towards her even while they enjoyed her hospitality.

"I'd now like to invite Megan to join me."

Flustered at the unexpected turn of events, Megan made her way to the podium. Jenna and Lowenna followed.

"As a farewell gift from the greater Trevallyan family

– and I use the term in its broadest sense," James explained, "please accept this token of our friendship and appreciation."

Lowenna hugged Megan as she handed over a small parcel.

"For all you folk who can't see what it is," boomed James while Megan unwrapped it, "this necklace and earrings are a Cornish knot design, to match the garden she dedicated today. They are made from ancient tin taken from the Trevallyan mine and set with a small diamond.

"And now to our next presentation," James continued, silencing the comments as he warmed to his role. "Megan admired one of the paintings from the collection in this house, thought to be of Isabel and Constance when they were young, and offered to buy it. The combined trust and board have decided to gift it to Megan, in the hope that one day she may return to us."

Spontaneous applause broke out as Jenna handed Megan the painting. Flabbergasted that the board would let her have it at all, let alone gift it to her, she was humbled by her reception. Her friends had worked hard on her behalf.

"Thank you," she mouthed to the crowd but was too choked up to say any more.

"That's the end of the formal part, everyone," announced Tristan, stepping up to the microphone. "Let the dancing begin!"

Isabel's Journal
27 November 1910 — Paris

At last, Paris, the city I have heard so much about, the city of youth and excitement. It seems nothing is impossible here. Everywhere I look, I see so many modern things. Mother would be shocked with the fashions, the length of the skirts, and the lack of corsets. Rather forward, but so much fun. I like the new Empire line by a designer called Poiret.

I want to go everywhere and see everything! There are lots of automobiles and funny little two-wheel thingies, like motorised bicycles with fat tyres. In the streets, one must be careful where one walks but they are able to dart around the traffic very efficiently.

I must also buy a few new hats, as I'm seeing feathers everywhere on people with obvious style and class, and a fur to wrap around my shoulders. They look very elegant. There is so much to see!!!

CHAPTER 19

Megan's Diary
13 February 2011

At last, my search for Isabel starts in earnest. I'm in Paris and as excited as she must have been. Isabel spent a lot of time going to house parties, which I won't be able to do, but I can go to the theatre and the cabarets, Montmartre, the artists' quarter, and the galleries. I'm not sure what I would have thought back then.

Some of the artwork of the time doesn't appeal. It looks very tortured and unrealistic, but I like the early impressionists. La Belle Époque – the beautiful era – is my favourite. French imperialism was at its height, and life for the wealthy was full of optimism. It wasn't as good for the poor and peasant underclass, but it was full of new opportunities. The whole period was about new ideas – new artists, new styles and new designs, about haute couture and haute cuisine.

It must have been exciting to be in Paris — the city of love and romance and the epitome of glamour. No wonder it has enchanted people for centuries, including me. I can't wait.

Eager to fulfil the choices ahead of her, Megan stood in the Champ de Mars beneath the Eiffel Tower, as Isabel and Mrs Baragwanath had, a century earlier. Tilting her head back, she looked high into the blue sky of an out-of-the-box winter's day. She tried to imagine what the two women would have thought about it in their day. It must have seemed like science fiction.

Isabel had written a few impressions of the famous tower but often only listed the places they'd visited. One entry ran, '*Today, we went to Notre Dame. We had morning tea in a cute little tea shop. I rested in the afternoon before dressing.*' Not a single word about where they stayed, how she got anywhere, the weather, or what she thought of the cathedral! Isabel spent more time describing what she wore to the evening house parties, balls, the theatre or cabarets than to what she saw during the day.

Thinking back to when she had been eighteen, Megan admitted that endless monuments to dead people would not have thrilled her either. For the fashionable Isabel, Paris must have been wonderful. A city that offered fulfilment for her interest in art, fashion and having a good time. Life then was all about freedom, modernity and experimentation.

Megan had booked an apartment hotel for a month and planned to explore Paris the way Isabel had described, by choosing random pages from the journal.

Mrs B is putting a damper on everything. We are not to go to the Folies Bergère or the Moulin Rouge as those places are considered below our class even though I've seen the posters and read the reviews. Pity. They look such fun with lots of music and dancing.

We may visit the Ritz and Maxim's - Paris's newest and best restaurant - she says, if I behave myself. How insulting. I have a mind not to go - just to be difficult. But that would be silly, as only I would miss out.

So far, we have mostly visited monuments and buildings: Notre Dame, the Arc de Triomphe, the Panthéon, the Palais-Royal, the Tomb of Napoleon, the Conciergerie ... The list is endless and much of it wearisome.

The Eiffel Tower, I admit, is impressive in its height, but it was only built as a temporary entrance for the 1889 World's Fair and was due to be dismantled last year. It's very odd, if you ask me. It looks temporary with all that open fretwork but I'm told the radio mast at the top, which helps guide the aeroplanes, saved it. I don't really care. Neither do I care that the River Seine flooded earlier this year. What is everyone so bothered about?

This evening, on our way to the theatre, we are to witness the latest invention, a neon lighting *display. I wonder what I should wear. It is cold, so I will need my new cloak with the fur-trimmed hood and my new gloves. And tomorrow we will walk Rue Saint-Honoré, THE street in Paris to be seen, and the home of every fashion house of note. That sounds far more interesting.*

🔺 🔺 🔺

Megan had been to Paris before, with Tony. Now that she was here and looking forward to reliving Isabel's time, she hoped she wouldn't 'see' him at every turn. The city was busy and lively. Despite the late winter chill, Megan found it easier to share in the everyday lifestyle of Parisians without the tourist throngs of summer. Going to the markets to buy fresh food to take back to her little kitchenette was something she particularly enjoyed. She also enjoyed riding the Metro, sipping coffee on the sidewalk and strolling the most famous streets as she visited gardens and admired the statues.

Every day she ventured out to soak up the atmosphere and rediscover sculptures and paintings so numerous, so alluring and so famous it was impossible to choose between them. Montmartre was exactly as she remembered – and as Isabel described. She bought a painting and had it shipped home. She read snippets of information from the guidebook and admired the architecture and beautiful stained-glass windows of yet another great monument to Paris's historical past.

One afternoon, relaxing in the relative quiet of the garden at Rodin's museum, she listened to the muffled cacophony of horns amid the roar of traffic in the not-so-distant distance. How different it must be from the slow-paced clip-clop of hooves on cobbles and jingle of harnesses of a century ago.

To begin with she'd been glad Isabel's journal had brought her to these places. After all, no one could look at Rodin's bronze and marble sculpture *The Thinker* – beautiful, elegant, rugged, every muscle shown in detail – and not be captivated, but as time passed she seemed less sure.

At one time, she had looked forward to the French nightlife Isabel had written about – the food, the wines, and the music – to see if they were anything like they were when Isabel experienced them, but by day's end she was drained. Unable to convince herself to go out again and dine alone, she preferred to cook something simple and sit in her apartment reading and writing.

Although thoughts of Tony had not intruded the way she first feared, so far, she hadn't felt the elation she had expected either. Reliving history through Isabel's eyes must make it seem more important, more authentic, mustn't it?

Isabel's Journal
12 December 1910 – Paris

I've been on the Metro, an underground rail system that takes you to different parts of the city! I'm not at all sure I liked being underground, but it is a fast and easy way of getting about. We took the Metro when we visited Sacré Coeur, the basilica being built on the Montmartre hill above the city. The views are breathtaking and the building, once finished, will be a fine edifice indeed.

What interested me most were the artists in the streets behind the basilica. I love seeing them at work. To see them create a picture on a blank canvas, that looks just like what I can see, is inspiring. The more modern works – impressionism, I'm told they call it – where the viewer must discern their own story, I find very exciting. I cannot understand some of the newer styles – cubism and art nouveau and the ones that look like daubs of paint splashed everywhere mean nothing.

I would like to talk at length to the artists about their thinking. How do they do it? I doubt Mrs B will give permission, but I will try.

Someone may know Wil.

I do love him so.

Megan thought Isabel was being overly romantic about this Wil, but until she knew something more about him, it was hard to be certain. With the painting from Isabel's room at Trevennick Hall safely locked inside a specially made padded case, she hoped Trina might be able to tell her something more about him when she got to Florence. She wanted to know more about this nameless artist.

Who was he? This Wil ...

One day, Megan's wanderings took her to Montparnasse where she found many of the places

Isabel had listed turned into private homes and modern office blocks. Newer style bistros and cafés had popped up everywhere and the huge modern tower intruded on the landscape, which gave Megan a totally different perspective of Paris life from anything Isabel and Mrs B would have known. Disappointed, she couldn't quite put her finger on what was missing.

Maybe some of these places were the ateliers *where the artists used to work*, she thought. *Had Isabel ever come here on her own?*

Whatever Isabel saw was not there now.

Megan shivered in the cold air and looked for somewhere to have lunch. Soon warmed by some *vin de pays* served in an earthenware jug, she sat contemplating Isabel's journal entries over a leisurely lunch, making comparisons between their lives.

Megan knew enough of art history to know that, like Montmartre before it, Montparnasse had grown into an intellectual breeding ground full of artists – musicians and composers, singers, and dancers, poets, and writers as well as painters and sculptors.

Isabel had loved it. She wrote about them often. Art seemed to be a magnet for this sheltered young woman. Was that her passion? Did she understand art enough, or was she simply captivated by the lifestyle of these nonconformist people?

Centuries ago, art was the only way people could see any sort of world beyond the small village they lived in. Photography and modern travel changed all that, and painters were free to let their imaginations run wild. In their shabby, chic clothes, the bourgeoisie would have attended the various balls and soirées looking for patrons to pay the bills, which is where Isabel would have met many of them.

The buzz surrounding these artists would have been romantic and titillating to a young girl. Megan understood how Isabel had been mesmerised but could not conjure up the same level of enthusiasm. In another century or two and looking back to the rush and bustle of modern twenty-first century society with its thirty-second sound bites and 'flash-fiction' genres, Megan wondered whether today's artisans would be granted the same level of respect and reverence as those of the eighteenth and nineteenth centuries. Did today's artists gather like they once did, to share ideas and develop schools of thought? she wondered.

Isabel's Journal
16 December 1910 – Paris

It seems we are to leave this city soon and travel to Nice in time for Christmas. Pity. I was beginning to know my way around, and I enjoy going to all the balls and the theatres. The nightlife is so lively here that we sleep in the mornings, have lunch, and go shopping or sightseeing early afternoon. Then we rest in the later afternoons before dressing for dinner and our evening out again. I am rather weary of all the sightseeing. I don't want to see another monument. I'd much rather go to the soirées where I'm meeting the artists I crave.

I've met M. Toulouse-Lautrec, a very eccentric character, and the rather odd M. Degas. He argued with everyone about the littlest thing, although he was happy to speak at length about the dancers at the music halls and nightclubs. I'm not sure I understand M. Degas' views on the Jewish people. He was very rude about them. I must ask Mrs B what she thinks.

I also met M. Matisse. He says I should visit him in Montparnasse. He is strangely conservative in appearance but his paintings are bright and colourful. They are not quite 'real' looking, not like M. Renoir's, but have more lines and colours in the right places giving the impression things are as they should be. I like them very much.

CHAPTER 20

By early March, Megan found she was increasingly disillusioned. Isabel's month in Paris had been full; Megan's was running low after a couple of weeks. Isabel had places to go and people to see; Megan talked with no one. Paris had also turned really wet and cold.

On such days, Megan preferred to stay in her apartment reading, writing emails and checking *The New Zealand Herald* website to keep up with events at home. She ventured out less and less and then only when something from the guidebooks or on the Internet stirred her imagination. Being alone in a foreign place was nothing like being alone in your own home. She'd been happy with her solitude in New Zealand; now it felt like a chain holding her back. From what, she wasn't sure, but she felt unreasonably restless and disturbed.

One afternoon, while she was thinking she should move on to Isabel's next destination, there was a knock on the door.

"Surprise!" shouted Jessica, as she rushed into the room and threw her arms around Megan.

"What are you doing here? Oh, am I pleased to see you."

"I've taken two weeks off. I've always wanted to see Paris, and since you were here, it seemed like a good idea. You also sounded a bit low in your last email, so I've come to cheer you up."

Once Megan had worked out Jessica was booked into a nearby backpackers, she insisted the young woman take the foldout bed in the living area and share with her. They had a lot of catching up to do.

Megan discovered Jessica had never been to Paris before.

"Somehow it never happened. I made it to Switzerland once, skiing, and another time a quick visit to Monte Carlo ... but Paris was always on the 'to-do' list. Now I'm here, I'm dying to visit the Ritz – Coco Chanel once lived there. I love her as a designer."

They booked for afternoon tea with a small glimmer of hope they might be able to visit the famous suite. The concierge proved completely unhelpful, so they made do with photos of the magnificent rooms, hanging on the walls.

For days, Jessica dragged Megan out to walk the Champs-Élysées, taking delight in the upmarket shops or wandering the famous Rue du Faubourg Saint-Honoré, still *the* street for fashion. Excited by a find at the antiques market, Jessica bought a set of iconic vintage Chanel buttons complete with the trademark interlocking Cs. But she was more excited to learn Chanel had opened her first hat shop in 1910.

"Did Isabel visit there by any chance?"

"If she did, she didn't mention Chanel by name, obviously the famous Chanel was yet to become famous."

It took them two days to go around the Louvre.

"I never realised this place was quite so extensive," laughed Jessica as she turned the pamphlet upside down trying to work out which gallery they should head towards next. Whilst Megan's energy was waning, Jessica's was not.

The day they took a Seine River cruise turned out brilliantly fine and crystal clear. In the late winter sunshine, everything shone brightly, especially the gold on the Alexander III Bridge and the cupolas on the domes of the many churches and important buildings. The cool wind off the water kept them inside to view the passing scenery through the expansive windows that curved over their heads. The riverboat glided under the numerous bridges while lunch was served to the sounds of French jazz singers. Jessica was almost jumping up and down with excitement and understood why Isabel had been smitten. Paris in springtime was a self-explanatory cliché for romance, even if Constance described Isabel's writings as silly nonsense.

Jessica brought new life and new meaning to Megan's stay in Paris. Evenings were now spent tasting French food in all its splendour, from the simplest of brasseries to the best of fine-dining restaurants, where the waiters wore white gloves. The subtle expectation that diners would change from sightseeing clothes into dressier attire was one aspect of Paris life they enjoyed.

"I like the idea of dressing up. It's fun and adds that certain ... how do the French say it? – *je ne sais quoi* – to the whole 'going out' thing." Jessica twirled in her new dress. "And a brilliant excuse to buy new clothes."

"I agree. Dressing for dinner turns the most basic of human needs into an event worth celebrating. And I can't think of a better place to celebrate eating than in Paris."

Their forays to Isabel's haunts had, once again, left Megan cold. She found them false in their modern form. Maybe in Isabel's time they were the epitome of style, but they weren't to Megan's taste.

One evening, over an elegant dinner with several exceptional wines at Le Grand Véfour, one of Paris's oldest and most exclusive restaurants, Jessica started to talk. Surrounded by restrained grandeur, regal, plush and smart with museum-quality mirrors, tapestries and paintings, its calm and unobtrusive atmosphere suited Jessica's mood.

"Megan," she began tentatively. "Since our time in Paris is coming to an end, I think I must say thank you. I really appreciate not being plied with questions about why I wanted to come."

"No need, Jessica. I've enjoyed your company. It makes evenings like this worthwhile. I wouldn't have come to a place like this on my own."

Megan had not mentioned her growing concern that her decision to follow Isabel was not turning out as she'd expected. At times, she was quite depressed with the whole journey.

"I'm glad I've been of some use then, because you have helped me enormously," said Jessica.

"Looks like we're having a mutual appreciation moment." Megan chuckled and raised her glass. "To us ... in Paris ... today."

Jessica clinked her glass against Megan's and took a sip before suddenly launching into her life story. "I was only seventeen when I took up law, mostly to spite my brothers. Looking back, it was a stupid reason to commit to a career. My father virtually disowned my two brothers when they opted not to take law and carry on the family firm forever, ad infinitum. That was when Mum was diagnosed with cancer."

Her voice was filled with sadness as she explained when her mother died, and afterwards, she had carried on living with her father. "Then, when grandfather died three years ago and Dad moved us to new premises, the business boomed ..."

Jessica took another sip of wine and fiddled with her fork, pushing a piece of parsley around the plate. "Oh, I don't know. I got so embroiled in everything there didn't seem to be a good time to make a break. I began to worry about whether I would end up like Constance. Lonely and unloved."

Megan decided not to interrupt. There was obviously something simmering, something the young woman needed to put into words.

"A while back, I started to panic. Had I really made the right decisions? Did I definitely want Dad to change the company name? Would that lock me into a future I couldn't get out of? With Mum gone, I suddenly felt I had no one to talk to, and I was scared."

Megan was at a loss as to what Jessica was saying. "And now?"

"I've discovered something about myself in the last months, but especially in the weeks we've been here."

Another long pause.

"And what is that?"

"I like strong women who make a life for themselves by going against the trend."

Megan listened as Jessica talked of how Chanel had ignored her critics and forged ahead regardless, and Julia Child, despite the setbacks, made cooking her life. She spoke of political leaders and scientists, of suffragettes and human rights activists and of authors and philosophers. Whilst impressed with the young woman's knowledge, Megan wondered where she was going with this list.

"Great women," said Jessica. "Women who stood up for what they believed in."

"And what do you believe in?"

"That has always been my problem. I don't have any strong beliefs worth fighting for."

Another course arrived, served by a helpful, friendly waiter who answered Megan's appalling French in much better English. They listened to his description of the giant langoustine fricassee with zucchini and mushrooms in almond milk and orange blossom, which made their mouths water. For some minutes nothing more was said, while they savoured their meal.

"I've been trying to work out what I like, what I'm good at and what I want."

"And do you have any answers?"

"Sort of. I like clothes. And art, well some of it anyway." Jessica filled her mouth with another large prawn, trying not to drip sauce over her. "And food."

"Don't we all," laughed Megan. "That's a good start."

"I don't mean just eating food, but this." Jessica pointed to her plate and waved her hand around the room. "The whole thing. Coming to Paris has opened my eyes. I doubt I would have discovered any of this living in a small Cornish town."

"Well then, what are you good at?"

"My job."

"That's good, isn't it?" Megan was truly baffled now. She thought Jessica was going to come up with something far-reaching, not status quo.

"Yes. It is. And in some ways, it's a relief. I'm twenty-nine, single, no kids – and no prospects at the moment either – and … well, you see …" Jessica fidgeted in a most un-Jessica-like way as her eyes wandered around the room.

"Goodness, Jessica. What is it? After all this talk about strong women why beat around the bush now?"

Jessica visibly relaxed and smiled. "You are right. Again. And I couldn't have done any of this without you."

Megan acknowledged the compliment. "So, you are good at your job, you like high-quality fashion, art and top-notch food. That I understand. But what aren't you good at, and what is it you want?"

"I'm a hopeless cook," she laughed. "But that's not the point, nor really what I want to say. I want to say that I include Constance and you in my list of strong women."

Somewhat surprised to be included in such a list, aware of her weaknesses and how lost she felt, Megan quietly accepted the praise. "That's very generous of you to say so, but why, exactly?"

The question broke the last of Jessica's hesitation. She believed they owed Megan a debt of gratitude. Few people had known anything about Constance – other than they had a job because of her – until Megan willingly travelled halfway round the world to show them.

"You've done such amazing things. You had the courage to leave everything you knew and set off on your own, not at all sure what you might find – while I've been worrying if I had made the wrong decision in the safety of my own backyard."

Megan held back from offering advice. Jessica had obviously worked through her dilemma and reached a conclusion.

"You have no idea what a difference it has made for me to talk openly without criticism, without you telling me what to do, but accepting me for who I am."

"I understand what a terrible loss it has been for you, losing your mother so young. I also understand your sense of loyalty to the family firm. I think you realise doubting yourself isn't going to provide answers. It seems to me you have managed to reconcile many of those worries and are looking forward. Am I right?"

"See. That's exactly what I mean. Wise counsel without suggesting a thing! And yes, you're right, and yes, many of my doubts have gone away. I realise now I don't have to fight the world to be successful. I don't have to be a famous figure to make a difference, and I don't have to be unloved or lonely because I'm not a wife and mother – yet. My life is what I make of it. You and Constance taught me that, and I thank you from the bottom of my heart."

Megan's Diary
12 March 2011 – Paris

I found what Jessica said both humbling and rewarding. I've never seen myself as a strong woman. I don't think I would have done any of it without Tony … but then he always did tell me I could do anything I set my mind to. All he ever did, he said, was turn me round so I was looking in the right direction.

Jessica's take on things has given me something to think about. It never occurred to me someone as young as her would see strength in my ordinary life, but if she has been inspired by me being me, then I'm pleased.

She seems excited by my ill-defined schemes looking ahead. They need a lot more work before anything can come of them, but I think they are starting to make sense to me. Now I've got Constance's inheritance I have to do something worthwhile with it. Some things in life you can control by your choices, others are handed to you by fate. How you deal with them is what is important, something Jessica has learnt. I'm glad I could help her reach that conclusion, however inadvertently I managed it. She's a bright, intelligent woman. She'll find her way. She will happily return to Cornwall with a new spring in her step and a determination to enjoy every moment of her life.

I wonder what she meant by her parting comment? 'She had something she wanted to pursue.'

I have to rethink my views on Isabel. Much of her journal is lightweight and girlish, but what happened later? Was she a strong woman, making choices she was prepared to live by, to the point of leaving everything she had ever known? Or had circumstances dictated the direction her life would take? That is something I need to find out.

The last pages are missing from her journal, right at the point where she might have said. Did she rip them out, or did Constance?

CHAPTER 21

As the train sped along the tracks taking her to Venice, through towns and villages and past fields and distant scenery, Megan's thoughts were of things past not present.

Her travel diary lay open, untouched, on the table in front of her.

Over the last few weeks she'd been much more diligent about recording places visited and scenery observed but journals needed something more. She'd learnt that much from Isabel's. They needed descriptions, observations, and impressions. As interesting as it may have been, Isabel mostly wrote about frivolities, leaving huge gaps and Megan with an endless list of questions.

Missing from Megan's diary were her day-by-day emotions. Unlike earlier happier entries, she didn't want to write about her dark days. The black cloud of emptiness that had followed her spiral into depression after Tony's death was creeping back, and her time of solitude was not working out quite as she expected. She was constantly beset with doubts.

After Jessica left Paris, Megan took time to map out where she wanted to go. She'd enjoyed Bath and

London and, in the end, loved Paris – thanks to Jessica. Eventually, she had to accept the places Isabel once visited were so altered there was no point in trying to replicate the young girl's experiences. Not the buildings, nor the monuments or scenery, they were all still there and as amazing, but the essence – the things Isabel enjoyed because of the people she met – was quite different.

No closer to finding Isabel than she had been back in New Zealand, Megan began to question her reasons for following her great-grandmother's footsteps. Instead, she took Isabel's journey and drew up a new itinerary. If this was to be her journey rather than a reflection of Isabel's, then a week in Provence – a holiday cliché if she'd ever heard one – was top of the list. The route Megan chose zigzagged across France before she finally arrived in Nice, just like Isabel's had.

Megan left Paris with high hopes of enjoying the passing scenery and small towns. Instead, the train trip proved to be far more difficult than she anticipated. Porters were a thing of Isabel's era, not hers. Despite a request for her hotels to send meet-and-greet drivers, the task of hefting her suitcase up and down the steep, narrow steps of the train was almost beyond her. The need to ask strangers to help left her feeling vulnerable and inadequate.

The excitement stirred by Isabel's journal when it first arrived had diluted to the point where Megan's adventure was becoming a trial. The emptiness suddenly engulfing her had come out of the blue.

In the weeks before she left New Zealand, she had often woken with a feeling of lightness and freshness. Several days, and sometimes a week or more, could go by without her thinking about Tony. In Hawaii, when Jason introduced Trina into the family, Megan had keenly felt Tony's absence, but in between, especially in Cornwall and then in Paris, he'd faded into the background as people and activities swept her along.

Travel with Tony had been exciting and interesting. They'd talk endlessly about their discoveries and shared experiences, but Megan unexpectedly found drifting around some of the most beautiful places with outstanding scenery – hilltop castles, churches, palaces, craggy villages, and stunning gardens – unfulfilling. No amount of inner discussion or imagined talks with Tony shifted those feelings.

Neither had she expected to miss Jessica. Her visit was a happy interlude, but within hours of her leaving, Megan felt bereft. Not necessarily for Jessica, but because she had no one to share anything with.

Thinking of Jessica and the girl's description of her as a strong woman simply added to Megan's misgivings. In no way did it describe the individual living within her skin.

Stop feeling sorry for yourself, she'd commanded, frustrated with herself. *Think what a wonderful trip you're on, seeing so many amazing places, surrounded by living history, finding your past ...*

At that point, she'd run out of amazing and wonderful things and instead brooded on how aimless she had become. For several weeks, she'd struggled with an irrational sense of isolation. None of these thoughts appeared in her diary. Megan wrote about what she saw, not how she felt. By the time she arrived in Nice, she was shattered.

* * * * *

Determined to make the most of her time in the south of France, Megan hired a driver and car – anything to avoid driving on the 'wrong side' of the road. Her guide was knowledgeable and informative, doing his job professionally and with great efficiency. He drove her through valleys and mountains, into wine country and along the coast, to enjoy the flavours on offer. Together they toured the back roads into ancient stone villages built into near vertical cliffs offering the usual retail outlets that attracted tourists and were places to live – places Isabel and Mrs B would have known. Places like the walled town of Vence and the historic village of St Paul de Vence, and Grasse, the perfume capital, or Eze, a medieval village overlooking the Mediterranean.

Megan lived the tourist life, chatting with the driver who spoke enough English for them to communicate freely.

She loved the food markets with their flower stalls and the enticing aromas of fresh bread, herbs, spices, and charcuterie products that permeated the air. She enjoyed the antique stalls and the friendly banter, but after a few days that dogged feeling of being detached from everything returned. Once, she could have furnished several houses with the number of armoires, linen presses, whitewashed tables, light brackets, and chaises longues she saw. Now she wandered past them, disinterested. There seemed no point. She found it harder to resist the fine linens and eventually bought a small hand towel as a reminder.

If eating alone at home was unsatisfying, suddenly eating alone three times a day in hotels and cafés became unbearable. "I can't stand this any longer!" she screamed.

"I'd like to enrol in a live-in French immersion cooking and wine course, please," she said to the woman in the tourist bureau, determined to fight the encroaching darkness.

That week life began to change. Her hostess and the family treated Megan as one of their own. She found it productive, restorative, and more enjoyable than expected, and full of laughter amid lessons on cooking, ·on having fun and on life. Her cooking skills improved immensely, but her French remained poor. Some things they couldn't teach her. But all good things end and, energised again, she packed her bags.

"*Au revoir.* Take care, madame. Good luck on your journey. I hope you find what you seek."

For the next leg of the journey, Megan conceded defeat. For no apparent reason, Isabel's journey had taken them from Nice to Genoa, then north to Geneva, Bern, and Zurich, turning south again to Venice before reaching Florence. Isabel hadn't said why they stopped, only where. Megan didn't want to travel all day in a train to spend another night in another town simply because Isabel had once been there – not any more. Megan flew to Zurich.

Isabel's journey had been about visiting people and participating in the social calendar. With no social calendar to follow, Megan could go sightseeing anywhere. She saw a poster for a luxury train tour through Switzerland that offered 'the world's most beautiful locations, first class hotels, spectacular mountains, dramatic bridges, and dazzling lakes' and instantly booked the nine-day trip. It sounded like bliss.

With only ten people and the two guides to escort the party, Megan had plenty of opportunity to share the sights and experiences with other people. Not once was she disappointed.

On board she teamed up with Rosemary, an Englishwoman also travelling alone, and an Australian couple. They laughed and ate and drank together a lot. Rosemary, a good decade older than Megan, exhibited such joie-de-vivre that Megan felt ashamed, her gloomy mood unworthy. Like the folk she'd left behind in Cornwall, Megan was unlikely to see these people again, but she was grateful for their company. They broke the dark spell she had been under, and Rosemary taught her a new lesson to take forward into her new life.

"The memory of love will remain, always. Grief is simply the price we pay, but the beauty of life continues. Love and laughter are what makes it fun. Always remember the saying: *We don't stop laughing because we grow old; we grow old because we stop laughing.*"

Megan had heard the saying many times before but had forgotten its message.

The change in speed as the train slowed for a station dragged Megan's attention back to the here and now. They were nearing Venice, her favourite city out of all the places she and Tony had visited. For that reason, she'd chosen to come back, rather than because Isabel had stayed there. For the next week, she would enjoy Venice in all its uniqueness before meeting up with Sarah and Trina in Florence.

The loud whistle penetrated Megan's thoughts enough to realise she should pack up and make ready to get off. Looking around, she spied a young man in the seat diagonally across from her. She would ask him to help lift her suitcase down.

Megan's Diary
10 April 2011 – Venice

My journey has been one of discovery: of new people, new experiences, and new places. I've learnt more about myself on this pilgrimage than I expected. Some of it I like and some I don't, but at last I have a growing sense of purpose.

My higgledy-piggledy response to these new discoveries has been as varied as the places and people – sometimes good, sometimes disappointing. But I am grateful to those I've met for showing me the art of living life to the full.

I've learnt shutting myself away is not living and neither is wandering around aimlessly looking for something to do. I need to find a new meaning for my life. I want to use Constance's money to help people, as she did in the end.

The flurry of constant movement is starting to defeat me. Maybe I'm getting old, or maybe New Zealand has a slower pace of life where people notice one another. Here, I feel lost. Isolated and removed from everything I know and understand, and some days I'm lonelier than I care to admit, but my journey continues and I'm beginning to understand why following Isabel was the right thing to do, for far more reasons than I realised. I am learning so much, even though it's been a bit of a wild-goose chase so far, but I'm sure I'll find Isabel somewhere along the way.

I'm starting to wonder if her spirit will be found in Florence where I think her story really begins, or back home in Auckland where she spent most of her life.

CHAPTER 22

"Happy Birthday," said the voice when Megan answered her cell phone.

"Jessica! How wonderful to hear from you. What a lovely surprise."

For a few moments, Megan answered her questions. "Yes, I had a great time. I've visited a few of the usual tourist sights but Mario has mostly taken me to places away from the regular haunts and shown me a different side of Venice. It's been wonderful."

"Mario! Who is Mario?" Jessica sounded doubtful. Sometimes she acted like one of Megan's own children, chivvying her to take care.

"My guide. I met him on the train. Well, not actually met him. I asked him to lift my suitcase down. He was such a nice young man and so helpful, he carried it all the way out to the street."

"You let a stranger take your bag?" squeaked Jessica. "What if he had run off with it?"

"Don't be silly. Everybody does it. How else am I going to manage? In fact, he asked me where I was staying and helped me all the way here – up and down steps and over little bridges, and down alleyways, until he found the doorway. I doubt I could have found the place by myself, let alone managed my case. It's a quaint, out-of-the-way, old-style pensione. He wouldn't take any money, so I hired him as my guide." Megan finished her story feeling rather pleased with her innovation.

"You're sure it's safe?" If anything, Jessica sounded more doubtful.

"You haven't travelled much, have you?"

She assured the girl of her safety and began to relate some of her adventures, which included walking for miles and cruising up and down canals in his speedboat. Mario was her constant companion. She'd seen and done things she wouldn't have known about, like visiting small community markets and even smaller eateries that served the most authentic Italian food.

"Just delicious, some of it. Mario took me to some of the outer islands to see the lacemakers and glassblowers. I've eaten fish cooked straight off the boats and managed to learn a few words of Italian. I hope Trina will be pleased with me."

"Sounds like you're having a ball."

"Yes, I am. Now, tell me about you. What have you been doing?"

Jessica launched into her activities since her return to Cornwall. They were very busy at the office, and her father had completed the name change and installed new signage. "I enrolled in a cooking course when I came back," she announced. "I'm really enjoying it. Much more than I expected ... and ..."

Megan detected the hesitation in her voice. "And what?"

"I've met someone," Jessica whispered.

"Fantastic. That is the best news I've heard."

On the first night, she'd shared the cook bench with Max. Since then, they'd developed into quite a team.

"It's early days, but we get on really well."

"That is the best birthday present you could have given me."

"Actually, I think I can do better than that."

Jessica explained how their conversation in Paris about Constance's book collection had started her thinking. She remembered seeing a small key with a ribbon attached in the old Trevallyan files. "When I got back I made some enquiries. Starting with Mabel."

"Good old Mabel. What did she say about it?"

"She didn't recognise the key, but she did say I should try the library."

"Really? Why?"

"A hidden drawer, she reckons."

"A hidden drawer! That sounds more like something from a farce or murder mystery to me," laughed Megan.

Jessica had thought so, too. Although sceptical, she'd wanted to check it out. Mabel insisted on going with her to show her where to find it and had talked non-stop all the way. 'I was only a youngster back then, of course, but sometimes I would help my mother, when she were housekeeper. I seen Constance use that drawer behind the false panelling in the library more than once. What with Constance gone 'n all, I reckon there's few other people would remember 'bout it.'

Mabel had been right. One piece of the decorative strip-panelling that ran around the library shelves Megan had admired, did move. Behind it, they found a small drawer.

"And the key fits," Jessica added.

"And? What's in the drawer?" Megan wondered how many more surprises Constance could keep springing on her from the grave.

"Letters."

"Letters?"

"Yep. All tied with ribbon and neatly filed into decade lots."

"That's incredible. What sort of letters?"

"Personal ones by the look of them, and all from one person." Jessica hesitated. "Isabel."

"Isabel!" Megan thought she sounded like a parrot, repeating everything Jessica said. "What did they say?"

"I don't know. I only opened one to see who it was from and didn't read any of them. The handwriting on the envelopes appeared the same, I assumed they were all from the same person. The first one was dated 1912 and the last one 1959." Before Megan could answer, she could hear another phone ringing in the background. "Hang on a mo, I must get that."

Megan couldn't hear what was said but less than a minute later Jessica was back on the line. "Can you do me a favour, please? Go to your window and tell me what you see."

"What? Why? Never mind that, tell me more about the letters."

"I will, but right now I'd like to know what you can see from your window," insisted Jessica.

Megan crossed the room and slid up the sash window. "My room overlooks a courtyard. There's an old marketplace to one side and a café and gift shop to the left. An alleyway leads ..." Megan broke off her description with a shriek as her gaze dropped to the people below. "It's Sarah. And Trina!" she shrieked in disbelief at the two girls grinning and waving up at her. Trina was carrying a large bunch of flowers. "You set this up! Didn't you!"

Jessica laughed. "You can go now. We'll talk later."

"Hang on, the letters ...?" But it was too late, Jessica had hung up.

Megan grabbed her room key and dashed down the stairs to meet the girls. "What are you two doing here?" she wanted to know as hugs and kisses were shared.

"Isn't it obvious, Mum? We decided to help you celebrate your birthday ... So here we are," added Sarah needlessly, twirling around like an excited puppy chasing its tail.

"I know we were due to meet up in Florence after the weekend, but I couldn't let you keep Venice to yourself now, could I?"

"And I couldn't think of any reason why I shouldn't join in the fun, too," Trina chimed in.

Feeling fit to burst with a grin across her entire face, Megan buried her nose in the flowers pretending to sniff their perfume to hide the sudden tears threatening to embarrass her. "This is the best of birthday surprises. Between you two and Jessica I can't imagine anything better."

Back in her room, she put the flowers into water while Sarah filled in some of the missing details from Mabel's story that she'd got from Jessica.

"It was a miracle Jessica found it at all," concluded Sarah.

Megan agreed wholeheartedly.

"I can imagine Mabel saying she was all cock-a-hoop when they found the letters. It would be so like her, and Jessica got her exactly right."

They laughed at the way the girl had mimicked the old woman.

"Wasn't it lucky Jessica put two and two together about the key, Mum?"

"Yes, amazingly so. I won't be able to stop thinking about them now."

There was little more to be said until she could read them, but if the first one was dated two years after Isabel's visits, they wouldn't help her here in Italy. She sent a quick email to Jessica, to ask her to send them home where she would study them at leisure – and with any luck learn much more about Isabel's life in New Zealand.

That evening, escorted by Mario, who was extremely disappointed, he said, to find the two beautiful signorinas already spoken for, the small party was ready for a birthday feast.

"Tonight, ladies, I have special treat for you." Mario spoke in delightfully accented English and kissed Megan's hand. "It was intended for Megan alone, but now she has company," he shrugged nonchalantly, "... and such pretty company, too ... we all go. We visit my auntie. She cook for you."

He and Trina exchanged some quick-fire conversation. Mario raised his hands in supplication once, before Trina finally nodded in agreement.

Turning to Megan and Sarah, she said, "*Andiamo.* Let's go. Mario says his auntie is waiting."

Bypassing his boat, Mario led them to a gondola while Megan pondered what had just gone on.

180

"This my cousin, Ricco; he take you. I meet you there." Elegantly he assisted the women down the steps and onto the gondola. "Wrap up warm, ladies," he advised, pointing to the rugs provided for the cooler April evening, and he waved them off as they disappeared along a narrow canal.

Unlike his talkative cousin, Ricco said nothing. He steadily poled the craft along the narrow canals turning into one then another and another. From this vantage point, their view of Venice was quite different. They glided past ochre, pink or cream coloured buildings, their rooftops pointing up to the narrow strip of dusky sky, and passed under a series of bridges. The lights from windows reflected on the dark, oily water that lapped the ancient stones resting on wooden poles driven deep into the depths of the marshy islands below. Megan thought there was something quite mysterious to the whole affair. Another turn and they entered a larger canal. Suddenly Ricco burst into song and serenaded the women as their journey continued.

On cue, Trina reached under the seat and pulled out a basket containing glasses and a bottle of champagne. "Mario told me when Ricco started singing I was to pour the bubbles. Don't ask any more. Just wait and see." Now Trina was being secretive, but Megan didn't care. She was happy to trust in whatever was going to happen.

"To you," said Trina.

"Happy Birthday, Mum." Sarah raised her glass.

Megan touched her glass with theirs, indescribably happy the girls were with her. But she secretly wished Tony could have been with her, too. When she was busy, Tony often faded from her daily thoughts, but occasions like this made his absence all the more noticeable.

They'd hardly finished their wine when Ricco glided towards a set of steps. The recessed door opened, and a short Italian woman stood welcoming them profusely at the entrance. Megan had no idea what they were saying, but Trina was instantly deep in conversation.

Ricco held the gondola steady as they stepped onto dry land and followed the woman wearing an incongruous floral apron over her beautifully cut red dress.

The short passageway led to a heavy wooden door with ancient iron fittings, which opened into a warmly lit trattoria decorated with scenes of Venice. Piped music blared from speakers set high on the walls, and two Italian flags flew above a doorway that led to a narrow alleyway opposite.

The aroma of tomato, garlic, herbs, and rich wine sauces assailed their senses. Candles burned in empty wine bottles on tables set with red checked cloths. Mario's auntie showed them to the largest table, shouting and gesticulating towards the kitchen. A low hum of conversation filled the room and wrapped itself around the new arrivals.

Mario materialised with bottles of Italian wine and glasses balanced between his fingers and poured copious quantities into the large balloons. "Megan, Sarah and Trina, may I present to you, *mia zia*, Rosa Bianchi. She is the best cook in all of Venice, in my opinion." He kissed his fingers and threw the kiss into the air. "And here, that is all that matters." He waved his arm around the room and bowed low with a wide grin.

Rosa gave him a friendly clip over the ear. He grinned even more.

Dish after dish appeared on the table while Trina quickly explained to Megan and Sarah what they were. As Mario had promised, each course was delicious, but Megan only tasted a small amount of each one, having been warned about a dessert.

"And now, Zia Rosa's speciality, her home-made tiramisu," announced Mario as Rosa set a plate before her. "A common Italian dessert found everywhere these days, I know. But ruined, I tell you, ruined. They are all pretend. Here, this is something you will never have tasted anywhere before. I promise you."

Megan's first bite, anxiously watched by Aunt Rosa and Mario, was exquisite. Her face said it all, as she finished every mouthful, allowing the creamy texture to melt away.

She couldn't have wished for a better birthday.

* * * * *

"Mum! What were you thinking?" demanded Sarah later back at the hotel. Neither of the girls trusted Mario's intentions, especially after learning Megan had paid for everything over the last three days. Sarah was sure her mother's honour was at stake.

"You're too trusting, Mum. Didn't you think he would want something in return for his attentions?"

"No, I don't think so. You've got it all wrong, surely." Megan was shocked. "Apart from kissing my hand, he's not made any advances like that. He's been very good to me."

Trina thought her money was more at risk. "Give him time. I'm sorry to say there are a few of my countrymen who have a reputation for flattering foreign women who look lost. After a few days, they come up with some story about needing money. If they get enough the first time, they disappear. If not, they hang around until the right opportunity comes up. You've been lucky. It sounds like we arrived at the right time."

After the girls had gone to their rooms, Megan stayed up to write in her diary. As she was preparing for bed, a soft knock rattled the old-fashioned door latch. Thinking one of the girls had forgotten something she opened it.

"Mario?"

Before she could say anything further, he ducked into her room and shut the door behind him. "*La mia bella signora*," he whispered, as he took both her hands in his. "Your girls have got me all wrong. I don't want your money. It is you I want. I have fallen in love with you."

Stunned, Megan took a step backwards and nearly fell over as he tried to wrap his arms about her. She twisted away and managed to put a chair between them as he advanced.

Dressed only in her nightgown Megan felt vulnerable. The girls had been right after all. How stupid could she be?

"Please, Megan," he begged. "Please believe me."

He made a grab for her and caught her wrist as she moved away. He pulled her close to his chest, trying to kiss her. The burning pressure of his hand on her back as he held her against his length stirred emotions she had nearly forgotten. Mario's other hand cupped her breast through her thin nightdress. Only Tony had ever touched her there.

Loathing coursed through her. She pushed against him, finding strength she never knew she had, and broke

184

free of his hold. "Mario. Stop!" she ordered, panting to catch her breath. She held her hand out in front of her. "Stop right there. I need you to leave. Right now."

"*Cara signora*, I don't mean to upset you." His hands spread fan-like before him, he shrugged as if to accede.

She stepped back to put some extra space between them and shook her head. "I appreciate all you've done. But I can't believe you have fallen in love with me in three days."

"We Italians are hot-blooded. It can happen. *Si?*" He moved towards her again, and she slipped around the small table. How could something this silly happen to her? It had gone beyond bizarre and now bordered on farcical.

Megan tried a different tack. "I don't think you realise how old I am," she began.

"All the more experienced, my dear," he answered with a husky tone, raising one eyebrow.

Megan nearly laughed as an image of the wolf from Red Riding Hood entered her head, but this was no laughing matter.

Spotting her cell phone on the dresser by the door, she grabbed the ladder-back chair to hold in front of her and edged her way towards the door. What she thought she would do with the chair she had no idea, but it gave her a degree of comfort. Even as she measured the danger, she felt like she was playing a part in a movie scene.

"Mario, what has got into you? What do you want?"

"I want only you. Please stay in Venezia with me? I show you how a man can love a woman. We take time." His voice was smooth and oily.

"What about my girls? Do you think they would let me, even if I gave it a moment's consideration?"

"Send them away. You are mama. What you say goes, doesn't it?"

This time she really did snort. She put the chair down and grabbed her phone. "We'll see, shall we? I'll call them."

"No. Don't do that." He reached out to grasp her wrist again but having manoeuvred her way to the door, she quickly lifted the latch and stepped into the corridor. She'd be safe now.

"Out!" she cried, pointing.

"Okay, I leave. I come back tomorrow and we talk. Yes?"

"No, Mario. It's best we part ways."

"No, no. I already make bookings and paid for special surprises I plan for you. You can't do this to me. You owe me."

He wasn't really a threat after all; he simply wanted money.

"That is your problem. You'll not get any more money from me. Now leave. Before I call the police."

He raised his hands in supplication and shrugged his shoulders. "OK, OK. I go." He grinned his cheeky grin. "It was worth a try. *Non?* No hard feelings?"

Megan watched until he disappeared from sight, then she relaxed. The whole scene had taken only a matter of minutes. She retreated to her room and locked the door.

Leaning against the door and closing her eyes, she said a silent thank you to Tony for appearing when she needed him. He was still her rock, her strength. Watching out for her as he had always done.

This little incident would not appear in her diary, nor would she tell the girls. She couldn't bear to think what they might say.

Something in the back of her mind clicked. Something about Isabel and that art tutor.

She must remember to read Isabel's diary again.

CHAPTER 23

Megan's heart thumped loudly in her ears as Trina rehashed the events of the previous evening. "I hope you enjoyed your birthday dinner, Megan. I didn't want to do anything to spoil it, but people like Mario let the whole country down."

Megan assured her she did indeed have a very enjoyable dinner. "And it was particularly lovely having you two girls with me."

Trina was clearly quite cross about the whole affair and unable to let it pass. "I'm absolutely certain he was going to hit on you last night, and I told him so. He of course denied it, but it was a classic plan. Romantic gondola ride - except with him, not us. We were an unpleasant surprise - then a wonderful dinner to flatter you, and afterwards he would escort you back to your room. Need I say more?"

Megan hoped they couldn't see her discomfort. If they knew their suspicions were warranted neither girl would let her out of their sight again, and they would want to do something about it, whereas she wanted to forget the whole matter.

"So, we agreed," said Trina. "Dinner as planned,

and I wouldn't tell the *polizia* about his little schemes. Needless to say, he won't be bothering you any more."

"I'm glad to hear it, girls. Now, what shall we do with our time?"

For the rest of the week, they talked, laughed, ate, and shopped their way through Venice, but their time there was over and Florence waited. The three women boarded the train at Santa Lucia Station laughing and acting like a bunch of teenagers going to their first ball. She felt blessed by her children and her newfound friends and thankful for her good fortune. Every person she met had taught her something new and given her strength – even Mario, if she was honest. Any lingering doubts about her life had disappeared.

Trina was especially excited about the impending visit to Florence. "I have so many things to show you and people I want you to meet, I don't know where to start."

Their adventures began at the station.

"Trina, *mia cara*. Over here. Quick. Hurry, hurry." Zio Giacomo met them on the platform and rushed them through the crowds. "We need to hurry. I want to avoid the *polizia*. They will give me a ticket if they find the car where I left it."

He and Trina talked non-stop until Trina found time to explain. "He's taking us to a place he's found. The padrona has offered rooms with full board. Zio Giacomo says you don't want to stay in that modern hotel with fake Italian food. You need to experience true Italian hospitality, family style."

There was no arguing with him. Squashed in his tiny Fiat with their luggage tied on the roof, they set off. After a few hair-raising spurts between traffic and tyre-squealing twists and turns into the hill above Florence, he pulled up at a typical Mediterranean house with painted stucco walls, terracotta roof tiles and small windows. At the door a wizened old lady, whose stature belied her vitality, stood in welcome. Their hostess gave Giacomo orders in rapid Italian, and with much pointing the three women were soon settled into their rooms.

Megan was grateful for Giacomo's consideration. Her room was charmingly decorated in well-worn furniture that could have graced any antique store and a pleasant change from some of the modern, characterless hotels she could name. Lace curtains billowed at the window, and a handmade quilt adorned the foot of the wrought-iron bed. A beautifully painted ewer and bowl, usable as well as decorative, sat on the washstand to complement the shared bathroom.

Frenzied tooting from a horn attracted Megan's attention. She went to the window to see what the noise was about and glimpsed Trina leaning out of the adjacent one. Below them, Giacomo was waving and shouting. "*Arrivederci*. I go now. *A dopo*. See you later."

With a final wave, he buzzed off down the road on his Vespa, leaving the car with Trina.

* * * * *

Dinner that evening was a feast. Quite different to the regional delicacies Rosa served in Venice and nothing like any of the food Isabel had detailed in her journal. Earlier that day, Trina had briefly explained the intricacies of her family, complete with its mini feuds, now many of Trina's family had turned up to meet her and Sarah.

How everyone fitted around the table in the tiny enclosed courtyard was a mystery to Megan – and not all of them were there, according to Trina, who'd introduced her to so many people she'd lost count.

"Zio Giacomo's head of the family and everyone's favourite," flattered Trina unashamedly, shouting above the chatter. She put her hand on her uncle's shoulder and stood on tiptoes to kiss his bristled cheek affectionately.

"He's the leather man I told you about. He runs the shoe and handbag factory and Zia Teresa runs the store." Trina put her arm around the older woman. "She was my guardian angel when Mama was sick. I couldn't have done it without her."

"*Primo*," announced Carmela, as she broke through the crowd. The delicious aroma of her creamy risotto had mouths watering.

Giacomo held Megan's chair out as they took their seats. Sarah ended up at the other end of the table with a group of young ones. Above the hum of conversation, plates clattered back and forth and were replaced as more courses arrived. Megan could smell the chicken cacciatore in its creamy sauce and the rich beef ragù with tomatoes, onions, herbs, and garlic, which had spent all afternoon baking in the oven. A stream of vegetables and the freshest of salads to cleanse the palate were crammed onto the table wherever a space appeared.

The wine flowed, music played and the chatter grew louder. People changed places to talk to other people. Wrapped in the warmth of a family who were pleased to see her, Megan felt welcome. Food was the Italian way to please, to be inclusive, and mealtimes were a chance to heal any wrongdoings. She hoped her pain would heal,

191

and soon, but this time it wasn't Tony she was thinking about, it was Jason.

As she watched Trina's face, alive, happy, and exuberant, Megan couldn't help feel resentful. Tony and I should have been there, she almost screamed. Why were we shunned? Her son had talked about how he had been welcomed into this family and how new and exciting he'd found it. Megan was terribly hurt to think Jason had rebuffed his own family and chosen to be here amongst these people without them; but she mustn't blame Trina's family for Jason's behaviour.

To take her mind off Jason, Megan tried comparing her experience with that of her great-grandmother. Isabel had said the English community kept to themselves. The locals were useful as servants and guides, but the expats preferred to dress and eat to their traditional mores. If that were true, then Megan thought they had completely missed the heart and soul of Italy.

"You look sad, *mia cara*," said Giacomo, making her jump as he appeared by her shoulder. He came and sat in the empty chair beside her. "You watch our Caterina, I see. It is good she is happy again. She was not, for such a long time. My sister, Francesca, when she came back from America with her little one over there," he nodded in Trina's direction, "she was changed."

Giacomo told a story of a sad and disillusioned woman. Francesca committed the rest of her life to making sure Caterina had everything she never had – skills, strength, education. When Francesca fell ill, she wouldn't let anyone tell the girl until it was too late. Those last few months were terribly hard on them both.

"You did a good job bringing up your boy, Megan.

Such a thoughtful, caring *giovane*. You must be very proud of him."

Megan listened as her son was described in glowing detail she could never have imagined.

"Jason is a perfect match, exactly what our Trina needs," said Giacomo. "We were sorry you and your husband couldn't share in their wedding. Was he ill long?"

What lie did Jason tell them? thought Megan. Not that she wanted Giacomo to know the truth. That hurt was private.

"And then we learn your husband dies, not long before our Francesca. Such sad times we share, is it not?"

Megan agreed. "Yes, we share similar heartaches. It is hard to come to terms with loss sometimes."

"But now you are here, it is wonderful. *Si?* We can celebrate family, big family, across the world."

"Yes, if that's possible," she agreed again, hesitant to accept his easy tolerance.

"I want to thank you, Megan, for giving us your Jason. He was a gift from God and came at the right time."

Now Megan really didn't know what to say. She had called Jason many things, especially of late, but she would never have put him on that level.

"Such a small ceremony it was. A special service by Francesca's hospital bed, with only Teresa and me as witness. But a festival nonetheless, celebrating a life about to depart and two lives about to begin."

Megan was surprised by this news. She hadn't asked Jason about the ceremony, imagining a huge party rather than the subdued affair Giacomo described. A rush of guilt surged through her as she remembered Jason had spoken of returning to New Zealand for a proper ceremony and party. She hadn't understood what he meant at the time. "I'm glad Jason and Trina are happy together. I wish it will always be so."

"Those two are bound by tragedy." Giacomo shook his head.

No honeymoon for them. Jason flew home, heartbroken, to his father's funeral, only to return in a matter of days because Francesca had slipped into a coma from which she never recovered.

"Our children, they suffered together in mourning, but they are strong. They will survive and flourish." Giacomo stood up and put his hand on her shoulder. "Don't be sad, *mia cara*, for what we cannot change. We have both lost and we both gain. Our hearts, they get twisted into knots, *si*? But we gain strength from our pain."

He disappeared into the crowd, while Megan wondered how much he truly knew of what had happened and how she felt. His words of wisdom were uncannily well timed.

* * * * *

Next morning, Trina arrived with plans for the day. "Before we get too engrossed with all the famous sights, I'd like to take you somewhere first. I have something special I want to show you."

A short time later, having traversed their way far more calmly than Giacomo down the winding hillside road and through the narrow streets, Trina parked the little Fiat in a space Megan thought impossible.

She led them to a narrow, four-storeyed building with a plain entrance. They walked past the main gallery into a high-ceilinged, airy space forming part of the famous art school – Accademia di Belle Arti – and stopped in front of a group of smallish paintings hung in a cluster.

Trina pointed to one slightly larger than the others. "My great-grandfather, Luigi, was a student here once, tutored by Luciano Rossi. Luigi painted this portrait when he was about seventeen or eighteen. He won the prize that year, and his painting has hung in the gallery ever since."

Megan barely registered the name of Trina's great-grandfather, even though she'd read about someone called Luigi in Isabel's journal. Instead, she stared at the painting, wide-eyed and open-mouthed, as if she'd seen a ghost. The portrait showed the head and shoulders of a dark-haired, dark-eyed girl, wearing a peasant-style blouse. Unless Megan's eyes were playing tricks on her, the young girl staring back was the same girl as the one in the portrait in her suitcase. The one she hadn't yet shown Trina.

"Mum, are you all right?" asked Sarah anxiously. "You've gone as white as a sheet."

Trina retrieved a chair from near the door. "Here, sit down. What's wrong?"

Megan sat, taking a few deep breaths to collect her jumbled thoughts, her eyes focused on the portrait. The set of the head and shoulders was the same, she was sure, as were the eyes, but she couldn't believe what she saw. "Trina." Her voice faltered. She cleared her throat. "What do you know about this painting?"

"Mum, don't worry about that now. We should go, you need to lie down or something." Sarah sounded perturbed, but Megan reassured her. She wanted to hear what Trina would say.

"Not a lot. Much as I love it because Great-grandfather Luigi painted it, his style wasn't that good. The face is exquisite, but it's like he got tired; the background is careless.

"He never became famous, he only painted a few commissioned portraits early on in his career. Those commissions soon faded away and he turned his hand to frescoes and street art to make ends meet. I don't think he ever reached his full potential."

"What about the model? What do you know about her, or the tutor? What did you say his name was?" Megan's eyes remained on the painting as Trina talked.

"His name was Luciano Rossi and from what I understand he wasn't a native of Florence. I believe he arrived a year, or maybe two, before this painting was done. Other than that, I don't know much about him. I don't think I've ever seen any of his work either, but he must have had a portfolio or at least a reputation to get the position. Nor do I know anything about the model. In those days, models were often urchins or peasants pulled off the streets at random. It was a way of earning a few extra lire. Life was tough back then."

Megan knew enough history to remember Italy, as a nation, had not been formed until the 1860s with Florence briefly its capital in the 1870s. It was a very poor country with huge debt, inconsistent government, and strong regional factions. Many people left to find a better life in America or wherever they could find work.

"Does the painting have a title?"

"It's called *Study of a woman 1911*, I think. The art school did the same thing every year – a portrait or still life. The students all painted the same image and the best one was chosen."

"Shall we go now, Mum? Get some fresh air," urged Sarah.

"I'm OK, honey. Really, I am, but I do think we should go back. I have something to show you that will explain everything."

Retracing their route up the hill, Sarah and Trina followed Megan into her room where she pulled her suitcase out from under the bed and tossed it on the covers. Megan lifted the lid then unzipped the hard-bottomed, padded case she'd had specially made to protect the painting she'd carried halfway round Europe.

Without a word, Megan lifted the canvas, instantly questioning if she had imagined the resemblance after all. Her painting was much smaller, only half the size, and the overall composition was its strength rather than as a portrait. She turned around, holding the frame so it caught the light from the window behind them and waited for their reaction.

Sarah gasped, the puzzled expression on her face mounting. "It's beautiful. Where did you get it?"

Trina looked similarly stunned. "Is that a Singer Sargent painting?"

"Actually, I'd hoped you could tell me who painted it. It's unsigned."

Trina took the painting from Megan and tipped it further towards the light. Then she propped it up on the dressing table to study it more closely while Sarah peered over her shoulder.

"It's the same girl, isn't it?" said Sarah doubtfully. "How could that be?"

"What do you think, Trina? Is it the same girl?" Megan clutched her hands together tightly knowing her voice betrayed her emotions. Had she found Isabel here in Florence?

Another moment or two passed while Trina continued to study the painting. "Yes. I think it is. No wonder you were shocked."

"What are we saying here?" asked Sarah, looking from one to the other. "That the portrait painted by your great-grandfather Luigi is of Isabel? The same Isabel as in this painting and the same Isabel of the journal?"

Megan nodded. "Looks like it."

"That is unbelievable." Sarah shook her head in bewilderment.

"You're getting a taste of what I've had for months," declared Megan, her sense of humour returning. "One shock after another. Most have been good news, but it does leave your head spinning."

A tumble of questions and answers followed. Megan explained how she first saw the painting in her room at Trevennick Hall, how she'd matched it up with the entry in Isabel's journal and how it came to be in her possession. "I can't believe I've actually found Isabel so soon." Megan took the journal from the bedside drawer, turned to the page, and handed it to the girls to read. "I really need to know more about both paintings."

"I'm not qualified enough," said Trina. "Zio Giacomo might be able to help with Luigi's paintings and the models he used. But as for this one of yours, my first instinct said John Singer Sargent painted it. He was one of Florence's leading lights, but what Isabel has written here doesn't add up. I need to ask some other people, but I think the Wil she talked about could be Wilfrid de Glehn. He was a great friend of Sargent. Either way, this will be a highly sought-after work of art – even unsigned."

"I'm so glad you're here, Trina, and I can't thank you enough. Meeting your family last night was a great privilege, and now this ..."

"They're a bit exhausting, I know, but I'm glad you've met them all now."

"I think the English expats missed out on a lot if they didn't mingle with the locals. I detected quite an undertone of rebellion in Isabel's writing about the strictures of expat life. She was far more interested in spending time with the artists' factions and models."

"That's it!" exclaimed Trina. "The artists. Of course, they're the clue. I've got an idea. I might know of someone who could possibly help us."

Isabel's Journal
15 May 1911

We've been here a month, and I think I've seen every sight there is to see in Florence and still Mrs B and her friends want to show me more. I want to meet people, different people, not visit endless buildings – again. Here I will secretly admit to admiring their beauty but I'm not going to let Mrs B have the pleasure of knowing. It is better than teaching piano to some of the bad-mannered

English brats. I think the heat must be getting to them. How I allowed myself to be persuaded, I do not understand – it's all so frustrating. Still it has its uses. I pretend to be teaching while I visit the artists.

We visited the beautiful cathedral in Piazza del Duomo with its intricate marbles, bell tower, baptistery, and famous golden door. All spectacular. The church of Orsanmichele was another gorgeous edifice. But mostly I like wandering around the piazzas where I can talk with people. The Piazza della Signoria, or the Loggia dei Lanzi, and around the Palazzo Vecchio, is where people gather the most.

The statue of David is enormous and most enlightening. I had been told to avert my eyes from the area unsuitable for young ladies and to concentrate on the whole image. I didn't, of course. In conversation afterwards, I talked about his hands being so large as to seem almost out of proportion, yet when viewed as a whole he looks perfect. That pleased the ladies no end.

The walk across the Ponte Vecchio, down narrow alleyways, and along wide avenues to the Palazzo Pitti is a very nice promenade. There are often street artists lining our way, and when Mrs B isn't looking I like to admire their work and talk to one in particular, my new friend Luigi. The Boboli Gardens are cooler with their many fountains but crammed with tourists. Why do English ladies like gardens so much?

I prefer to walk along the river on the way

back and through the Uffizi courtyard where I know I will find the ladies 'practising their art'. They call it modern and say its message is in the eye of the beholder – so one of the ladies told me as she splashed more colour on the canvas, to the apparent delight of their Italian tutor. More like making appalling shapes with horrible daubs of colour, if you ask me.

I suspect their tutor was just humouring them. He has to, after all. He gets paid to teach them. He's hardly going to tell them what he really thinks, now is he?

But he interests me. It's the same one from the art school. He's rather attractive, but old – maybe 30-something. His eyes twinkle and his laugh is irresistible. He spoke to me briefly while his eyes looked me up and down in a most brazen manner, but his smile ... his smile could melt a mountain of snow. I will accidentally meet him again tomorrow. I am quite taken with him and would like to know him better.

CHAPTER 24

Professor Paul Rosse was a total surprise. Trina had said little concerning the professor of art history she'd heard about. Megan expected to meet an ageing man in a baggy suit with grey hair and craggy skin, rather than this smartly dressed, commanding individual who strode along the echoing corridor of the Accademia di Belle Arti.

Megan shook hands as Trina made the introductions. The man wore his hair slightly longer than the norm and sported a neatly trimmed beard. Megan estimated he would be about sixty, but what most captivated her was the energy he radiated. His smile lit his entire face, reaching into lively, intelligent eyes.

"Welcome to Florence. I'm pleased to meet you." He spoke in perfect English, although his accent was instantly recognisable, despite its acquired nuances.

"You're a Kiwi," came Sarah's surprised comment.

"Yes. I am. Like you." He smiled again. His eyes twinkled, and Megan immediately warmed to him. Someone from home, an ally in an uncharted sea.

Suggesting they all join him in his office, Paul guided them down the long corridor. "I've missed the place. Stanford has been good for my career, and I have enjoyed my role as visiting professor in Florence, but it's time I returned home." He opened the door and allowed the women to enter before him.

Once seated in studded leather chairs around an ornate, heavy desk, Megan explained the purpose of her visit. Paul listened attentively, occasionally asking a few questions of his own to help clarify their tale. Megan was certain the way he looked at her showed he had as much interest in her as in her story.

"As I see it there are two aspects to all this. One, finding out more about this tutor and his models at the Accademia delle Arti del Disegno, as it was called then, and second, identifying the artist of your painting and linking the two together."

"Anything you could tell us would be helpful. Thank you," said Megan.

"Do you know anything about this Luciano Rossi?" asked Sarah.

Paul steepled his fingers, elbows on the desk, while he pondered his answer. He smiled. "As a matter of fact, I believe I do. But I'd like to check a few things before I comment. Mrs Marsh, could we meet again later when I've done some research?"

After they had agreed on a time and place to meet, Megan and the girls made their departure. He walked with them to the entrance and held Megan's hand slightly longer than necessary as they said farewell. Once outside Trina said she was impressed, and his Italian when he addressed her was impeccable.

Sarah didn't share Trina's enthusiasm. "He was a bit full of himself, wasn't he? I've never seen a Kiwi guy so immaculate, especially not any uni types, and why didn't he want to tell us what he knows?"

Megan kept her thoughts to herself about this surprising man. She instinctively knew Paul was someone she could trust. She had the feeling she would see a lot more of him and he would have much to say when the time was right. "I expect he needs to be careful."

"Careful of what? We were only asking for information." Sarah was unreasonably rattled.

Trina was eager to show her new family the sights and haunts of her home town. "Don't worry about it, I'm sure he has his reasons. Can we be tourists now?"

With Trina in the lead, Megan looked back to find Paul still watching her.

* * * * *

"My feet are killing me. Don't tell me there's more?" Sarah sank into a chair at the bar they'd chosen and pulled off her shoe to rub her aching foot. For the last three days, they had tackled the list of all the places Isabel wrote about during her lengthy stay. They had walked and walked, dodging traffic and people as best they could, until blisters formed.

"Heaps," teased Megan, knowing from previous visits the vast numbers of statues, paintings, frescoes and domes Florence had to offer.

Trina laughed when she saw Sarah's face drop. "Sorry. I didn't mean to scare you. None of our visits have taken us to my usual haunts. I've not visited half of those places for so long I'd almost forgotten. Seeing them through your eyes has helped me appreciate how wonderful they are."

"I think we need to pace ourselves better," said Megan, who had plans of her own. She needed some private time for an evening with Giacomo to talk about Luigi, plus another meeting with Paul.

By the end of each day, even though the sights of central Florence did not cover a particularly large area, Megan and Sarah were mentally and physically worn out.

"It strikes me it's much harder to get around now than when Isabel did all this," said Sarah.

"Much more," agreed Trina. "There wouldn't have been those pesky Vespas dodging in and out around the place making life difficult, that's for certain."

"I thought they were going to run me down more than once."

Trina smiled. "What do you say to some shopping and eating instead?"

Sarah immediately brightened. "That sounds more my cup of tea."

"Pardon? You want tea?" queried Trina, completely misunderstanding the very English expression.

Megan laughed while Sarah explained. "It means that's more to my liking. So yes, shopping, please."

Over a carafe of ice-cold white wine, Megan listened while the two girls planned their shopping spree. Top of their list was another visit to Zia Teresa in the family shop, which catered for high-end wealthy tourists, and one to the factory so they could see what Trina's mother had created.

"The leather markets are also a must. I know the best places to find handbags, shoes and coats at excellent prices, and if you want cashmere jumpers and scarves, or pashminas, there's this delightful little shop that offers the best quality."

Megan interrupted her flow. "I don't need to do much shopping. I'm happy if you girls go off without me."

Trina also wanted to take them to her favourite cafés and bistros, to taste the best bruschetta, *arancini* risotto balls, and pizza. "Not the ones catering for the tourists, of course, but genuine, traditional pizza prepared for Italian taste."

For the evenings, Trina had plans for other restaurants and bars.

As did Megan. With Paul.

Isabel's Journal
20 June 1911

We've been here a little over two months now. My reputation as a piano teacher has spread, and I now have several students – I hate it. It's boring, boring, boring! Still, it's an opportunity to get away from Mrs B and the ladies. They have long since decided I was safe to go about unescorted during the daytime.

The evening routine never changes. It's a musical evening, or cards evening with the ladies. I never get to dance any more, there are no balls like in Paris and I won't meet any young men of interest if I rely on them.

I've taken to calling into the art school. I'm sure Mama would be horrified if she knew. Mrs B I'm not too sure about. I don't think she would have given me permission so I didn't ask, but I wouldn't mind guessing she would have gone if she'd had the chance. I have to say I was very clever inventing another student so I could get away.

The first time I went there I was petrified I might get caught out, but nothing happened so I've been going for weeks now.

I couldn't believe my eyes that first day. My friend from the street artists and other students were sketching a model sitting on a chair in the middle of the room. Their tutor was with them – the same gorgeous man I saw in my first week here.

When he saw me, he was very welcoming and encouraged me to talk about the students' work. He's very theatrical – exuberant one moment, dark and brooding the next. The students seem to adore him but his language leaves much to be desired, if my poor Italian is any judge.

I was quite flattered that he asked my opinion. I told him I knew nothing about art but wanted to learn. He said it didn't matter. Beauty was in the eye of the beholder, and I was very beautiful. I was embarrassed by his forthrightness but am getting used to it the more I see him. It's the Italian way, after all.

CHAPTER 25

Their days and nights were filled with endless activity. Whatever doubts Megan had back in Hawaii about spending extended time with Trina in Florence had vanished. Her new daughter-in-law was in her element, showing off the city of her youth and generously sharing her family.

The two girls got on well, considering their unusual start, and shopped till they dropped. Trina often invited her cousins to join them when they went out at night, and they had avoided any underlying tensions. The tension now was between her and Sarah.

"Why do you have to go to dinner with him? Again," asked Sarah as she showed Megan her latest purchases. "Why can't he tell you what he knows during the day at the academy?"

One evening, the girls had gone out nightclubbing leaving Megan to her own devices and – Sarah thought – alone, but Megan had had other plans.

While she and Paul shared a quiet meal and a bottle of wine at a candlelit table, the two girls walked in. Megan could tell by the look on Sarah's face she was not happy.

Sarah said nothing at the time, but later she tackled Megan about it.

"Because, my darling girl, he has lectures during the day. And I happen to enjoy his company."

"That was obvious the other night," she snapped. She stepped out of the dress she had been trying on, without waiting for Megan's opinion, and began to pull on a skirt and top.

"Not that long ago you encouraged me to go out and make new friends; now you object to me going out. What's the matter? What don't you like about Paul?"

The girl made no response as she looked over her shoulder in the mirror to see the back.

"That looks nice. Sarah, there is no point pretending nothing is wrong. What's upsetting you?"

"After your near run-in in Venice, I thought you'd be more cautious. That's all."

"Paul is hardly a Mario." Megan preferred not to think about that man, but because of what happened, Megan was sure her judgement was right this time. Paul was genuine, and there was a natural rapport between them.

Sarah ignored her comment and pulled the top off over her head.

Megan tried to dig deeper into why Sarah was acting out of character and had taken such an active dislike to someone she'd only just met.

"It's none of my business," she answered, zipping up another dress.

"Whether it is or not, you clearly have something on your mind."

Her normally forthright daughter was proving evasive. Megan wondered if Sarah was jealous. The two of them had spent a lot more time together over the last year – had Megan not spent enough time with her daughter here? Was that the problem?

Megan knew something was wrong. The pair had always been close and the ability to talk to one another had been their strength,

Worried she was missing something, Megan tried to narrow down the possibilities. "Is it Trina? Are you getting on OK with her?"

"Trina's fine."

"Are you mad with Jason? Is that it?"

"Yes, but I'll get over it."

Surely, Sarah couldn't be jealous of Paul?

"So, it's Paul that's bothering you."

Sarah shrugged again. "Like I said, it's none of my business. If you want to spend time with him, I can't stop you. But I don't have to like it."

"No, you can't stop me, but I would much prefer it if you were happy for me. It's not like you to take a dislike to someone you don't know. Give him a chance."

"Why? I don't think you should be seeing him. And that's that!"

Megan didn't know what to say in response. Sarah was not normally intractable. She'd have to think about the cause. "I really like that skirt," Megan commented, changing the subject. "Do you want us to get some things for Bella or Nick while we're out today?"

Sarah merely shook her head. "I've already bought more than enough for Bella. I've got Nick a few things, but there's no point getting him anything more. He's such a down-to-earth basics man. He doesn't care whether it's Italian or Chinese – as long as it's comfortable."

"We'd better go and meet Trina, then," said Megan, eager to relieve the tension.

In addition to all the ancient monuments, buildings and artworks, Trina was keen to show them some of the contemporary art galleries, the likes of which she coveted, selling work by new artists. Megan went along to some but found much of the work tortured, confusing or inexplicable. Her tastes were entrenched in the natural and real.

"You don't have to like it," Trina laughed at Megan's comments. "You just have to recognise its potential. Works like these will fetch hundreds of thousands in years to come. The sort of work you like would once have been radical to many people of the times."

Trina sounded as informed as any art historian and loved every moment. She explained how religious works gave way to romanticism, realism, and impressionism. Nudity, she said, was revered by some cultures and in some centuries, to then be despised in others, which often explained why the fig leaf was added as a covering to many statues.

Sarah was excited by some of the new works and, with novel ideas of her own, wondered if she could change her style.

"Depends on whether you want to work for yourself or someone else," said Trina.

"I'm going to leave you two to carry on," interrupted Megan, looking at her watch. "I need to get changed. I'm meeting Paul early this evening."

"Have fun," said Trina.

Sarah simply glared at her.

* * * * *

"Have you got anything new to tell me?" asked Megan over a glass of Chianti as they sat replete from dinner. She hoped the candlelight softening the scene would put Paul in the mood to talk.

"I've a few bits and pieces that could interest you."

Megan found his melodious voice easy to listen to and encouraged him to talk. "Go on, enlighten me then."

"Let me start with the formal bits. Wilfred de Glehn was indeed a friend of John Singer Sargent. They met in the 1890s while de Glehn was a student in Paris. De Glehn met his wife Jane, also a painter, in America while he helped Sargent paint the huge decorative mural cycle for the Boston Public Library. De Glehn and Jane married in 1904, and your friend Wil took his bride to visit his sister who lived in Cadgwith in Cornwall."

"I've been to Cadgwith," exclaimed Megan. "It's a sleepy coastal village. I remember now, their one boast to fame was a visiting artist I'd never heard of. Are you telling me this is the same one?"

"Probably. There can't be that many artists in Cadgwith," confirmed Paul. "The pair visited Cornwall regularly. Somehow, de Glehn and Jane ended up as guests of your Isabel's father. I can't find any record to prove it, but I have a strong suspicion the painting you showed me is a Wilfred de Glehn."

"That's amazing! What Isabel said in her diary is true? Wil and Jane came to stay, and Wil painted Isabel."

"Looks like it, but a word of warning. Since the painting is unsigned, its provenance relies solely on the diary entry, and unfortunately your Isabel doesn't mention his name so it could be difficult to prove."

"I don't mind if it's proven or not. I love the story. Tell me more."

"The three of them, de Glehn, Jane and Sargent, travelled together frequently, and Wil's style has often been mistaken as that of Singer Sargent's, which is why young Trina thought it a Sargent to begin with. Good eye, that girl has."

Trina had said the painting could be significant. Paul confirmed it.

"What about Luigi's painting here in Florence? What's the connection?" Excited by yet another story about her ancestor, Megan urged him to keep talking.

"That connection is more coincidental than absolute. Singer Sargent was indeed born in Florence, and Florentines claimed him as their own, but there's no record to show the de Glehns and Sargent worked in or visited Florence together. It's extremely unlikely they would have met Luciano Rossi or his student Luigi. So far, it's a dead end."

Megan noticed how Paul's eyes glowed as he talked about his favourite subjects – art and artists. For the first time since she'd met Tony so long ago, a man held her interest. She had no need to interrupt or contribute to the conversation, she was content being with him.

They strolled through the streets of Florence as Paul told her the historical significance of this building or that, before they stopped at a bar for a nightcap. "Can we talk about things other than art and history?" he asked.

"Of course," Megan replied. "We are friends now, aren't we?"

"I hope so." He raised her hand to his lips in a much

more Italian than Kiwi manner. "I'd like to get to know you a lot better. Can we meet again tomorrow?"

His seriousness unsettled Megan a little, but hesitantly she agreed. "But not tomorrow evening. I'm having dinner with Giacomo and Teresa."

"Lunch it is, then."

Isabel's Journal
25 June 1911 — Florence

I hesitate to put this on paper, but I think I must or else I will never believe it happened. I have met the most romantic and adorable man one could ever wish to meet.

I am in love.

But I will not use names in case someone reads my musings. It is enough for me to know whom I am talking about.

CHAPTER 26

"It is good to see you again, *mia cara*. *Vieni*, come in," Giacomo invited.

"*Buona sera*, Megan." Teresa busied herself in the kitchen and talked non-stop about what she was cooking that evening, while Giacomo poured the wine.

"It is fascinating, is it not," he said, as he handed Megan the glass, "that our grandparents knew one another – your Isabel and our Luigi. You, me, we of similar age, but we not of same generation. Luigi, he my grandfather. Your Isabel one generation more."

"Oh. Of course. He must have been, I didn't realise until now," said Megan. "Not that I ever gave it any thought. Luigi was simply a name in Isabel's journal until I came here. But yes, it is a fascinating coincidence. Do you remember him?"

"*Si*. Of course, I was eldest, Francesca, the youngest, *si*? You understand?"

Giacomo outlined the whole family tree, which Megan tried to follow but frequently got lost. There were too many of them. He finally got back to the days of Luigi. Even though Luigi and Isabel were the same age, Luigi did not marry until much later, hence the

215

generational discrepancy. He lived until he was nearly ninety. Giacomo remembered him well.

"Luigi was a romantic. He see good in everything, and he love everyone. His wife, his children, his grandchildren, he never happier than when surrounded by people.

"Before I knew him, before he got old, when the mood took him Luigi would go off and paint; sometimes he disappear for days or weeks picking up work wherever he could. When he was in that mood, nothing would disturb him. If he worked in his studio, they said he would not eat for hours, he would slash a painting if it didn't go right, or he could painstakingly rebuild a portrait from nothing, or so my father told me. I knew him as an old man, sitting in front of the fire, praising Nonna's cooking and telling stories to the little ones. He was a good storyteller. He could read people."

Giacomo told her a few of his funnier ones about people who wanted portraits done. Luigi would paint what he saw in the sitter and then another one how he believed the sitter saw themselves. Often, they were quite different, but Luigi knew how to flatter people and make them feel good.

"He learnt to draw fast and enjoyed doing the street portraits the most, especially as he got older because it kept him at home more often. He met many people that way and had stories to tell about a lot of them. He would draw little cartoons of his children and grandchildren even when his hands had become too arthritic to do justice to the images. He couldn't keep still. Let me show you."

Suddenly, Giacomo got up from the table and disappeared, returning a few moments later. "Look what I have here." He handed Megan an old-style artist's sketchbook with a cloth cover. "This belonged to Luigi."

Fascinated, Megan began turning the pages. Charcoal and pencil sketches filled each page – faces, a jawline, an eye, an ear, and neck, half a face side on, a full face. Always the latest sketch at the beginning; Luigi believed in starting a book from the back. Giacomo would point out one or two and put a name to the child. These were not works for sale, these were experiments, memories, works of love.

Careful to handle the pages with respect as each one layered upon the other, she began to recognise a face or two from an earlier page. A girl who looked a lot like Isabel appeared on several pages with other sketches of small children, but Megan dismissed it as unlikely.

"What a wonderful heirloom." Tears brimmed in her eyes as she shut the book. The man had been a master, and Megan thought his drawings were exquisite. "Thank you for showing me. They are such wonderful sketches. I think he must have been a special man. I can see his love of people. Such strong lines and fine detail."

Giacomo took the sketchbook. "Si. He was special." His voice was warm and gentle. "Special to whole family. He liked faces, but he knew he was not quite good enough to be famous."

Teresa started clattering plates and setting the table. "Soon we eat, but first, Giacomo, show Megan the old one."

Giacomo took one sketchbook away to replace it with another cloth-covered book with yellowed, fragile pages, wrapped in a pillowcase for safekeeping.

He refilled the wine glasses. "These are mostly of my nonna, his wife and their *bambini*, when they were little ones. And then the *nipote* – their grandchildren. Pages and pages of them."

Megan was honoured he would show her such personal and clearly romantic images. Handling the pages with infinite care, she looked at the sketches. Again, they often showed only part of a face, but all of them captured an emotion: laughter, a smile, sadness, a frown, love. Megan could see love in every line of the woman's face as she looked at the child drawn next to her, or when she stared straight at the artist. The drawings were beautiful. She was beautiful.

Towards the back of the book another face appeared – young, enthusiastic, and energetic. Dozens of drawings of the one face, some partly completed and started again. Others, almost perfect, covered page after page. He had captured every expression, nonchalant, demure, and alluring.

"Who is this?" Megan asked Giacomo, her heart starting to race.

"She has no name," he replied with a shrug. "Nonna used to laugh and tell us she was his first love. His muse, his art. She was a model at the academy."

Megan was sure this girl had a name. She had seen her face before. Had Trina not told him what they'd found at the Accademia?

She was Isabel.

Megan's Diary
12 May 2011

Finding Isabel in Luigi's sketchbook was fantastic. It's another link in the chain of discovery into who she really was and what she wanted out of life.

Once I'd told Giacomo and Teresa that they were looking at Isabel, they were over the moon and more excited about our ancestral connections. The girls were also enthusiastic. It's amazing to think that Isabel and Luigi knew each other so well. I wish Isabel had written more about it in her diary, but she didn't, whatever her reasons – unless it's all in those missing pages. It's another thing in this journey I can't change.

Hard as it is to believe, those sketches confirmed Isabel did model for the art school. How a well-brought-up young English girl managed to do such a thing seems incredible. In those days she really would have brought disgrace on the family. Was it to fulfil her mother's prophecy or the other way around? Had her mother been right after all?

I've been back, and we've searched through the other sketchbooks to see if there were other later images of Isabel but couldn't find any.

Still, it gives me leads, something to follow. Isabel was clearly fascinated with art, infatuated with the artists, and rebelled against everything she had been taught.

Am I one step closer to determining her passion in life?

I still don't know what happened to her once everyone knew she was pregnant. Where did she live? Did the expat community support her, or was it the father of her child? Or Luigi? And when did she leave Florence?

So many questions with no answers.

CHAPTER 27

"Bye, Mum." Sarah gave her mother a hug as they stood together in the airport lounge. "Thanks for everything."

Megan couldn't believe how quickly three weeks had slipped by, but this time she was less apprehensive about being on her own.

Since her discovery, Giacomo and Teresa were more insistent Megan share a meal with them and encouraged her to stay in Florence; she could help in the shop, they said. Or maybe they would open a second shop for her to run.

Not only did she have them, there was also Paul.

Sarah had continued talking. "It's been great. I wouldn't have missed it for the world."

Was it only last week when she and Sarah heard the same words from Trina, as *she* reluctantly returned to work? Trina had promised them a fun time, and fun was exactly what they'd had. Between Liberation Day on 25th April and Labour Day on 1st May, it was party time with a lot of music and dancing at ceremonies, historic reenactments, fairs, concerts, and food festivals.

They'd watched street parades, attended plays and concerts and overindulged in the food. The music and street parties were especially good, although Megan got a little upset when she got briefly separated from the girls. The atmosphere seized her imagination – quite formal in some aspects and completely uninhibited in others. Megan knew she would remember it always.

Not that Trina had spent the entire time with them as promised. One of Jason's flight schedules unexpectedly included Rome. Trina couldn't resist the opportunity and took the express train to spend one day with him. Secretly delighted at being abandoned in favour of her son, Megan hadn't yet shared with Sarah her suspicion that Trina was expecting. She wasn't sure Trina knew for certain. There was something about the look of the girl and gut instinct that told Megan it could be so.

Now she was back at the airport to say goodbye to her daughter.

"Do take care, won't you?" Sarah put both hands on her mother's shoulder and looked her squarely in the eye. Megan knew exactly what she was referring to.

They'd had a terrible row, worse than the first and one that Megan regretted, but it broke the tension between them. Sarah finally admitted her initial qualms: she'd thought Paul too suave and too elegant to be true. She thought him far more fit for the role of Don Giovanni than a stuffy art historian and had simply wanted to protect her mother.

"He's not Dad," she had said, confirming Megan's suspicions. "I'm not ready for someone to replace him."

"No one could ever do that, sweetheart," Megan had assured her.

After their spat, Sarah had relaxed towards Paul. The three women would meet up, and while he escorted them around some of the endless galleries, Paul would talk about the artists and models of the time. He and Trina hit it off, and sometimes their discussions were more technical than either Megan or Sarah could follow. Yet somehow his knack of making the subject come alive meant Sarah had been captivated by his enthusiasm. And, she said, she'd learnt a few things from him about graphic art.

The final call came. Another hug and a reminder from Sarah, "Don't do anything silly, will you," and it was time to part.

"Have some confidence in my judgement. I'm not that gullible," laughed Megan, thankful Sarah had no idea how close she and Paul had become, or what truly happened with Mario. Which reminded her, she hadn't checked up on what bothered her about Isabel during that farcical moment.

* * * * *

Megan was suddenly glad she had agreed to meet Paul that afternoon and drive into the countryside to visit a vineyard. Saying goodbye to Sarah had left an empty feeling in the pit of her stomach.

"May is a perfect time in Tuscany," he said as he manoeuvred the car around the winding corners. "Lots of sunshine and almost perfect temperatures. And before all the tourists arrive and cram the place out."

Megan was relieved he hadn't asked how much longer she would stay. She hadn't made up her mind yet and didn't want to be pressured. For the time being, she was happy to enjoy his company.

"There's Castello Banfi – famous for its ancient Etruscan castle," Paul announced, as they chatted amiably about the passing scenery. "These days the estate wins many wine awards, but the place is huge. I thought we'd go somewhere a little quieter and more exclusive but with equally good wines."

Megan pointed out all the villages tucked into hillsides or workers in the fields that took her eye as they drove by. A while later Paul pulled into a long driveway that led to a two-storeyed building exuding old-world charm. A tracery of cracks spread across the crumbling terracotta wash on walls draped in ivy and festooned with flowering window boxes.

"Oh, Paul. It's beautiful."

"It's better inside." He guided her past olive trees, surrounded by low *Buxus* hedges that edged a pathway to the door. As they walked into the cool interior, the owner greeted Megan effusively. He led them through to their table on the terrace, promising to bring an array of wines and a tasting platter of local products.

Megan sat admiring her surroundings. Grapes dangled from the framework above their heads, filtering the bright sunlight, as a gentle breeze touched her skin. The view was breathtaking, overlooking rolling hills planted with vines and olive trees as far as they could see. Softly splayed branches hung heavy with fruit, and the cypress trees looked so perfect they could have been topiaried. Dotted here and there in the garden were the usual array of statues and urns expected at every turn throughout the region.

Their host reappeared. "*Si. Si. Benvenuto.* See what I have for you."

For a while, conversation was limited as their host described the various blends and ages of the wines poured into tiny glasses for them to sample. Megan left the final choice to Paul.

Their sommelier quickly brought fresh glasses and a full bottle. They gently swirled the dark red liquid and savoured the rich flavours before nibbling at the crusty breads, assorted olives and cheeses. Once that platter had been cleared another one appeared layered with bruschetta, a ripieni of stuffed zucchini and another of seafood wrapped in vine leaves, all of which were exceptional. Megan relaxed and settled into the comfortable camaraderie they shared.

"You spoke once before of a desire, a need, to return to your roots. Why do you think this has come about now?"

Paul, having developed his own version of Italian nonchalance, shrugged eloquently. "Who can say?" He paused to test the nose of the wine in his glass. "I think maybe ..." He shifted his position awkwardly. "My father died quite young – I'm older now than he ..."

Megan sipped on her wine and waited for him to continue. She didn't want to pry if he didn't want to tell her.

"I think you reach a stage in your life when it's time to weigh up your priorities. I've dedicated my life to my work, and I've ended up an eccentric old recluse," Paul admitted. "But I don't want to end my time on this earth wishing I'd done something I could have done and didn't."

Megan shared his viewpoint. There were things Tony had still wanted to do when he was struck down and, in part, that had a lot to do with her decision to search out her roots.

"Did you get to see your father before he went?"

"No. He went too quickly; like your Tony." A look of regret passed over Paul's face. "I didn't return for the funeral. I couldn't face it. It was too soon after Susan passed away."

Megan remembered the evening he'd talked about how he'd lost his wife after a long, drawn-out battle with cancer. How he'd thought he'd go mad. They'd had no children, so with nothing to focus on he buried himself deeper in work, travelling anywhere it took him as long as it was far away from New Zealand.

Paul ran his hands through his hair, plainly bothered by painful memories. "I know I behaved badly – selfish and cowardly. It wasn't fair on my mother, but I hope she understood. She said she did."

"I'm sure she did. Mothers have a knack of understanding their sons," she told him, knowing Paul wouldn't understand the irony of her comment. "And forgiving them."

In that moment, she knew: after what Giacomo had told her and his wise words of comfort, deep in her heart, she had forgiven Jason.

"Is your mother still alive?"

Paul shook his head. "No, she died some years ago. I went back long enough to arrange her funeral and sort out the paperwork on her estate. I left again as fast as I could. Sorry, this is a bit heavy for such a delightful evening."

"I don't mind," Megan reassured him. "It was my fault for asking such a leading question."

"Enough of the past for now – how about a toast to the future?"

They clinked glasses.

"I thought my question was about the future. But maybe instead of asking why you wanted to go home, I should have asked what you want to do, once you return."

"I'm not sure. Retire maybe?"

"Retire? You aren't ready for that, are you? Take the summer off and go sightseeing. Get to know the country again, but you must have better ambitions than to stop everything you do."

Paul accepted her rebuke with a nod. "Perhaps you're right. My dream has always been to have my own art collection. But I've never had the necessary fortune to own anything, and I wouldn't know where to begin with a gallery that sells art. I know about art but not about commerce, so it's never happened."

Megan stored that piece of information away, knowing Trina was the opposite. Trina knew about the commerce of a gallery that sold art more than she knew about how to buy art. Maybe she could put the two of them together somehow, in the future.

"That sounds more interesting," Megan commented, but not ready to say anything further, decided to return to an earlier conversation. "I've been thinking about what you told me before, about my artist Wil. Can you explain again how you thought he was connected with New Zealand?"

Paul was in his element. "Your Wil, as you put it, was a peripheral player. There's nothing to show he went to New Zealand. Like I said, I can't be certain, but this is why I think Isabel ended up there."

With words, Paul painted an intricate picture of the Florentine art world of the late nineteenth century into the early twentieth. A scene where artists collaborated, with much shouting and waving of arms over wine and pasta, to come up with new ideas, and where they argued and debated styles, brushstrokes and colour and developed new schools of thought. Everyone knew everyone else. They shared garrets, models, pigments, tools and – if one is to believe the stories – wives, girlfriends and sometimes men friends, although that was not so openly discussed.

Astounded, Megan broke in during a lull in his discourse. "Do you think Isabel was part of that scene?"

"Very much so."

In Paul's mind, one Florentine artist, Girolamo Nerli, was of particular interest. "He spent a decade in New Zealand from 1893, setting up his own Otago Art Academy in Dunedin briefly, to take private pupils; then three years later he went to Auckland to open a studio and exhibited with the Auckland Society of Arts in April of the following year."

Megan interrupted. "I'm sure he was an interesting character and important to New Zealand art history. But I'm confused. This was all more than a decade before Isabel was in Florence. What's Nerli got to do with anything?"

"Sorry. I'll try to simplify things." Paul admitted his weakness for getting bogged down in the detail and his habit of lecturing when there was a story to tell. "De Glehn drops out of the picture completely. His only involvement seems to have been with the painting of Isabel in Cornwall. It's Luciano Rossi that matters."

Paul told her about the artist, Louis John Steele, who married the daughter of Giulio Piatti, a Florentine artist. Steele moved to Auckland around 1886 on his own. Within eight years, Steele's studio was described in the papers as 'a combination of art gallery, museum and general curiosity shop, with himself as a genial showman'."

Megan listened intently while Paul added more details and linked dates and people together.

"This is how the whole thing ties together," he said eventually. "Steele was quite well established internationally and ran an important studio in Victoria Arcade in Shortland Street. He and Nerli exhibited together at the Auckland Society of Arts. C F Goldie was Steele's most famous student and co-collaborator.

"There is no doubt Nerli, Piatti and Steele knew one another. The art world in Florence was small and intimate. And that," concluded Paul, patting the table with enthusiasm, "is how I believe our friend Rossi knew about New Zealand."

"That's amazing. I think I followed it all, and maybe you're on to something. But, you believe Luciano knew artists living in Auckland?"

"Yes, I do. They would have been a drawcard."

"Really? I wish now I'd got Jessica to send those letters of Isabel's here instead of back home. I'm sure they will tell us a lot of what happened. I can hardly wait to read them."

"I'm sure they will." Paul's mood suddenly changed. "I've something else to tell you, now we're alone. I didn't want to share this with Sarah and Trina. You can decide what to tell them when the time comes."

"My goodness, you are sounding mysterious. What's this all about now?"

"I've had my suspicions for some time, but I needed to put the whole picture together before I told you."

Megan wondered what could be so bad that Paul had withheld it.

According to Paul's research, Luciano Rossi really was a mystery man. "Rossi arrived in Florence with no history to speak of and charmed his way into a role with the Accademia. The dons weren't happy, judging by the written complaints I found in the archives. But, since his students achieved quite remarkable work under his tutelage, he had been allowed to stay. Until one day, he disappeared."

"How odd. Have you discovered what happened to him?"

He pulled a piece of paper out of the inside pocket of his jacket that hung on the back of his chair. "This might help."

Instinctively, Megan sensed something big was coming.

Paul spread the paper out before her. "It's a passenger list of a ship that left Hamburg late in 1912. Many Italian families, especially from Tuscany, left for better conditions elsewhere – including New Zealand. See here."

He pointed to some names partway down the page.

Della Rossa, Isabel Trevallyan, widow, aged 20.

Della Rossa, Julia Trevallyan, infant, aged 6 months.

Further down *Rossi, Luciano, male, single, artist, aged 34.*

Megan couldn't quite grasp the meaning of any of it. Gordon at the London records office had been unable to find a marriage certificate for Isabel, yet here she was shown as a widow. Nor had a father of the child been named, but this document showed Julia with an Italian name.

"I don't understand. What is this saying?"

"At this stage, it's evidence Isabel and her daughter left Italy for New Zealand on the same ship as Luciano."

"But their names are spelt differently."

"That's quite common. Don't take any notice of that. My own family were originally of Italian heritage and went to New Zealand in the 1880s. Our name has been spelt many different ways including Rossi, Russo and Rossa, finally ending up with Rosse."

"I didn't realise that. How interesting."

"What I think happened here is one of two things. A transcription error – someone has misread or misheard the name Rossi, turning it into Rossa; 'Della' means 'of the', or ..."

"But this shows Isabel as a widow, not his wife, and Julia's father is unknown."

"Or, more likely, Luciano told the shipping clerk what he wanted them to know."

"You mean he lied?"

"Probably. Whatever it all means; the record is what it shows. But I don't think your Isabel was a widow either."

Megan's Diary
15 May 2011

I was speechless when Paul told me about the passenger list, but at least I now know when Isabel left Florence and roughly when she arrived in New Zealand. And I have a name to follow - Isabel Della Rossa. I don't understand why Grandma Julia carried the name Trevallyan as Gordon told me, in that case. What is it with people who change their name and disappear off the face of the earth! It's frustrating.

What I have learnt is that Italy in those days was notoriously regional. Similar names, spelt differently, would identify whether the family came from the north or south, which might have explained something of Luciano's mystery. Like with Paul's family. That was an unexpected revelation. I'll enjoy finding out more about his history. He said he'd been concerned they may be related and had spent some time trying to trace Luciano's family, but could find nothing — and nothing that linked him to Paul's family in any way.

According to various records, most of the Italian passengers went straight to the Hutt or Nelson, to join other Tuscan families in the booming market gardens and tomato trade, while Isabel remained in Auckland. I wonder if she made friends with anyone and if they wrote to each other. Paul has doubts. I have no idea how well Isabel spoke Italian either, if at all.

Whichever way we look at it, we can say with certainty Luciano travelled to New Zealand with Isabel. The question is, was Julia their baby? The birth certificate didn't name a father. Was it Luciano or someone else? Luigi? I hadn't thought of that possibility before.

Did Luciano betray my great-grandmother? Had Isabel been separated by choice or abandoned? Did he plan to leave Isabel and the baby alone in a strange country or did something happen to them once they'd arrived? Paul is convinced Luciano lied.

He is also sure they would have had something to do with the art scene in Auckland.

It's a starting point, but again, I'm left with too many unanswered questions.

Still, something good has come from all this. I am suddenly itching to get back home and read Isabel's letters. Maybe they will fill in the gaps.

CHAPTER 28

Megan never did get the knack of touting to the tourists wandering around the marketplace, like the Italians could. As a favour to Teresa, she'd agreed to help man a stall, where they could sell their seconds. Not that Megan saw anything wrong with their so-called 'seconds' but she knew Teresa would not tolerate anything less than top quality. Most of the family found themselves roped in during the summer tourist months. The task could be quite tiring, with long hours and, on some days, little return. Calling out about the best deal Florence could offer would possibly attract more people, but it wasn't her style.

Despite the clamour and crowds surrounding her, Megan had time to think while she sat on the high stool beside the stall. In the six weeks since Sarah's departure, Megan had spent many hours with Paul, but as the academy's Spring Quarter neared its end, they had spent less time together. Their easy friendship had shifted. She couldn't quite explain how, or on whose side, but something was different. He appeared distracted. In some ways, she didn't mind – things were happening too fast anyway. She wasn't ready for any sort of relationship; she wasn't sure she ever would be.

Thinking back, Megan remembered occasions when she'd caught sight of Paul in the corridors seemingly in high spirits, laughing and joking with a student or fellow staff member, to find his mood changed by the time he'd joined her.

One day, before he'd noticed her, she saw him place his hands on a student's shoulder and kiss her on either cheek, highly excited about something, yet he never mentioned it. But then, why should he? It was none of her business, but it left her wondering about his past relationships and, for that matter, current ones. It seemed impossible a man with his appeal would not have had any dalliances since his wife died. She realised how little she knew about him.

Towards the end of June, Paul announced he needed to return to the States. His reasons sounded vague, something to do with his tenure and requirements to teach.

"Don't rush back to New Zealand while I'm gone. Summer in Tuscany is amazing," he said. "Let me show you. Stay in Florence. I'll try not to be away too long."

Megan was non-committal. Winter in New Zealand held little attraction, but with the second anniversary of Tony's death coming up at the beginning of September, she wanted to go home, regardless of Isabel's journal and its timetable. Waiting around Florence all summer would be pointless.

Thinking it through, Megan decided it was best for her to leave before Paul returned. She could hardly believe she'd nearly got caught up in a silly spring romance, if what they shared could be called a romance. Had she become a little too desperate for company, as Sarah had warned, and fallen for his suave sophistication?

The phone call from Jason, confirming her earlier suspicions about Trina, bolstered her decision.

"Hey, Mum! Guess what? You're going to be a nana again. A Christmas baby they reckon."

"How wonderful! Congratulations to you both."

"Trina's contract with the art gallery finishes at the end of July, and she's not going to renew it, so I'm looking at a change in my routes. If I'm successful, and I think I will be, we want to go home."

Megan held her breath. *Does he really mean what I think?* "Home ...? Do you mean ...?"

"Yes, Mum. I mean Auckland."

"Jason! That's the best news I've heard all year – and I've had quite a bit of news in that time. That's wonderful."

"See. I told you I would make it up to you one day. Are my stakes a little higher now?"

"Yes. They are," she laughed. "You back in Auckland and a new grandchild will just about do it, but don't get too cocky."

He couldn't go into any more detail or give her any idea of a time frame; it would depend on the outcome of his application, but they wanted the baby born in New Zealand.

Teresa and Giacomo couldn't stop talking when Megan told them the exciting news. Megan had trouble keeping up with their torrent of words and gestures, sometimes in Italian and sometimes in English. They were disappointed, though not surprised, that Trina would not return to Florence. They understood.

"The young. *Bambini*. They make their own way these days," said Giacomo, shrugging, and waving his hands. "Never do they listen to their elders."

"So different to my day." Teresa sounded cross. "We never dreamed of such a thing. To move away from our mamas ... But then ..." Teresa shook her head sadly, aware she could not take the place of Trina's mother.

Megan added to their sadness when she told them her news about leaving as well. Such terrible news, they said, and pleaded with her to stay longer.

"At least until *Ferragosto*, Assumption Day, on 15th August," Teresa begged. "It holiday time, celebration time. Festivals and parties, you know. You stay. You have good time. People go to beaches. It quieter then and the students – they won't come back until September."

Megan laughed along with Teresa. She had learnt much about their theatrical manner of speaking in the past few months and knew not to take them too seriously.

"I can't thank you enough for the way you welcomed me into your family. I'm sorry to leave but I must get back."

Megan didn't tell them Paul texted to say he would return early August. It was too complicated to explain. She did agree to stay until the end of July and help as much as she could for the next month. "Trina's job will finish then; I'm sure she will come to visit."

With that, Teresa and Giacomo had to be thankful and gave Megan their blessing.

* * * * *

For once, Megan wished modern communication didn't make it so easy to get hold of people on the other side of the world. Now she had made up her mind to leave, she didn't need Paul sending emails or texts every other day. She became distant with her responses, and sometimes didn't respond at all, which made his emails more insistent. Finally, he phoned.

The first time Megan saw his name come up on the screen, she ignored it – with some difficulty. It went against all her instincts and training not to answer a phone, but she knew this conversation would be a difficult one – one she preferred to have face to face, or not at all.

She thought her behaviour more fitting to a silly teenager than a mature woman, but feeling decidedly foolish, she couldn't think what to say to this man. To tell him it was over would assume something more between them. Could she think there was something 'more'? Yet to ignore him and pretend nothing had happened between them would insult them both. Sarah was right. She was totally inexperienced at this relationships lark. Oh, how she missed Tony.

Goodness, I haven't thought about Tony like that in ages. Just as I thought I was ready to move on and remember all the good times, he is suddenly back reminding me of the yawning gap he left.

Megan knew why Tony suddenly sprang to mind. She needed advice and she always went to him when troubled. Who could she go to with this dilemma? No one came to mind. Her daughter would be horrified, her son embarrassed, and Teresa would tell her, in true Italian style, to follow her heart, and encourage her further.

Paul came next in her list of choices, but that thought was the silliest of all. She found herself in this position because of him in the first place. Why, even the word silly had become a descriptor of her thoughts and behaviour of late. Something she'd never been called in her life before.

Her cell phone rang.

"Hello, Paul."

"Oh Megan. I'm glad I've got hold of you at last. Look, I just had to talk to you about this. It wasn't something I could put in an email." He sounded flustered and out of sorts.

"Goodness, Paul. Whatever is the problem?"

"It's that ... Well, what I mean to say is ... Please don't ask for explanations at the moment. I can't give you any – nothing that would make sense anyway – so it's better not to try."

Megan's heart thumped, a sense of foreboding tugged at her while she waited for Paul to finish.

"It's that after all I've said to you, it turns out I won't be back in Florence after all."

"I see," said Megan, suddenly disappointed even though his return to Florence would not change her plans.

"Yes. Sorry. I have to stay here. Look. I'd better go now. You may not hear from me for some time. But I'll get in touch as soon as I can."

All her concerns were wiped away in one very short and, for Paul, totally out-of-character phone call. She had no idea what he was up to, but something had him rattled.

Isabel's Journal
12 July 1911

For the last few weeks, my friend from the art studio has taken me to all sorts of different places to meet his fellow artists, and I've got to know some of the models. We share a meal sometimes, if I can make an excuse to Mrs B.

It's so very exciting. I'm happy to sit in the studio and watch the students. Some paint only hands or feet; others are studying the face. Some leave a face floating on the canvas with no visible means of support, some add a dark background. Some of the students have progressed to full-length portraits but, shocking as it seems, the girls are almost nude. If they are lucky, some are partially draped in a length of cloth or clothed in revealing costumes, standing beside a fake column or statue. The first time I saw this, I was horrified and embarrassed but am surprised to find myself interested in the human form.

I told him he was using the girls to his own benefit and it was degrading. He just laughed, telling me I would understand when I grew up. I wish he wouldn't treat me as a child sometimes. I blushed as he put his hand under my chin and kissed me gently on the lips. I was all a muddle after that.

The next time I called the studio was empty except for my friend.

He asked me to model. I refused. He argued; I refused again. He asked for a kiss, I refused. He chased me round and round the room. We were laughing as we played cat and mouse. He caught me. His Bella, he called me.

Then he kissed me: long, slow and oh, so gently. I agreed – but my face only.

He said someone else could paint my face. And he knew who.

He's promised he'll paint me – properly – one day. My image was embedded in his mind forever, he said. He is so romantic I feel quite giddy in his company. I do hope he will paint my portrait. I would sit for it if he asked me. He will ask me, I know, and I will sit for him.

Déshabillée or not.

Megan's Diary
12 July 2011

I have read the last entry in Isabel's diary today, one hundred years exactly since she wrote it. I find that extraordinary. Her diary doesn't tell me much, although I have found that entry I was looking for – the one about being chased around the room. She was young and in love but I find her story rather sad.

So, the things I know: Isabel spent time with a group of artists and their models in their homes, just as Paul described; Isabel did have her portrait painted, and I know who painted her face – Luigi – the portrait still hangs in the art school. And I know what happened next with Isabel and her 'friend', and not too long after either, given the dates. She gave him a lot more than a kiss. The extra three words at the end were added later. I wonder what the significance of that might be? Did he ever paint her? Is there another portrait of her somewhere?

Whether Isabel ripped out the last pages – however many there were – to keep it private, or because the entries were too risqué, even for her, or whether Constance ripped them out after having read the diary, I will never know.

It's frustrating not knowing – who was the friend? It had to be Luciano, surely, given the passenger list Paul discovered. But some things can't be found in official documents, never mind how hard one looks and interprets the possibilities.

One thing is becoming clear though – Isabel loved art. She was fascinated by it, drawn to those who created it and clearly loved one of them enough to throw all caution to the wind and have a liaison. What an old-fashioned word that is, but it fits with the times, so I will use it with amusement.

Is the art world in New Zealand something I need to find out more about? Will I find Isabel there? Was that her passion?

CHAPTER 29

Megan had not realised how much she had missed home until she landed. The moment she'd arrived in the familiar Auckland Airport and worked her way through customs to the arrivals area, she knew she'd made the right decision. She felt at peace, happy to have cut her trip short. Nowhere was quite like the New Zealand she loved, despite August's damp chill.

The windscreen wipers swept back and forth while Sarah kept up a constant chatter about the latest happenings: Nick's boss was driving him to distraction and she was trying to persuade him to break out on his own; she was pleased with Jason and Trina's news and looked forward to their return, and Bella waited excitedly at home, along with a pile of mail.

"As I was saying, Mum," continued Sarah, drawing Megan back into the conversation, "you know you're welcome to stay with us as long as you like. Don't rush any decisions about renting or buying until you're really sure."

Megan listened as Sarah explained how she'd cleared their spare room and retrieved some of Megan's things from storage to make the place more homely. "Sounds wonderful, darling. Thank you."

For now, Megan would accept Sarah's home as hers.

Glad to be back, the near hour-long journey to Albany was more like a pleasure trip than a necessity, even with the rain. As they drove along roads, with gardens of midwinter green, she appreciated the beautiful country she called home. With its mix of standalone houses and taller buildings, sea views and lush parkland surrounding Maungakiekie, One Tree Hill Domain, and Cornwall Park, the whole place looked splendid.

As they drove across the harbour bridge, Megan had the chance to admire her city and harbour with its bays, boat moorings, volcanic peaks and headlands. Rangitoto Island, which normally stood sentinel in the gulf, now appeared as a shadowy dark shape in the gloom, the water between them like slate, but Megan had no trouble recalling its summer face. She remembered the trips with Tony; when the sun shone, the trees were a vibrant green, the sky a clear blue and the Waitematā lived up to its name: sparkling waters. They had climbed the boardwalks that protected the volcanic stone and native trees from harm, until they'd reached the summit and breathtaking views far and wide. She must go there again this summer and take the whole family ...

"Nana. Nana!"

Megan could hear Bella's excited screams before the car had come to a stop in their driveway. She hurriedly got out, beaming with delight as Bella threw herself into her arms. Oh, yes, she was so glad to be home.

* * * * *

The next morning, an hour of noisy helter-skelter reigned. Sarah apologised profusely every few minutes as they rushed through their routine to get ready for work and Isabella off to day care.

Bella didn't want to go, she wanted to stay with Nana, but Sarah was adamant. Nana needed time to get over her jet lag and do all the chores and other things adults had to do. None of the explanations washed with little Bella who continued to throw a sizeable tantrum.

"You're not going to win with that sort of behaviour, my girl. Do as you are told."

Megan agreed with Sarah. "I'll see you later, sweet Bella. Be a good girl now, and do as Mummy says."

After a lot of hugs and kisses, Bella was buckled in her car seat, and two cars disappeared out the driveway, leaving Megan in peace. The first thing she wanted to do was read her great-grandmother's letters. She had resisted opening the parcel from Jessica last night, feeling too tired to give it her full concentration. In the last three months, Megan had learnt a lot about Isabel and felt she was a step closer to finding the real woman at every new discovery. The letters, she hoped, would provide the last links.

Megan made herself a cup of coffee and some toast, and sat comfortably in the armchair by the window. The rain of the day before had stopped, but the sky was grey. The scudding clouds, with the occasional glimpse of blue, reminded her of Clovelly as she reflected on how much had happened since then – and how much she had changed.

She found some scissors and cut open the fat, bubble-wrap envelope and withdrew the first bundle of letters, tied with ribbon as Jessica had described. Excitement swelled inside her as she recognised the handwriting, despite the faded ink on aged envelopes. Megan laid the four bundles of letters, sorted into date order, on the small table beside her and unfolded the first letter.

Isabel's words, barely filling the page, floated before her eyes. They were strange, formal yet childlike. Megan read them twice hoping to discover hidden depths but the letter simply asked Constance to inform their mother she had arrived safe and well, and now lived in Auckland, New Zealand. She had met some people and was teaching piano.

That was it.

Megan checked the date – April 1913.

Bitterly disappointed the letter lacked the information she expected, she wondered why Isabel had written nothing about a husband or lover, or whatever he was at that stage, or about the baby, and how she'd got to New Zealand. Neither did she write about her impressions of Auckland or anything about where she lived – nothing of significance about her new life at all. Megan quickly read a few more of the letters seeking the details she craved, but they held nothing of interest either.

Disheartened, she picked up her notepad and started to jot down dates and ideas from what she already knew:

Isabel left home, shortly after her eighteenth birthday, at the end of October 1910 as companion to Mrs Baragwanath.

Mrs B returned home in late September 1911 as arranged, without Isabel. Did Mrs B know Isabel was pregnant? Unlikely. The dates are wrong, but she might have suspected Isabel was having an affair and chose to ignore it.

Isabel returned home when her father took ill; he died December 1911.

She was noticeably pregnant by then.

Her mother Eleanor banished her for bringing shame on the family.

Isabel returned to Italy either late 1911 or early 1912.

Where did she live? With the expat ladies? Unlikely.

With her lover? Luciano? Or could it have been Luigi?

Grandma Julia was born early June 1912 in Florence.

They left Italy December 1912 with Luciano.

April 1913 Isabel aged twenty – and alone in a country far away from her home.

What about the baby? Ten months old?

Constance was ten years younger, so ten or eleven. Isabel could hardly pour her heart out to a child. What would you write to a child in those circumstances?

Isabel clearly didn't write to her mother, given she asked Constance to pass on the message in her first letter.

Who were the friends she mentioned?

Why would Constance keep the letters all these years?

That last entry gnawed at Megan.

The relationship between the sisters was odd and definitely fraught. She scanned a few more letters. They were in a similar vein – short, with hardly any details. A few lines about the seasons and how different they were, how Isabel enjoyed the sunshine but it could rain just as much as in Cornwall. The houses were mostly built of wood not stone, and they used horses and carriages or walked.

Megan fiddled with her pen as she considered the missing links.

The letters in the first bundle contained little to quench her thirst for information – except one. Isabel lived in a boarding house called Arncliffe, in Symonds Street. It was a start but not much. Megan resisted the temptation to read the letters out of sequence. Later letters, to an older Constance might be more informative, but Megan believed it important to follow her great-grandmother's lead.

The morning disappeared as Megan read more letters and jotted down more notes, or rather questions without answers. Her head dropped back as her thoughts drifted.

She woke with a start an hour or so later with a fuzzy head and feeling weighed down. With her body clock out of sorts, Megan decided to put the letters away until later. As she went about her chores she wondered how she could find what she wanted to know. A trip to the council archives might help, but then, she argued, what difference would it make? She knew where Isabel had once lived and was certain that whatever building now occupied the space would look nothing like the boarding house that once stood there. Kiwis didn't seem to have the same sense of history as the United Kingdom and Europe and tended to knock down old buildings and build new ones. Perhaps because wooden houses didn't have the same timelessness. Whatever the reasons, Megan knew Arncliffe would be long gone.

The fact Isabel once worked as a piano teacher could be significant. If nothing less, she'd earned her keep in what would have been considered a ladylike manner. What more did Megan really need to know about her distant ancestor? Except she was charged to 'find Isabel and honour her name'.

Shrugging off thoughts of Isabel, Megan decided she had better start on her own plans. She needed a good lawyer here in Auckland who could work with Jessica, and a property advisor of some sort, plus a good accountant, people who would look after her interests and explain things in simple language. Thoughts of Jessica reminded Megan she must reply to her latest email. The relationship with Max had developed considerably. There was no talk of marriage yet but it could well be on the cards.

After writing up a list of possible candidates, Megan made appointments for the following week and then checked the clock to see if there was enough time before the family arrived home to face the one thing she had managed to avoid for two years.

It was time to visit the cemetery.

Megan stood in front of the headstone and read the words chiselled onto it. She waited to feel something. To feel Tony still with her, wanting to talk to him, but she felt only emptiness.

As she ran her hands through her hair to release some of her unease, Megan realised Tony was always with her in the back of her thoughts. They had never been together here. She would never find him in this cold, sad place, which only brought back memories of the worst day of her life.

She got back in the car, turned around and drove to their favourite beach. She sat on the seat under the trees where they had sat many times and watched the ocean in the bay change its mood according to the wind and the light. Today, although slate in colour with the odd sparkle as the faint winter sunshine peeked between the grey clouds, the water was calm, with waves softly lapping at the sand. Something about the beach filled her with joy and gave her peace. One day she would like to live right on a beach like this. The sounds and smells were familiar and comforting and she breathed in the salty air and closed her eyes.

And Tony was sitting right beside her as usual. Megan smiled. At that moment, the sun burst through the cloud and lit up the section of water in front of her.

Whenever she needed to talk to Tony this would be her haven, the place where she would find him.

* * * * *

"What are you looking so pleased about?" asked Sarah a week later after Megan had returned from her meetings.

"I've had a rather successful afternoon."

"Doing what?" Sarah's tone was sharp.

Megan noticed how Sarah avoided any eye contact as she continued to prepare Bella's dinner.

"Nothing much." Megan paused, wondering why Sarah might be cross with her. "Not yet anyway. Can I help?"

"Throw some mushrooms in with the chicken pieces and pop them in the oven, please."

For a few moments, the two women worked silently side by side in the kitchen.

"What sort of nothing much?" nudged Sarah as Megan finished seasoning the chicken and put the lid on the casserole.

"Just engaging some personnel to set up a trust and a company." Megan shut the oven door and began to cut up the vegetables.

"Personnel? What sort of personnel? What company?"

"Oh, you know, lawyers and suchlike. I told you I needed to set up a mechanism to manage Constance's money. I'm making sure I've got it all covered."

Now Megan avoided eye contact. She smoothly changed the subject. This was not the time to tell Sarah about any of her ideas. "Jason tells me his application to change routes has been approved."

"I heard. That's good news, isn't it, Mum. And much nicer for you – to have us all living in the same city, I mean. All of us together again – except for Dad, that is."

Megan thought Sarah's rapid speech and insistence on them being 'all together again' a little strange. She'd never been much bothered about her brother in all the years he'd lived overseas. What was bothering Sarah now?

Megan hoped she sounded comforting and reassuring. "Yes, it is, sweetheart. Good for us all, I think."

"When are they due to arrive?" Sarah's voice wobbled.

"Not till early October. Trina promised to stay with Teresa and Giacomo over the summer."

"Oh. Okay. What did you say the name of your company was?"

"I didn't." Megan smiled impishly. "And you'll have to wait until I can talk to you and your brother at the same time, to find out."

Megan poured two glasses of wine, handed one to Sarah and gave the girl a quick peck on the cheek. "So don't ask."

"Okay, Mum, I won't nag, but any hints? That's a long time to wait." Sarah took a sip of wine, her raised eyes sought answers over the brim of her glass.

251

"Maybe it is. But it'll take that long to get everything sorted, and you have enough to do without being bothered with legal details. I won't do anything rash without talking to you first, I promise."

"Deal! Now, tell me what else have you found out from Great-great-grandmama's letters?"

A few hours passed before Megan had the opportunity to tell Sarah anything further. Nick arrived home and the end-of-day activities took over. Later that evening, over a late-night cup of tea, Megan happily took up Sarah's opening.

"I was disappointed with the letters. They were quite stilted and revealed little I don't already know. I expected outpourings about her new, exciting life in New Zealand with a husband and baby, but they were the exact opposite. They were so lifeless I found them disturbing."

"What did she write about?"

"Mundane things. As Constance grew up Isabel eventually started writing about Julia, but only in casual ways – how she was doing in school and that she played the piano quite well. There was never any mention of the father or how Isabel coped alone in a strange country. The sisters had little in common. I don't think they knew how to communicate with each other. Their lives were so different. As time passed, Isabel wrote about Julia getting married and her granddaughter Caroline, but nothing about the boys who had died. The last letter was about the car accident that killed my parents. But the letters held no emotion. They were statements of what happened."

"How sad, for both of them," sympathised Sarah. "But especially Isabel, with no family to talk to when such tragic things filled her life. She must have been a very strong woman, I think."

Megan found it remarkable that Sarah would use the same words to describe the women of the family as Jessica. Why did they think Constance and Isabel – and her, if Jessica was to be believed – strong?

Megan wondered whether her great-grandmother had ever given anything much thought. Isabel appeared to move through life in a progression of events. She never expressed any sentiments in her letters, and the girlish excitement of her journal had vanished.

"I think she was very young and resilient and just got on with life. She had no choice. There was no going back. In later letters, she dropped a few enlightening bits and pieces of information in here and there. It seems Constance used to send Isabel money from time to time. And two or three of the letters appeared out of character – one asked Constance to write, and one begged her to say she'd been forgiven. I assume Constance did not reply, since the tone of the letters returned to being formal and brief missives of facts."

"Except maybe that's why she sent money," said Sarah.

"Possibly. And I found one very formal letter that confirmed what Constance had written in her letter to me. Isabel knew she was dying and wanted Constance to keep in touch – and presumably to keep sending money although she didn't specifically ask – and be mentor to her great-grandchild, namely me. But we know that didn't happen."

There were so many missing pieces.

"But didn't you tell me you'd found out Luciano

"what's-his-name had left New Zealand without Isabel and the baby? How did you know that, if not from the letters?"

"Shipping records," answered Megan. "I found him listed on a ship headed for Sydney early in 1914. It looks like our dear Luciano knew how to look after himself and escaped any ties before war was declared."

"Did you or Paul find any records of him in Australia or Italy after that?"

The mention of Paul made Megan feel guilty. She'd not replied to his last email. He'd been chatty about all sorts of things without once telling her anything important. He said he was focused on writing a detailed and complex programme for the next year's intake of students. She didn't know what to say in reply.

"No. Nothing. Unfortunately. I haven't been able to find out what happened to Luciano Rossi after he got off the ship. There are no war records or a death certificate. He just vanished."

CHAPTER 30

The weeks flew by in the lead-up to Jason and Trina's return. Megan kept busy helping find suitable rental accommodation when she wasn't on the hunt for Isabel. With a little advice from the library and the local genealogy branch, her research skills improved, and she spent many hours searching the Internet for clues.

The day Megan found an advertisement on the Papers Past website for a Lady Isabel of Arncliffe House who taught piano was a real fillip. Another interesting find was a notice of a school prize-giving for a J Trevallyan for pianoforte. Megan knew it had to be her Grandma Julia. She had been a wonderful pianist and taught piano for many years, like her mother had. They were all good leads but nothing definitive. None of the variations of Isabel's name showed on any records or official documents, and Megan couldn't find her death certificate either.

Megan was feeling defeated by the magnitude of the task. There was so little for her to go on. She got up from the computer after yet another fruitless search and let her mind wander to the latest exchange with Paul.

Something about him niggled at her, yet why she should be thinking about him at all, she couldn't say. They hardly knew one another. She should have written him off as a passing friendship a long time ago. She didn't have a clue why he left Florence so suddenly, and he was being particularly secretive about his reasons.

They'd kept in touch by email and the occasional phone call, but often these were bland updates with general news rather than anything more personal. The distance between them, not only physically but emotionally, seemed huge. It was as if they each recognised the attraction between them and had made the decision not to get involved – without saying anything to the other one.

What was it about him that kept him in her thoughts?

The email alert sounded, drawing her back to reality. "Please go and see this place and if it's as good as it looks in the photos, then sign us up for it," wrote Jason, providing a weblink and an address.

Megan flicked through the information and thought the place had great potential. After making an appointment, she grabbed her keys and was about to head out to her car when she heard a vehicle pull up and footsteps. Megan peeked out the window but couldn't see anything. It must have been a neighbour, Megan decided. Picking up her handbag she walked towards the back exit when a knock sounded at the front door.

She hurried towards the door, seeing a dark shape through the frosted glass.

"Paul!" she cried as she opened the door, shocked by his extraordinary timing. How on earth did he find her? "What brings you to Auckland?"

Megan wondered what she would say if he answered 'you'.

"It's summer vacation in the northern hemisphere,

so with a couple of weeks to spare, I decided to get a taste of what New Zealand is like these days. I told you – I intend to return home permanently before too long." Something in his tone or the way he stood implied he wasn't telling the truth, or not the whole truth anyway.

"And is that all?" Why was she pushing him? What did she really want him to say?

As if to confirm her suspicions, he burst out laughing. "It seems you know me too well. I thought I could be all innocence and get away with saying, 'because I wanted to'. I do want to return, and I do have plans. It's just a question of when."

"So why are you here now?"

"I've a surprise and wanted to tell you in person."

Now she was intrigued. "Another one? I'm not sure I like all these surprises at my age. I'm not convinced they're good for my health," she teased.

He chuckled again.

Megan looked at the creases around his laughing eyes, the slight flush on his face and the warmth of his smile, and relaxed. In the space of one morning, she had gone from deciding to dismiss him from her life completely to being delighted to see him.

"Ah, Megan. I'm so glad to see you again. You do make me laugh. Something I don't do often enough."

Megan privately agreed; neither did she. Maybe that was his secret weapon – he made her laugh. Out of the blue, she remembered what Rosemary from the Swiss train trip had said about laughter: we grow old when we stop.

"I was on my way out, but there's no reason you can't come with me. Let's go, we can grab a bite to eat first."

Automatically, Megan headed the car towards the beach and her favourite café.

They chatted easily on the journey. Even though they had issues to resolve, it didn't stop them being friends in the meantime.

"What is this surprise you've come all this way to give me?" she asked, when their lunch had been ordered.

"I've found a drawing of Isabel."

"What!"

"I read a report in a scholarly journal about the recent discovery of a charcoal sketch. The authors were researching its provenance but had few clues to go on. They believed it might have a New Zealand connection. Of course, that alone stirred my interest. I phoned the gallery and the curator told me what she knew."

"I can hardly take it all in. Every time I think I've come to the end of the story, there are more surprises. Keep going."

"Well, there was a small motif drawn on the sketch. They thought it a Māori design, as it was similar to tattoos seen in C F Goldie's works. That was the gallery's sole clue."

"Was it Māori?"

"Yes, mostly, I think. Although it was clever. When I saw it, I thought there was also a small Celtic knot worked in the centre. But I'll come to that later. The curator said the woman was European and appeared to be either seated or possibly kneeling and holding an infant. The faces were detailed but the form was mostly free-flowing lines that gave shape without definition, which didn't sound typical of either Goldie or his mentor's work. At first, when she was describing the drawing, I thought it sounded very like a sketch by one of New Zealand's great artists, Frances Hodgkins – pity she had to spend most of her life in Britain – but the motif was not at all like her work.

"Anyway, by the time the curator and I had finished the conversation, I wanted to see this sketch. I took the next flight and arrived on her doorstop in Cornwall within twenty-four hours."

Luckily for him, his standing in the art world opened doors, and they had invited him into the inner sanctum of the gallery. In typical Paul fashion, he would not hurry a story. Megan was amazed how quickly they slipped back into their easy-going friendship as they talked, each ready to laugh at the smallest comment. Once again, she found herself happy to listen as he described the place in detail, not at all bored by his way of telling a story within a story.

"They gave me gloves and a magnifying glass so I could inspect the sketch laid out on the table. I recognised her instantly, but held my tongue. An unsigned painting of a cottage near Cadgwith, had been gifted to the gallery as part of a deceased estate. The art directors decided to clean the painting before putting it on display, which is when they found the packing inside.

"The beneficiaries believed the cottage painting had been in the family for a long time, but no one knew who the artist was, although there was some speculation it could be Jane de Glehn because of its location. There was nothing to say where it came from or what its New Zealand connections were."

"And you are sure it's Isabel?"

"Absolutely."

Megan was desperate to know more, but she'd been glancing at her watch for a while, conscious of her appointment with the property agent. She was running out of time.

"Look, I have to go. I'm meeting someone to see a place Jason is interested in renting, but ..." she tailed off, coming to a conclusion. "Come with me. We can talk on the way. I've got lots of questions."

On the way back to the car, Megan was preoccupied, and would have walked into a sign if Paul hadn't steered her around it. She stopped to take a second look up at the three-storeyed building beside her. She checked her watch again; there was just enough time if they hurried.

"Paul. Stop a minute. This property is for sale. I'd like to have a quick look."

Paul talked with the man at the door, while Megan rushed through the rooms noting the modern yet classic and stylish décor. The beachfront apartment had a comfortable, homely feel about it and she was quite taken with it.

"Nice place," said Paul once they were in the car on their way into the city. "Thinking of buying?"

"I wasn't. I've been quite happy living at Sarah's. It's worked out very well, but I will need somewhere of my own sooner or later. But that one caught my eye." The coincidence that she should find it today seemed extraordinary, but motivating. "But right now, I have to focus on somewhere for Jason and Trina."

Thirty minutes later, they pulled into a parking building and walked to the low-rise Newmarket apartment block that Jason liked.

If Megan thought her day unusual, it wasn't over yet.

An hour later, instead of signing Jason up for a rental agreement, she had bought a city-side apartment. Not for her to live in, but one she had different plans for. And she hadn't talked any further with Paul about his astounding discovery.

CHAPTER 31

"What do you mean, you bought it?"

Sarah had been bad-tempered and in no mood to talk for the best part of a week, but Megan couldn't leave it any longer. She had to tell Sarah or risk alienating her further.

"I know you've had a bad time lately, honey, with work not going well. And I'm worried about you. You don't seem your usual self," soothed Megan. "Now's not the time to talk about this in detail. Let's wait until you feel better."

"It's him, isn't it? You wouldn't have done this otherwise. What's he doing here anyway?" Sarah was being unreasonable, and both mother and daughter knew it. Since Paul's arrival a week earlier, Megan had seen quite a lot of him, and Sarah's antagonism had risen as each day passed.

"I told you because I thought you'd like to know. It's a good investment and will solve Jason and Trina's accommodation issue until they are ready to find something else. Now, how about you take a shower while I see to Bella? You might feel better after."

Megan knew the conversation was not over. She'd

not yet mentioned her liking for the beachfront property, but she hadn't forgotten about it, nor would it be the right time to tell Sarah Paul had, indirectly, influenced her decision to invest in the city apartment.

When she and Paul had met the agent, the one he showed them was a rear unit, much smaller than it appeared in the photos on their website and with less light. Megan turned it down as unsuitable for Jason and Trina, but as they were leaving, the agent had a suggestion.

"If you're not in a hurry, I may have something else for you. The owner of another unit nearby is moving. I could ask if they want to rent it out, if you're interested."

Megan agreed.

"Let me make a phone call."

A few minutes later, the agent escorted them to a neighbouring building and into a front corner apartment. Immediately the feel of the place was different. Of much higher quality, with full-length ranch sliders on both sides of the corner that opened onto a balcony, light filled the large, open-plan space.

"This would make a great art studio," Paul said casually, as he looked up at the white walls and high ceiling. "There's so much reflected light."

Megan stared at him in surprise. Unwittingly, he had provided an answer to her subconscious dilemma. She quickly checked the rest of the apartment to make sure it would be suitable for Jason before she made her final decision.

"I'm sorry. It seems I've wasted your time," said the estate agent, hanging up the phone, "but I can't persuade the owner to rent it. He wants to sell."

Megan never acted impulsively, but her instinct said 'buy it'. This time she knew it was the right thing to do. She put in an offer on the spot, complete with furnishings.

"I'm not sure what you've done or why," said Paul as they stepped into the street, "but I think you should celebrate."

A few minutes later, they sat relaxed in armchairs next to the fireplace at a nearby bar, with a glass of wine. "I feel I have to do something productive with Constance's money," she said, outlining her plans.

Paul liked her idea. "But how does buying the apartment help with that?"

"Your comment about it making a great art studio."

Paul listened as Megan explained. He raised his glass and clinked it against hers. "You are amazing."

* * * * *

Sarah certainly didn't think she was amazing. Despite the refreshing shower, a great dinner – from a recipe that Megan had mastered on her French cooking course in Nice – and Nick surprising her with flowers, Sarah remained down in the dumps. While Nick put Bella to bed, Sarah bombarded Megan with questions about why she'd bought the Newmarket place.

"We're just covering the same ground," said Megan, doing her best to appease her. "I gave you my answers. I don't know what you want me to say differently."

Neither did Sarah, apparently. "I still think this is all to do with Paul."

Whether it was partly guilt that she hadn't told Sarah

the whole truth or whether Megan was learning to stand up for herself, she didn't know, but she was finally tired of Sarah's distrust.

"I don't know what's got into you. You don't seem to agree or approve of anything I do these days."

Sarah's face changed and anger flared. "What's got into me? That's rich. It's more like what's got into *you*. All I hear about is Paul this and Paul that."

"So what? Paul is a friend, and I value his opinion. But this isn't about Paul. This is about me doing the things I want to do."

"So, you don't value my opinion now, is that it? His is more important, it seems. You never listen to anything I have to say any more."

"For goodness' sake, Sarah. Of course I listen, but in the end, I need to make my own decisions. I can't spend the rest of my life relying on you, or anyone else for that matter, to do it for me. I'd just like to be able to do something without it becoming a battle between us all the time."

Sarah started to say something in retaliation but plainly thought better of it. She turned back to the kitchen bench to finish clearing up.

"I think it's time I moved into my own place. Me being here is spoiling things between us."

"I should have known," snarled Sarah. "You've been back less than a month and you can't wait to move."

Megan couldn't quite understand. "Known what? What are you talking about?"

"You. Settling down."

"But that's the whole point. I do want to settle down, but I need my own place to do that. You and Nick and

Bella have your own lives to lead. You don't need to worry about me all the time."

"You promised."

"Promised what?"

"Not to do anything rash. But here you are rushing off to do who-knows-what with *him*." Sarah almost spat the word.

"I'm not being rash. Nor am I rushing off anywhere. And leave Paul out of this. He has nothing whatsoever to do with it."

Not to be placated, Sarah stormed off to bed in tears. Megan thought there had to be something more to why Sarah was behaving strangely. She hoped the girl would confide in her soon.

* * * * *

Megan decided not to ask Sarah if she could invite Paul to the house, even when she wasn't there. The disagreement between them bubbled away under the polite silences that avoided another outburst like the last one. In the meantime, Megan met Paul away from the house. If he noticed, he never commented. By the end of the second week of his visit, their easy companionship was restored.

They'd wandered along the beach in the late winter sunshine, chatting, as once she and Tony had done. Often, they found a café and ordered lunch, or later, wine and some nibbles, and kept talking. They had managed a pleasant couple of evenings together, conversing for hours over dinner. In hindsight, she realised they had discussed many of the things they had separately been uneasy about. Not least of which, what they expected from each other.

"I hope you understand, Paul, but the rawness of Tony's death is still too fresh. It hits me at unexpected times. I really can't consider a deeper relationship yet. I hope we can continue to be friends, though."

"Of course. I value your friendship too, but I'm far too set in my ways to change. I need the freedom to come and go as I please without feeling I've let someone down. We both have our own ways and need our own space."

Her money also stood as a silent barrier between them, and they didn't want to complicate matters.

"Here's to friendship and a few laughs."

"And the joys of sharing mutual interests."

With those ideals paramount in their thoughts, other tensions faded away.

But there was still one tricky conversation Megan hadn't yet sorted to her satisfaction – why he had left Florence so suddenly and never returned. And then there was that kiss.

Paul was clearly offended. "Kiss? What kiss? I have never kissed a student in my life."

"What you saw," he stated adamantly, after Megan explained further, "was my research assistant presenting me with some excellent news. I simply said thanks in the typical European way. Cheek kissing happens every day on every street corner. You should know that. You would have seen enough of it with Trina's family."

She conceded she had seen many such occasions and was reassured she had misinterpreted his actions. "What was the news that made you so happy?"

As soon as she had opened her mouth, she knew she

shouldn't have asked the question. It was none of her business. Paul suddenly became reticent again and only answered half of it.

"Something to do with work." He shrugged one shoulder and coolly changed the subject. "That image," he said, reverting to their earlier conversation about the sketch discovered in Cornwall, "could be one of the marks used by a student within a studio, to identify their work."

What was Paul hiding? she wondered.

"Didn't you tell me there is considerable conjecture about the authenticity of these marks as identifiers?"

"Yes. Some professionals dismiss the idea completely, but I wasn't necessarily interested in any one artist but rather in ascertaining whether Isabel was part of the studio in some way."

"Could Steele have been the artist?" asked Megan, eyes alight with possibilities.

"Unfortunately, no." Paul was adamant. "Steele's technique was quite different. By this time, he enjoyed painting early Māori scenes. In fact, if anything, the sketch looks more in the style of Nerli. But I think this one was drawn by someone seeking to find his own expression, or else by someone in love with this woman."

"You mean Isabel had a lover?" Megan found the idea Isabel may have had someone who cared for her after all, heartening.

"Perhaps. This one was sketched in a hurry, beautifully and with great skill, but I don't think the artist told her how he felt. If he had shared his passion, why did it end up as packing somewhere overseas?"

Megan, who really wanted to believe Isabel had a

lover, didn't agree. "I think Isabel was given the sketch. Why would he draw her, if not as a gift?"

"Who knows? I tried to trace how the sketch might have ended up in Cornwall, but none of the options seemed to fit."

"Could Isabel have sent it to Constance? That would explain it, even if it doesn't explain how it got in the back of another painting." Megan's idea had merit and made more sense than some of their other notions.

Despite or maybe because of their shared enthusiasm to find Isabel's friends of the 1920s, Megan was content when she was with Paul and worried less about the events happening all around her.

"I'm sure your family are there for you," reassured Paul. "From what I've seen of Sarah and Trina, you have two strong women in the family. Everything will work out perfectly. You wait and see."

Megan told Paul about the two remaining clauses in Constance's will and her despair at not finding anything useful. Paul had some ideas. Given all she'd learnt recently, Megan thought she knew a few things about researching the past, but Paul's knowledge and expertise left her agog, especially when it related to the art world.

Together they spent hours digging for clues. With numerous places to visit that might have a snippet of information, Megan could hardly keep up. Sometimes they went together to the art gallery, the archives, the museum library, or the council, and sometimes they went to separate places. They peered at faded microfiche and pored through endless files, sometimes coming up with nothing, sometimes with a gem worth following. He also visited the lesser and more obscure art contacts he'd discovered, in the hope of finding another connection.

The day before Paul was due to return to the States, he arrived at her place and spread the latest array of documents on the table. "See, didn't I tell you? Whatever she wrote, there's no doubt Isabel led an interesting life."

CHAPTER 32

On the second anniversary of Tony's death, Megan drove to the beach and sat on the bench exactly where she'd sat a month earlier after her futile visit to the cemetery. As soon as she started to think of Tony, his comforting aura eased her disquiet, giving her space to think.

In the months Megan had been away, her relationship with Sarah had changed. The girl seemed fragile and argumentative for little or no reason, and her ill will towards Megan's friendship with Paul was completely out of hand. While Sarah had relaxed a little in the days since he'd left, Megan began to wonder whether continuing any sort of friendship with Paul was worth the effort if Sarah was going to disapprove every time Paul was around. But another part of her defended her right to live her life the way she wanted. Two could play the stubborn game – except it wouldn't resolve anything. After half an hour of reflection, Megan got into her car and drove back to Sarah's ready to confront her.

Determined not to let their exchange turn into another argument, Megan kept her temper in check and chose her words carefully. "In the last couple of months, you have totally confused me. On one hand you say you want me to be happy, to get out more, make friends and enjoy life, but on the other hand, you don't want me to have my own home and you don't like my friends. Which is it?"

"Of course I want you to be happy, it's because ..." Sarah was clearly discomforted by Megan's question. "I want what's best for you."

"Why do you think I won't make the right choices?"

"Your decision to sell your shop wasn't rational, for starters."

"Goodness. That was quite some time ago. And maybe it didn't appear so to you, but I wasn't coping or enjoying being there any more. The business would have gone downhill if I'd stayed. I was in a very dark hole back then."

"I know that, Mum," Sarah acknowledged, "but I ... I'm not sure you really know what you want yet. And I think Paul is rushing you."

"I don't agree. Yes, I sold my shop without taking advice. What's done is done, and I know it was the right decision for me. Now I have other ideas of what my future might hold. Please give me credit for some decisions. I've changed since then."

"I know, which is why I was happy for you to travel, and wanted you to sell the house. Even if it hurt me."

Megan refrained from suggesting Sarah was being patronising. While the place had been Sarah's childhood home, without Tony it meant nothing to Megan any more. Neither did her old shop. "It's time for me to start being my own person, and I want your backing."

Sarah remained silent. Her cool, blue eyes stared intently at her mother.

"Sarah, listen. Perhaps I should have told you earlier, but I'm telling you now. I've seen an apartment on the Browns Bay esplanade. How about we knock on the door and ask if it's still available?"

Paul had told her the man at the door was the owner's son. It was a private sale, and he was over briefly from Australia to sell the place. Nothing had changed to indicate new owners, and Megan was hopeful.

"Sarah, will you come with me, please?"

"Why today? Today should be about Dad, not you."

Megan's temper was rising at Sarah's continued opposition to everything she suggested but was determined not to react. "It has been, honey. You'll never know how much." Megan paused. "It's time, Sarah. It's time for me to move on. To be my own person now, not as the other half of your father."

Sarah didn't respond to that comment, reverting instead to Megan's invitation. "How do you know this place is what you want?"

"I went to an open home. I was being nosy and wanted to see what the price tag might be." Megan had loved the place and immediately felt at home. She wanted to buy it, with or without Sarah's approval, but getting her daughter on side was uppermost in her thoughts.

"Hmph! Why didn't you tell me about it?" Sarah's tone was sharp, and she looked as though she was about to argue – again.

"Because you were upset with me. Because I was only looking then. Because I needed to think about it. You're still cross with me, but I'd value your opinion, and I want you to be happy for me."

Sarah's body language told Megan she had at long last made her point.

* * * * *

A tiny old lady answered the door, her back almost bent in half as she leaned heavily on a walking stick. When Megan asked if the property was available, the woman looked shocked and then tearful.

"I'm sorry. I didn't mean to upset you," Megan flustered and, apologising again, turned to leave.

"Oh no, my dear, don't go. It's providence. Come in. Come in. I'm Muriel, by the way." The place, furnished in soft creams, was as immaculate as Megan remembered it. A few antiques, a couple of landscape paintings and some fine porcelain gave the place the elegant, yet comfortable feel she remembered.

"Can I make you a cup of tea?"

"Let me," Sarah offered, while they chatted. Muriel told them she was a widow with a son living overseas, which confirmed what Paul had told Megan.

"I love this apartment, but with my arthritis getting worse, I can hardly do for myself any more."

"It's lovely," said Sarah. "You've looked after it very well."

"Thank you, my dear. I applied for a place at the retirement village but there was a long waiting list. I thought I could sell my home in the meantime. But the timing didn't work. A place came up before I'd sold. My money is all tied up here, you see, so I couldn't take it. But it meant I had to take this place off the market. Oh, it's all so complicated. But I'm not managing."

"I'm sorry to hear that." Megan glanced across at Sarah as she served the tea and wondered what to say next. She didn't need to. Muriel hadn't finished.

"I've now got a letter to say they have another place available for me next month. I do so want it, but I've been worried how I'm going to get through all that selling business.

"My son came over specially to complete the sale before, and he wasn't happy it didn't go ahead. I haven't dared tell him. He will be cross with me for bothering him again."

"Surely not?" Sarah sounded shocked.

"Oh, he'll handle the money side in the end, I know," Muriel said as she explained how he needed to countersign some documents before she could accept an offer. Talking more to herself now than them and voicing her doubts, she added, "I'm not sure he'll do what I want. Maybe he's right ..." Her voice faded away. "And then there's the selling and moving. He won't want to come here for that. It's too much." Muriel looked teary again and fished for a hanky in her cardigan sleeve. "Oh, dear. I don't know what to do."

"If it will help you, could I talk to your son?"

"You coming here ... it's my lucky day. Do you really want to buy the place?"

"Yes. It's perfect for me," Megan answered, without hesitation.

Sarah opened her mouth to say something, but the quick shake of her mother's head forestalled any questions.

Megan already knew the asking price, so she offered a premium. "To help cover your moving costs."

She also offered to get her lawyer to contact Muriel's to sort the paperwork. They would have it settled well within the time frame.

Muriel sat quivering. "Oh, my dear. Oh, my. You do make an old lady's heart glad. Thank you. Thank you so much."

* * * * *

"You'll never guess what Mum did today," said Sarah to Nick later that evening as they sat side by side on the couch.

"Probably not. I've stopped being surprised by what your mother does." Nick winked across at Megan with a grin.

"She bought an apartment!"

"Congratulations. Where and why?"

"On the beachfront. As a favour to an old lady."

"Sounds good to me."

"Will you two stop it?" Sarah glared at Nick trying to send the message she wanted to tell a story.

Nick wasn't taking the bait. "Stop what?"

"Oh, for goodness' sake, you two! You know what I mean."

Nick laughed. He put his arm around Sarah's shoulder and kissed her temple. "Okay. Tell me."

Megan jumped in ahead of Sarah. "I bought an apartment. A, because I need somewhere to live – I can't stay here forever – and B, because an old lady needed help."

"Still sounds good to me," teased Nick.

Sarah punched him. "Yes, but she paid way above the

asking price. And Mum offered to help Muriel – that's the old lady's name – pack up and move to her new place and … and …"

"And what?" Megan interrupted her flow, wondering where Sarah was heading.

"And … it's the nicest thing I've seen anyone do for a long time."

Nick kissed her again. "Couldn't agree more."

Between them, they filled Nick in with the details and talked about timing.

"Mum, there's something else. I've done a lot of thinking, and now since meeting Muriel today, well …"

Sarah took a deep breath. "I'm sorry for the way I've behaved lately. I only wanted to look after you, but I think I've been a bit of a roadblock. I'm sorry."

"Thank you, sweetheart. I accept your apology, but what's Muriel got to do with it?"

"It's all mixed up in my head, and the poor old lady absolutely needed help. Her son needs a good kicking, if you ask me, refusing to sign the papers and all that nonsense. I'm glad you sorted him out in the end. I was so angry at the way he treated his mother. She was too scared to ask for his help. Can you believe it? He shouldn't control her like that. But then I realised … I've done the same to you, haven't I? Differently, but I stopped you doing what you wanted."

Megan chose not to answer her daughter and let her talk.

"I keep thinking about how incredibly lucky we are to have each other and what happened to Constance because she had no one. Family is so important, and I want to leave Bella with that strong sense of loyalty." Her voice faltered. "It mightn't make sense to anyone else, but it does to me."

"Me too," agreed Megan with a smile as her heart sang.

"At last!" said Nick, pulling Sarah closer to him. "About time you two patched things up."

CHAPTER 33

On a fine but windy spring day in early October, Auckland turned on its best display to welcome Trina to the country. Megan paced the arrivals hall, peering around people to catch a glimpse of them as soon as they walked through the doors.

"Jason!" she called, waving her hand, and hurried towards him.

"Hello, Mum." Jason wrapped his long arms around her.

"You're looking well, Trina." After Jason let her go she hugged the girl. "Welcome to your new home."

Once the luggage was loaded into the car and they were on their way, Megan outlined some of her plans. "If you're not too tired, that is."

"I'm OK," confirmed Trina. "I managed to get some sleep on the plane."

"Great. In that case, I'll take you to where you are staying for the time being, and after you are set up, if you are feeling up to it, we're to have dinner at Sarah's."

Later that evening, Jason inadvertently managed to raise his sister's hackles. "Mum has excelled herself," he said, referring to the apartment in which he and Trina were staying. "Did you know about it?"

"Not until after." Sarah cast her mother a reproachful look.

The tension between them had eased since she'd bought Muriel's apartment, but with two weeks to go before possession date, Sarah could still be touchy.

"We've had this conversation," replied Megan. "Remember? And you were specifically talking about a place for me to live, not anything else."

"I didn't know you had anything else in mind. You left that bit out."

"Okay, ladies," interrupted Nick. "We get the point. But what's so bad about it anyway?"

"Actually, nothing," agreed Jason. "Mum's purchase is quite astute."

"I love it," added Trina. "It's perfect."

"You can stay as long as you want," said Megan cautiously. Did Sarah still object to her purchase or that Jason and Trina lived there? "But don't feel committed. It's up to you."

Over dinner they caught up with all the other news. Sarah talked about Bella's birthday next month, Nick complained about some of the dodgy shortcuts his boss took and Trina asked for advice on doctors and midwives.

"I've only got ten weeks to go, I'll need someone soon."

Megan noticed Sarah fidgeting uncomfortably and wondered what was bothering her.

"I'd like to see Dad's headstone," said Jason, "sometime before my new flight schedule kicks in."

"Go if you want to," said Megan, "but it's not somewhere I like going. I have a suggestion – if you're all up for it. I'd like to have a small ceremony and family get-together on your Dad's favourite little beach. It would be a great way to recognise passing the two-year mark and have a party to celebrate the future."

Everyone agreed. They picked Labour weekend, the week after Megan had shifted into her new home, with the hope the weather would be accommodating. After dinner, as they sat in the lounge relaxing as the evening wound down, tension crackled. Something was going on. Would it be a good time to tell them her news? she wondered. She didn't want Sarah to think Jason was the favoured one, if that was the issue.

Trina broke into an awkward silence and unwittingly solved her dilemma. "I'm feeling rather tired. Would it be all right if we went back now?"

"Of course, sweetheart," said Jason, suddenly concerned. "We should have been more thoughtful."

Once Trina had assured everyone she was okay, Nick picked up the car keys and ushered them out the door. "Back soon."

Left alone, mother and daughter finished tidying up.

"Sarah? Are you upset with me over something?"

"No." The evasive shrug said otherwise.

"What's the problem, then?"

"Who said there's a problem?"

"Sarah. This is ridiculous – and childish."

"I am not being childish!" Sarah sounded a lot like her child-self about to stamp her foot and, not for the first time, Megan's eyebrows rose in surprise at her daughter's reactions. She was becoming fractious.

"So, talk to me." Megan gentled her voice, trying not to perturb her any further.

The two women stared at each other for several long

seconds. Megan wondered whether Sarah would say anything.

"Why did you buy that place?"

Back to that topic again. "As an investment. I have plans."

"As you keep saying, but you never tell me anything about them. What are you hiding?"

"I'm not hiding anything." Megan paused at Sarah's disbelieving expression. "Well, yes, if I look at it from your side, I suppose I am – but I told you I wanted to talk to you and Jason together. Nick and Trina as well."

"Well, they were here tonight and you didn't say anything."

"That's hardly fair. It's their first night." Megan wondered how their simple conversation had escalated into another argument.

"Aren't you happy enough here?" The switch in her girl's thinking convinced her something deeper was going on.

"Of course I am! Why do you ask?"

"I thought you were going away again," said Sarah, confirming Megan's concern.

"Going away? Where? What made you think that? I've just bought my new place."

Sarah shrugged again.

"Spit it out, Sarah. What's bugging you?" Megan put her hand on her daughter's shoulder. The young woman immediately burst into tears, taking them both by surprise. A few hugs and several tissues later, she pulled herself together a little, while Megan poured two glasses of red wine.

She handed one to her daughter. "Come on. Sit

down and tell me what the matter is. Before Nick gets back."

"I'm being stupid," Sarah snivelled.

"Never that, sweetheart. But it must be important if you are this upset by whatever it is."

"I don't want you going away again. That's all."

"I have no plans to, but what else? There's more to it than that," pushed Megan.

Sarah fidgeted in her chair, heaved a sigh, and blew her nose again. Seconds passed. Megan wondered what her girl was leading up to.

"I've lost another baby." Her voice was deadpan.

Megan's heart lurched. Sarah had lost a baby the year after Bella; to lose another was a major blow.

Suddenly Megan felt guilty. She had been so caught up in what she'd wanted to do that she hadn't noticed her daughter was pregnant. She'd let Sarah down by not being there when she was needed. "Oh, my darling girl, I'm so sorry."

Megan recalled Sarah had complained of a stomach ache about a week before and disappeared off to bed early. Megan assumed it was her time of the month and had left her alone. No wonder the air had been tense tonight with talk about Trina's baby. Sarah must have been very upset.

"How far along?"

"Only six weeks. I'd barely taken the test when the cramps set in."

"Why didn't you tell me you thought you were expecting?"

Sarah shrugged. Megan worked out it would have been around the time of their last big row, when Paul arrived unexpectedly, and Megan bought the city apartment.

"I'm sorry I wasn't there for you, darling. I've been too wrapped up in my own plans."

"I lost another one before this, too."

Megan was truly shocked. "Oh, no. When?"

"While you were away. Before Hawaii."

"Oh, my poor girl!" Guilt, compassion, empathy, and regret washed over her. This was Sarah's third miscarriage. They had wanted a big family. It didn't look likely now. "Why on earth didn't you tell me? It explains so much. No wonder you've been out of sorts." She remembered now that Sarah had been touchy in Hawaii, almost impossible in Florence and difficult since Megan had been back in New Zealand. Hardly a surprise, now she knew. She wished the girl had confided in her earlier.

"You'd think I'd get used to it."

"I don't think it's something you'd ever get used to." Megan went to sit on the arm of the chair beside Sarah and gently rubbed her back as she used to when Sarah was a child.

"Let it out, sweetheart. We can't all be strong all the time. You're allowed to give in."

Megan let her daughter weep, relieved she could share her grief at last. When she felt sure Sarah's tears were exhausted, Megan said, "Do you want to talk?"

Sarah nodded again. "I've let things get on top of me and don't know where to start. But there's so much going wrong. I hate my job and want to change, but I have no idea what to do instead. We don't have the money for me to be out of work while I figure it out, because of the mortgage. And I'm worried about Nick. He's unhappy at work. We can't both make a change."

Megan's mind drifted, wondering how she could help take the young couple's minds off their latest tragedy. They would never forget, but they could fulfil other dreams.

Her daughter's words brought her back with a jolt. "... but then I suddenly realised what life would be like if I lost you, too."

Sarah's anguished sobs tore at Megan's heart. "Lost me? I hope I'm not going anywhere for a good while yet. You would never lose me no matter what happened. I'll always be with you." Megan wondered what else she could say to alleviate her girl's pain and worries.

"So you're not going back to Italy or to the States to be with Paul or anything?"

"No, I'm not." Comprehension dawned on Megan. No wonder the poor girl was beside herself. "I'm sorry if I gave you that impression. No. Never. I enjoy Paul's company very much, and I hope we will continue to be friends. I'll listen to his advice from time to time, but I don't want to live anywhere but right here."

A weak smile crossed Sarah's face. "Truly?"

Megan nodded. "Promise."

"That's a relief ... Oh, Mum. I miss Dad so much." Fresh tears flowed and a damp handkerchief did little to mop them up.

"Now *that* I can understand. You always were your Daddy's little girl."

Megan saw a small flicker of a smile.

"Yes, I was, wasn't I."

"He loved you very much. You know that, don't you?"

Sarah nodded. "The first year after he went ... I think ... I was too focused on making sure you weren't too miserable and, wishing I could do something to help you get your life back on track, I didn't let myself think about the void he'd left in my life. But this last year has been agony."

"Oh sweetheart, I really wished you'd told me. We could have talked about him, the babies, everything."

"I didn't want to spoil your adventure. And you were wrapped up everything ... in Paul, and finding your past. I was, well ... I don't know what it was exactly, but with you away ... and Jason not here either, I was so alone. Ridiculous, isn't it? I have Nick and Bella, and they are both so precious to me. Bella especially ... but ..."

"I understand. Really, I do, Sarah. Grief is an odd thing. There is no time frame and no pattern to how and when people grieve, but that is what you are doing. When Grandma Julia died, I thought my world had ended. She was the only one who knew me from when I was a little girl, and there was no one to share my memories with any more. The one and only link with my past was gone. I've had to build a new past. Pity she didn't tell me herself, but at least we know now."

"Yes. That's it," Sarah brightened. "I felt as though I'd lost another part of me somehow. People say Bella is like me but only you and Dad could tell me for certain. I see her do things or she gets this look or tilt of her head, and I have memories of me doing the same. But you weren't here to ask, and it brought it home to me that Dad would never be again. I couldn't even say to Jason, 'remember when?' "

"Now I've heard it all. You missed your brother!" Megan couldn't resist teasing her a little. "See, I always told you family was important."

"Yes, you have. I'm sorry I've been a right bitch to you at times lately."

"You're forgiven – now I know what was behind it all."

"Oh, Mum, what would I do without you? This journey of yours has proved it even more."

"And, for your information, Bella does remind me of you sometimes, and I saw a resemblance of you in the portrait of Constance in the Hall in Cornwall. I didn't recognise it at first, but, later, it made sense. Family traits and mannerisms often get passed through the generations. "

Sarah really smiled this time. "That's nice to know. Thanks, Mum. At least Constance and Isabel and Grandma Julia will live on in our hearts and minds, no longer lost and alone."

By the time Nick returned, the two women had finished their wine, Sarah had mopped up her tears and Megan had a new appreciation of her daughter.

CHAPTER 34

In a better frame of mind than she had been for a long time, Sarah offered to book the packers and removal vans for both Muriel and Megan.

"Your instincts were right, Mum. The place has just the right feel. I'm glad you made me come along with you."

They had gone to the storage shed together to remind themselves what Megan had kept and what she might need to buy in the way of furniture.

When they went to check on Muriel, another surprise was in store. The old lady considered she had far too much furniture for the downsized, one-bedroom apartment where she was going.

"Would you like to have some of these things?"

Megan stood in the middle of the living area and admired the items Muriel had offered – a tall antique cabinet fitting into the niche in the wall, the wing-back chair Megan had sat in and knew to be very comfortable, and the matching two-seater that faced the balcony and the view.

"I don't want to take the round table either. It's extendable so it might suit you."

"If you're very sure, Muriel. I'd be delighted. They're perfect."

In turn, Megan offered Muriel some of her smaller pieces. Between them, they soon furnished both apartments to their satisfaction and decided to sell the rest.

"The packers will be here early tomorrow, and you don't have to do a thing."

Megan promised to be on hand to help Muriel through the process and get her set up in her new place. By the end of the week Muriel was completely settled, already enjoying the facilities, and making friends. Megan promised to call in once in a while or take her to lunch. In a short space of time, they had become friends.

Megan's apartment fitted like a glove. She often left the drapes open so she could enjoy the view, and being walking distance from shops and cafés added to its perfection. Megan was truly home.

* * * * *

The day of their commemoration-cum-party turned out to be a typical spring day, sunny but with a sou' westerly blowing. The air was fresh with a sharp scent of seaweed. It wouldn't be warm enough to have lunch on the beach as first planned.

Megan clambered awkwardly out of the car clutching a cluster of printed balloons. Nick retrieved the fold-up table from the boot and carried it down to the beach, followed by a chattering Bella who fiercely held onto the one balloon she had charge of. Sarah gathered her carry bag from the car and checked they had everything they needed before locking it up.

"Yes, sis. I've remembered the bubbles and glasses," Jason answered Sarah's query, helping Trina out of the car. "And all the other things. And before you ask, yes, Trina has everything ready for later."

Megan smiled. Sarah's attitude towards Jason had changed now he and Trina lived in Auckland. Bit by bit she relaxed more around him, and Megan hoped it was a sign he was forgiven. The two young women appeared to get along, if a little tentatively. Today could well be the right time to tell them her plans, if everything worked out as she hoped. It had taken all her willpower not to concede to Sarah's earlier pleas to let her in on the secret.

Sarah took Trina's arm, and the girls wandered side by side down to the beach leaving Megan and Jason, carrying a large wicker basket, to tag along behind. Nick found a sheltered spot next to the sea wall, which helped deflect some of the wind. The ever-efficient Sarah quickly decorated the table, weighing the balloons down with a heavy glass base, before she pulled out a packet of standard balloons, scissors, a mini balloon pump and a pile of marker pens.

Nervous laughter followed the loud bang as the cork popped off the champagne bottle Jason opened. Nick helped fill their glasses, while Jason poured Trina a sparkling grape juice.

"Here you are, ladies. In celebration."

"What about me, Uncle Jason? Can I have a drink?"

"Of course you can, sweetheart." Jason crouched to her height. "I have something just for you. See?" He fished a coloured plastic wine glass from the picnic hamper and poured Bella some grape juice, finishing it off with a mini cocktail umbrella and a straw.

290

Bella's eyes bulged as she reached out to take it from him.

"Manners please, Bella," said Nick.

"Fank you," she said, concentrating on putting the straw, bobbing up and down in the bubbles into her mouth.

Sarah said a quiet thank you, impressed Jason had thought of Bella and had brought wine buckets and ice without being asked. She was satisfied everything was sorted. "Okay, everyone. Before the wind drives us from the beach, let's start. Mum, you wanted to go first."

"I apologise in advance if I get all emotional, but there's lots of things I want to say – bear with me, please. First. Trina, I'm very happy you could be with us today. You are part of the family now and we welcome you. I think we should start with those who are missing: your Dad and Trina's mother." She inwardly added Sarah's lost babies. "I'm sorry we didn't know her."

Trina, leaning back against the wall beside Jason, murmured her thanks.

"Now we're here, I think we should remember Dad the way he would have wanted. I have lived ever since by the poem read at the service. Remember it?

Do not stand at my grave and weep,
I am not there; I do not sleep.
I am a thousand winds that blow,
I am the diamond glints on snow,
I am the sunlight on ripened grain,
I am the gentle autumn rain.
When you awaken in the morning's hush
I am the swift uplifting rush

Of quiet birds in circled flight.
I am the soft stars that shine at night.
Do not stand at my grave and cry,
I am not here; I did not die.   (Mary Elizabeth Frye)

Megan paused to blow her nose. The silence lengthened as her family waited for her to pull herself together enough to continue.

"I hope you take those words to heart." She sounded husky and cleared her throat. "It's so true. Your Dad is with you in every breath of wind, in the waves that lap this shore, in Bella's smile, and his essence is part of Trina's unborn babe. He is still with you. The purpose of these balloons is so we can write our private words and release them. It might not be good for the environment, but I think it will be good for us," she said, trying for some levity. "Let's have some fun. As they sail into the sky, celebrate, whatever your thoughts."

Nick worked the pump while Sarah handed the markers around for everyone to write something on the stretched skin of the balloon. One by one, they released them into the air. Bella, understanding nothing of the grown-up's words, jumped up and down in excitement to see the balloons fly away.

"Okay, my turn," said Jason quickly. "I'm the only one who knew both of them. Their deaths so close together threw me into a spin and I reacted badly." He coughed to cover a sudden rush of emotion. "I wasn't there for any of you, not even you Trina, not really. I tried but ... well. I just wasn't. I know that now. I want to say sorry, Mum. For being selfish, for making you angry with me, for anything I did to upset you. And, ... I'm looking forward to being a dad, and I hope I can be as good as the one I had ..."

For a moment, no one said anything. Blinking back her own tears, Trina took his hand, kissed him on the cheek and surreptitiously wiped away a stray tear that threatened to fall.

"I probably need to send up lots of balloons to make up for it, don't I," he grinned, breaking the ice. Sarah threw a pen at him; Nick punched him in the arm, and Megan raised her glass and smiled while she fought to keep her emotions under control.

"Me next," said Sarah.

"Not so fast. I'd like to say something," said Nick. "I know you're keen to move on to other things, Megan, but I want to put my oar in here. I'm grateful I knew Tony. He was a good man. I liked him. I'm sorry Bella won't know him, nor your little one, Jason and Trina, but Megan is right. We honour him most by remembering the good times and being happy. That's it, really."

"Thanks, Nick. You're so right." Megan jumped in quickly – three of them speaking about Tony was enough. But Sarah wasn't to be denied.

"Hey, Mum. My turn. Don't worry," she said gently. "I'm determined not to cry. I just wanted to say I miss Dad – all the time and ..." Her wet eyes almost belied her promise. "I want to acknowledge family – all family, those close by, those far away, those almost forgotten but retrieved, thanks to Mum, and those to come."

Nick quickly refilled glasses and everyone raised a toast.

"Can we let off more balloons now, Mummy?"

Bella's innocent question destroyed any lingering

gloom and brought laughter in its wake.

"Yes, Bella. I think we can. Come on everyone, more balloons!"

Nick, pump in hand, could hardly keep up with the numbers as they scribbled words on the bits of coloured rubber. Jason started blowing some up with old-fashioned puff. The mood had turned to party mode with every balloon released, as Megan had hoped. This was a celebration, after all.

To Megan's surprise, Sarah's bag and Jason's picnic hamper were stuffed with hidden presents.

"Help yourself," instructed Sarah, "and give the gift to the person whose name is written on the tag."

"Sarah and I came up with the idea," added Jason, "to put right some wrongly spoken words."

"And for missing too many family events," Sarah reminded him.

Jason handed his mother a gift. "I promised to make it up to you, and bit by bit I hope I am."

Megan opened the gift to find a framed photo of him and Trina on their wedding day. But this was no traditional wedding photo nor was it a professional shot. Trina looked stunning with her hair clipped back and adorned with flowers, her simple summer dress of exquisite fabric draped perfectly, standing next to Jason in an open-neck shirt.

The camera had captured a spark of electricity between them. The look on their faces as they gazed at each other was an intense moment of intimacy and unity.

Megan wrapped one arm around his neck as tears blurred her vision.

"Love you, Mum," he whispered. He quickly let her go and walked off to talk to Nick before she could respond.

Megan unwrapped her gift of an art book from Trina and a crystal hanging from Sarah, both of which were beautiful. She had no words. She was far too choked up and needed time to collect herself.

When all the gifts had been exchanged and words and ideas exhausted, Megan picked up the scissors. "Thank you so much for today. You've really made it very special. This is exactly what I hoped for. Oh, this is too much," she said, wiping away tears she pretended were caused by the wind and changed tack. "But enough. I'm getting cold and we need to go – lunch is calling – but before we do I want to let off the last of these balloons. Bella, come and help me, love."

She held Bella's hand as one by one she cut the strings to the printed balloons.

"Goodbye – to sadness; Hello – to the future; Welcome – to new family; Happy Anniversary – to Jason and Trina: I hope you'll be as happy as your Dad and me. Okay, Bella. Three more to go," encouraged Megan as she guided the scissors. "Best Wishes – from me to you; Congratulations – on a life well lived, and last but not least ... Happy Birthday – for next week, Bella."

* * * * *

The warmth of the house and smell of hot soup greeted them as soon as they opened the door back at Sarah's.

"Mmmm. Smells delicious," said Megan, glad to be inside out of the wind.

"I'm starved," said Jason as he took off his jacket and pulled a lump of bread off the freshly baked loaf.

"Me too," said Nick, copying him.

"Wait." Trina slapped Jason's hand. "Both of you," she added, while helping Sarah set the food on the table. In good spirits after their mini festival, they took their places and devoured Trina's colourful Italian antipasto platter with the same speed and intensity as the soup and breads.

"Cake, Mummy, cake please," demanded Bella, who had insisted it was decorated with five birthday candles.

As they cleaned up after coffee, Megan watched the four of them relaxed and happy. They were enjoying each other's company in a way they hadn't quite done before, and jokes were flying. Sarah and Jason threw banter about things they remembered from their childhood, Trina joined in telling them of some of her antics, and Nick, well Nick was the quiet anchor to Sarah's exuberance. Megan couldn't have wished for a better mix.

"All done?" asked Megan as Sarah came to sit by her later.

"Yep, all done. Thanks, Mum, this was a great idea." Sarah took Megan's hand in hers. "Today, I said my final goodbyes to 'what might have been', too."

Megan knew exactly what she was talking about. "I think now might be a good time to let you all into some secrets, don't you?" Sarah beamed. Megan couldn't describe it any other way. "Just give me a minute to set Bella up with a colouring-in book and a DVD to watch."

Before long, with four sets of enquiring eyes trained on her, Megan began her story.

"The first year after your Dad went, I know I hid from life." She shuddered and flapped her hands as she remembered the dark emotions of those lost days. "The second year threw me into the unknown. Thankfully, I met a lot of wonderful people who helped me and taught me much about life. Now I want to give something back."

She reminded them how quickly time had passed since she'd left to trace her great-grandmother. "It's close to a year to the day, and I've learnt a lot along the way, and I know I've changed. I found so much of it startling and frightening: startling because of its unexpectedness, and frightening because I felt a great sense of responsibility and didn't know how to fulfil it. But now I have some ideas.

"Firstly, I want to give you both a sum of money. No strings attached." Passing envelopes to her children, she held up her hand to stop the comments as the first 'buts' came spluttering forth. "Let me finish, and no arguments. Please – it's my gift to you, let me do this. I've got more than enough," and she told them about the trust she'd established, which would cover her grandchildren's future education.

"Thank you, Mum," said Sarah, looking at the cheque. "That's more than generous, and I won't say no. It will be a lifesaver for us at the moment."

"I hope it helps."

Sarah hugged her mother.

"Yes. Thanks from us too, of course," agreed Jason, casting a jubilant look between Trina and his mother. "I told you I was willing to help you spend it."

"Jason, don't be mercenary," Sarah scolded but Megan laughed.

"And now," continued Megan, "to the reason I bought that apartment you two are staying in. I want to create an 'Artists in Residence' programme for women portrait artists."

"The fine details will need to be worked out with the art school. That'll be up to the administrators. I won't get involved. But I think it will satisfy my pledge to Constance."

"Wow, that's wonderful, Megan," cried Trina. "What an amazingly generous thing to do."

"It's a great idea," agreed Sarah. "I wish I'd known what you were planning, Mum, then I wouldn't have given you such a hard time. I should have trusted you."

A message of reconciliation passed between them.

"Not so fast, you two," said Jason. "This needs thinking through. What're you doing, Mum? You mustn't give all your money away."

Not him, too? Megan sighed. *Can't I do a simple thing without someone telling me I'm wrong?*

"Not my money, Jason. Constance's."

"What's the difference? It's all yours anyway."

"My money is mine: what I have from the sale of the house, from your father's insurance, from years of working. Mine to spend on my new home, holidays, and other personal things. Constance's money, I believe, has to be used for the good of others."

"Why? You said it was family money. Why not use what you want and invest the rest? You could live another twenty or thirty years. You'll need money."

"I appreciate your sentiments, Jason, but I have more than enough. I have to do this for my own conscience. Constance was without doubt a feminist – and before her time, when they were a rare and strange breed – this programme will continue to fulfil those ideals. I still have to satisfy the rest of her wishes and honour Isabel in some way – when I find her."

CHAPTER 35

In her new home, Megan's search for Isabel continued. Summer arrived early and pōhutukawa trees blossomed through the warm, sunny days as November evolved into December. Their distinctive red stamens looked striking against that startling blue sky all Kiwis know and love.

Megan regularly walked the beach and revelled in the sounds and smells of the ocean – the susurration of waves at her feet, birds cawing and squawking overhead. She loved the way the seaweed gracefully danced in the waves but didn't turn her nose up as it curled and dried on the beach. Every day she would pick up another shell to add to her collection of joy markers, as she called them. Days when life now had purpose, when she knew what she wanted to do and was doing it.

In the months since Paul left, she had followed every link and possible lead she could from the papers he had left with her and, like the pōhutukawa, an alluring picture of Isabel was emerging. A contact of Paul's had given Megan her most meaningful insight into her great-grandmother's life.

"You believe she was a professional artist's model?" quizzed Megan.

"Yes, I do," said Dr Clare Turner, the Auckland-based art historian.

The idea that Isabel had been a life model was now becoming clearer in Megan's mind. In Florence, she had assumed Luigi's drawings Giacomo had shown her were simply expressions of puppy love, but now it seemed more likely she modelled for the students at the accademia. There was much to learn about dear Great-grandmama.

"Tell me, more about these models, please," said Megan.

"Strange as it might seem to us today," said Clare, "artists back then valued their models and treated them with great respect, regardless of the general view that women should be pure and decorous and women who were not were somehow lesser citizens. These girls were often without any other means of support, thrown out by their families because of poverty or in disgrace. They found modelling an honourable way to earn a living. It was far better than begging and often better than being a servant, especially for single mothers. Even if they'd pretended to be a widow, without means of support, they wouldn't have been much better off. At least modelling was honest and open, and sometimes the girls would become the lovers or wives of their patrons."

Clare's explanation rang true with Megan.

"Unfortunately, the names of many of the girls of the time you are asking after were never recorded. Only by their faces can we be certain how popular they were, or whether they belonged to any particular studio or school."

Clare had unearthed numerous documents and several books on the history of artists' models and explained how artists would use the body of one model and the face of another. Their drawings were not always a complete image of one person.

"Your friend, Professor Rosse, told me about the sketch of a young woman and child he discovered in Cornwall. I've since contacted the gallery and seen a digital copy, and I think I have something to show you."

"I didn't realise it was online." Why hadn't Paul told her? Was he hiding something again?

Clare put one of the large books in front of Megan and opened it to a pre-marked page. In keeping with all things Trevallyan, Megan was once again stunned. The double-page spread of black-and-white photos of charcoal drawings were all of Isabel. Just like in Luigi's book: part of the face, an eye, a turn of the head, one scenting a rose, but, undoubtedly her.

"Is that your Isabel?"

"Yes. Yes, it is. But how did you find her?"

"By chance. A student doing research on the usage of charcoal and pencil in preparatory sketches brought the book to me to ask about these very images. Until then, I knew nothing about her, but after my discussion with Professor Rosse, and when I saw the digital image, I wondered if this could be her. I investigated further then wrote to tell him what I'd discovered. Hence your visit today, I believe."

"Yes, Paul emailed me. Tell me what you know ... please!"

"Very little, unfortunately, except her name."

At last! Megan edged forward in her seat and bit her lower lip.

"I believe she was known as La Bella Rosa Bianchi, meaning 'my beautiful white rose', and nicknamed Bella. She seems to have been a popular model."

Megan, overcome, could hardly believe her ears.

* * * * *

"You'll never guess what I've found!" Megan exclaimed to Sarah later that month when the certificates she'd ordered finally arrived.

"Is this about Isabel?"

"Who else? I couldn't wait and had to come around and show you. I've sent emails off to James and Jessica in Truro, and to Paul telling them all about it. I've found her. I've really found her."

"Whoa, slow down. What've you found this time?"

Sarah had already seen the images of Isabel from the book Clare Turner had shown Megan. She had also read every snippet of information her mother had gleaned from every newspaper clipping and archives record.

Megan had tracked down many articles about exhibitions, descriptions of paintings and stories about the artists and their models. Their bohemian lifestyle had clearly appealed to the reporters, who believed such stories gave readers a frisson of excitement in their mundane lives. Some of the most famous models were named but mostly the reports described the paintings in terms of 'a girl seated on a chair with her hair flowing and a sheer veil slipping from one shoulder' – any one of whom could have been Isabel.

"After I found out her modelling name, I went searching for records under any variation of it I could

303

think of." She waved a piece of paper in front of Sarah. "Look what I've got here: a death certificate for a Rose White."

Sarah read the form while Megan explained. "Unfortunately, whoever completed this didn't know much about her. They left all the information about where she was born and her family blank. The doctor estimated her age at late sixties and stated the cause of death as heart disease."

Megan pointed to the name of the person who gave the information, which meant nothing.

"And you're sure this Rose White is Isabel?"

"Not entirely, but it's highly possible. I need to find burial records and the headstone. They might tell me more. What I don't understand is where Grandma Julia was when her mother died."

"Are you thinking your Grandma Julia and Isabel were alienated?" Sarah handed back the form.

"Looks likely. Isabel seems to have had two lives –Bella the artist's model, and Lady Isabel the piano teacher. Any sign she was also a mother is missing."

Megan searched electoral rolls to find Isabel's address, but nothing. Nor had she been able to find out what Isabel did in her later years, which, she assumed, would not have been modelling – but she did find Julia Trevallyan.

Julia was sent to boarding school in Epsom, presumably to allow her mother free rein, or else to shield her from her mother's notoriety. Either way, they didn't live together.

"But do you notice something else about this certificate?" asked Megan. Sarah shook her head. "Check the year."

"1959?" Sarah was puzzled.

"The same year my mother and grandfather died, Grandma Julia also lost her mother. She lost everyone who ever mattered to her. No wonder she shut herself away from everything and there was only ever the two of us. But I'm curious now about how close those two were. I had assumed very close, since Grandma Julia and I were, but the records show me another possibility I hadn't thought of."

Images of Grandma Julia flickered in Megan's memory. The times when when Megan found her sitting quietly staring into the garden as if in another world meant something more significant now. The times she saw her staring at a photograph, or when she would change the subject if Megan asked questions, and times when her eyes were red and, as a child, Megan had not thought it important. Old people always looked different, their skin and eyes wrinkled, reddened and sagging – nothing like young skin. Except at forty-seven, Julia wasn't old. The realisation that the young are indifferent, carefree creatures, who don't see what is in front of them until they, too, have suffered, is something only understood in hindsight, thought Megan.

Isabel had abandoned her traditional upbringing, her parents and everything she knew to become the lover of an artist, and remained an outsider to the conventional world her entire life. If what Megan had discovered was anything to go by, Isabel had likely isolated her own daughter to maintain that life. Only now, after losing Tony, did Megan begin to appreciate the price Julia had to pay for Isabel's choices but, as Megan's grandmother had shown, life goes on. There is life after tragedy and it can be rewarding.

305

Making up her mind on the next course of action, Megan picked up her bag and headed for the door. "I'm off to find the headstone for this Rose White."

* * * * *

Megan knelt beside the broken concrete on the side of the hill and stared at the moss-covered chiselled words on the headstone – name, date of death and an inscription:

> ART AS A MOTIF FOR LIFE
> IS AN EVOLVING CONTINUUM OF FORM
> HERE LIETH A GOODWIFE
> WHOSE LIFE ART TRANSFORMED.
> RIP LA BELLA ROSA

A lone tear rolled down Megan's cheek. She had reached her journey's end. A little over a year ago she had set out to follow her great-grandmother's footsteps around the world, and now she had found her here, buried under the trees in an old section of the Purewa Cemetery, close to a century after she had arrived in New Zealand.

Neglected since it had been erected, the headstone confirmed her findings. Her great-grandmother had arrived in New Zealand in 1913 as Isabel Trevallyan *in* Della Rossa and died as La Bella Rosa Bianchi, and was buried as Rose White in 1959. Engraved in the concrete beside her name was a Celtic knot, the last motif to link this woman with her roots.

In the shade of a large pōhutukawa, Megan sat down more comfortably to think about all she had learnt in her search for her great-grandmother – the history, the hurts, and the mysteries.

Isabel had written 'he' used to call her Bella. Megan assumed the 'he' was Luciano but couldn't be certain, and she may never know, nor where the name Bianchi came into it. The burial record had told Megan little. The person who had given the information only knew the woman by her professional name. Quite how or when Isabel's name changed would remain a total mystery.

Megan would have liked to know much more about her avant-garde great-grandmother, since Grandma Julia had been nothing like her mother. Nor had Julia been there when her mother died. Why, Megan had not discovered, and it was unlikely she ever would. Isabel virtually vanished.

If Megan's fruitless searches were anything to go by, Isabel, young and alone with a baby, had survived the deprivations of World War One, avoided the flu epidemic of 1918, got through the great depression of the early 1930s, bypassed any work that required registration during World War Two and lived into the boom years of the 1950s without appearing in any newspaper, on any lists (despite compulsory voter registration) or receiving government support of any kind. It seemed incredible someone so visible in the free-spirited world of art could be so invisible in the everyday world.

The title Lady Isabel would have given her an air of sophistication as a piano teacher, but how Isabel managed to keep her two identities separate in the relatively small city was another mystery to add to all the others. Given what Megan knew of her forebear's character, Isabel would have been in her element during the 1920s, a boom time for everything new. She would have adored being part of the set who enjoyed the latest in music on the radio, danced to records from around the world and went to the cinema, as well as experimenting with the new styles in art, clothes, hair, and make-up.

There were still many questions in need of answers that Megan would never have. She could only guess about Luciano Rossi, but he must be Grandma Julia's father, and Megan would probably never know what happened to him.

But finding that Isabel's life was inextricably linked with the world of art solved many riddles and gave Megan a solution to her problem. She was glad Isabel had friends, real friends, who valued her, and that she, in turn, valued her family ties and kept in touch with her sister Constance.

Megan decided she rather liked this Isabel and her unconventional ways – a strong woman who knew what she wanted and followed her heart. There was hope for her yet.

Megan stood up, wiped away the last of her tears and said a silent farewell, promising to return.

CHAPTER 36

The idea had first come to Megan as she sat next to her great-grandmother's headstone. As she wandered around her apartment looking at where she could hang the painting of Isabel and Constance at Trevallyan House, the idea took shape.

Megan had spent some time debating whether she should gift the painting to a gallery, to be properly cared for, or keep it. But rather than give it to a gallery, what about establishing a new art gallery? One in honour of Isabel? Thoughts spiralled in her head.

Fizzing with ideas and excitement Megan called the family together. "Here comes the tricky part. I want to make this gallery idea work, but I can't do it by myself."

Sarah sat pensive and thoughtful, Nick waited patiently, Trina perched on the edge of her seat, excited, and Jason didn't see how he could help with anything.

"I need partners. I need people with skills I don't have, and I want my family involved."

Megan decided to appeal to Nick first, knowing his life's ambition was to set up his own business. She thought she'd be on safe ground with him. "Nick. I want to buy your services, please."

"Of course, but you don't have to buy them. What do you want done?"

"No. Let's get this straight," insisted Megan. "None of this is to be done as a favour. It has to be on a business footing or it won't work. I would like to engage Nicholas Woodhouse Architects to draw up the plans for the gallery."

"Slight problem there, Megan. I work for someone else, I'm not a registered company and the boss wouldn't let me moonlight. He takes the cream – and far too many shortcuts for my liking. I'll find you someone suitable."

"Nick," blurted Sarah, "I think Mum is offering you the chance to set up your own company."

"Sarah's right. I don't want anyone else. I want you. I want to be your first customer. Will you accept?"

Nick hesitated. "Nice idea, but I need more than one client to make a viable business, Megan."

Understanding his reluctance, Megan explained her offer. "I'm prepared to put up the money as a silent partner in the company or, if it makes you more comfortable, provide an interest-free loan."

Nick listened to her arguments but didn't respond.

Megan pushed her case. "Think of this as the chance to tell your boss what you think of him and then leave him to it."

"How can I resist an opportunity like that? I'd love to tell him where to go. But I'm not at all sure about taking more money from you."

"You won't be. This would be a loan. And the company I've set up would be your client."

With her new sense of purpose and an instinct she was on the right track, Megan's confidence had grown to the point of certainty. She had thought out every angle and carefully planned how she could work to each of their strengths. Constance might have bought loyalty by tying everyone up in knots, but she wanted to do the opposite and give her family opportunities with no strings attached and no barriers. This money was as much theirs as it was hers.

"Okay. I'm a starter. Provisionally. But we will need to talk terms."

Megan nodded. One down. "Thank you. But remember, this isn't all about me. I want to do this for my family – the whole family – past, present and future. But I need you all to see it through."

She decided Trina would also relish the idea. Megan remembered how the girl had glowed in Florence when they visited the galleries and she'd talked about owning her own gallery one day.

"So, Trina, I'd like to hire you as the gallery manager. You know all about galleries and ..."

"That's not fair, Mum," butted in Jason. "We're about to have a baby. You can't expect Trina to work."

"Jason!" interrupted Trina, placing her hand quietly on his lap, and playing into Megan's hand. "Just listen, please."

Trina was hooked.

"There's nothing to do at the moment other than express an opinion. I don't have a property or prospect in mind. That's where you all come in." Megan thought that would put his mind at rest, but seemingly not.

"Mum! What's got into you? We've only just got here and you're planning our lives to fit your idea of what we want."

Trina clutched Jason's arm and shook her head, stopping him from saying anything further.

"I'm sorry, Jason. What have I done to offend you? I thought you'd like to be part of it? You don't have to, of course, but talk it over with Trina before you decide." Why was he cross with her? What had she done to upset him?

"Now, Sarah, my darling. I have a special request of you. I need a business manager – at least, I think that's what it's called. Someone to do the networking, establish our brand identity and do the advertising and promotional work. We can hire someone else to run the office and do the accounts. Would you do that?" She hesitated, uncertain now of Sarah's reaction after Jason's outburst. She gabbled on. "Or do you want to do something else? It's just … I know you're unhappy in your job and I thought this might be a good alternative for you."

Sarah sat silent while the seconds drew out.

"For once I agree with Jason. You've been going off half-cocked ever since you came home. You keep coming up with bright ideas and making plans without talking to us first and then expecting us to fit in. How do you know this will work? It's very risky."

Megan's earlier buoyant mood and self-confidence was slipping. The happy atmosphere of the day had shifted into wariness and unease. In contrast to what she had expected, only Trina seemed genuinely interested in her proposal. She didn't think Nick would refuse the chance of his own business, but he'd do nothing without talking to Sarah, and without her agreement, it would end there. "I wanted to have everything set up ready so I could …"

"But it's our lives, Mum. You're beginning to sound like Constance," Jason snapped.

Megan was horrified. She wasn't being like Constance. Just the opposite.

"Mum," began Sarah more gently. "I know you mean well, but you're organising us into things we're not sure we want to be organised into."

"No. No. You've got it all wrong. I only want to do what's best for you," flustered Megan.

She had listened for months to their wistful comments about what they would like from life and had gone about her plans with all these ideas in mind.

"I know you do, but *we* need to decide what that is, not you."

Megan's face fell and her heart lay heavy. It looked like she had a lot to learn about trusting in her own judgement after all. If she'd talked this over with Tony, he would have seen the pitfalls and never let her walk into them. "But I had such plans," her voice sounded deflated, and she felt rebuffed, "such high hopes this was the right thing to do."

Her dreams were crumbling, and she was lost in her own uncertainty again, at a time when she thought she was taking control of her life. But she would fulfil Constance's wishes to honour Isabel, with or without her children's support. She would find a way.

Trina had sat quietly throughout the exchange, hardly saying anything. "Can I ask a few questions, please?"

"Of course. Anything you like," answered Megan flatly.

"What sort of gallery? One that displays paintings, one that sells on behalf of new artists or one that sells prints?"

"I really don't know. I was looking to you all for advice and direction. I had hoped to display Wil's painting of Isabel and Constance somewhere special. The gallery could have used it as a feature, but it can live at home. I'd thought we could name the gallery after Isabel or one of her nicknames. Would the artist-in-residence programme work in somehow? I don't know. I'm not sure now. Maybe it's a silly idea after all."

"If I took this on, I would like to do further study to complete my qualifications."

Jason looked at his wife in astonishment. "Don't you think we should talk this over first?"

"And let Megan give up on the idea before it gets off the ground? No, I don't think so. Let's talk about it now."

Jason clearly didn't like Trina's answer. He immediately got up from the chair, poured a drink and went to stand on the balcony, within earshot but plainly with no intention of taking part in any further discussion.

Megan, while surprised Trina had been the one to support her, brightened. "Absolutely. I wouldn't expect anything less."

Trina continued to ask who would decide about the hanging, lighting, temperature control, security and how often the displays were changed, and a myriad of other questions beyond Megan's understanding. Trina even knew what should be in her contract.

From the balcony, Jason watched his wife. His face portrayed varying degrees of consternation, astonishment and admiration. Jason was learning something new about her, too. Paul had spotted Trina's potential back in

Florence; now they were all learning – she was a talented and capable art professional who knew her trade.

"Most of your questions are beyond my knowledge," Megan smiled shakily at the girl. "To me, the gallery manager would do all of that. Trina, I know nothing about art, other than what I like. You're the one with experience in this field."

"And what if it doesn't pay off?" Sarah challenged.

Megan shrugged. Her initial feelings of excitement and euphoria were so deflated she could hardly conjure up any hope that Trina's support alone would pull it through. "If it doesn't work, then it's a loss I can carry. I would still have the property to sell and other investments to call on if necessary, but there's enough anyway. I can do this. I know I can. We can use contract staff to begin with to limit our risk, and you would be the only one giving up a job. You could look at this as an opportunity, or a challenge, or you could retrain. It's your choice, Sarah."

Her daughter didn't answer. Nick decided to join Jason on the balcony while Trina, ignoring the conflict, voiced a few more thoughts.

"I think we should only offer originals to start with. People can buy prints anywhere, but if we are to build our reputation up to international standards, we need quality. I agree we need to support up-and-coming artists through the scholarship and residence programme. We will also need works by recognised artists, both New Zealand and overseas. But I wonder, did you have anyone in mind to select the international artwork?"

Megan shook her head. She hadn't given any thought that she might need such a person.

"I think you should ask Paul," said Trina. "He'd be perfect for the job."

Sarah's attitude towards Paul had become benign since he'd returned overseas, but the mention of him being part of the family business was like a red rag to a bull.

"Not you, too! Why him?"

If Trina was surprised at Sarah's outburst, she didn't show it. "Because he knows what he is doing. If we are to get this right, we need someone well known and knowledgeable, like him. Why not?"

Sarah didn't reply. She folded her arms and looked unimpressed.

"Sarah, this is none of my business, I know. I'm new to this family, but if I am to be a part of it ... I have to say I think your antagonism towards Paul is unfounded. He's a nice guy. He is not a womaniser, a fly-by-nighter, a drunkard or a crook. He has a really good reputation in the art world and in Florence in particular. He knows his stuff. We can trust him."

Trina's quiet, calm confidence gave Megan courage. "Trina's right, sweetheart." Megan changed seats to sit beside her daughter on the sofa and patted the girl's knee. "I thought we'd sorted this out?"

Sarah had the grace to look uncomfortable. She released a deep sigh. "Oh, all right. I give in. I seem to be the only one who has any doubts, anyway. I don't want to see you hurt, Mum. That's all."

"I know, darling. But by being anti-Paul, you've done what you accused me of doing – controlling me to fit your views. Can we forgive and forget now and move on?"

Sarah nodded. Briefly covering her mother's hand with her own, she suddenly stood up, shrugged her shoulders back and, patently taking charge, called the men inside. "Okay. Let's do this."

CHAPTER 37

A few days later, Sarah and Trina were in full flight about what needed to be done. Megan didn't know, and didn't ask, what had been said to the men and to each other to change their minds. It no longer mattered. In that time, Megan had made a few decisions of her own.

Slowly, she had come to the realisation that throughout her life she had relied on someone else to guide her: first her grandmother, then Tony and now her children. She had always let her destiny be determined by others. With Tony it was a shared experience, one she willingly engaged in, but no longer. Megan was determined to fulfil Constance's wishes to honour Isabel in the way she wanted to.

Thinking back, Megan knew she had come a long way since those dark days of black hopelessness that had dogged her. Her children would never understand, never having experienced it. Neither could she expect them to, but sinking into those depths had changed her. Megan told herself she would find a way, but in the end that way had come to *her*.

First task was to find a suitable property, and Trina was keen and full of ideas. Megan was glad to have Trina on her side. "Are you sure you're up to it?" checked Megan, knowing the baby was due in about three weeks. "What does Jason think?"

"I admit, Jason didn't want me to take it on. But I told him this was the opportunity of a lifetime and he couldn't take it away from me. I'll be OK. I won't do anything silly, I promise."

Rather than leading the charge, Megan ended up being swept along. Once Trina had given her approval, the change in Sarah and Jason was remarkable and provided the final seal of validity needed to prove this wasn't some madcap idea of their poor misguided mother.

Megan decided it was best for her to let them take ownership of the project. In the long run, it would suit her purposes better than they could imagine.

"I can't tell you how excited I am," said Trina, "and honoured you thought of me. It's exactly my ... what did you call it, Sarah? My cup of tea?"

Recalling their time in Florence, the three women laughed, happy to be of one accord again.

Sarah became as excited as Trina but chose to stick with her job for the meantime, so Nick could quit his. "Once Nick's finalised the set-up and legal details of the new company and started your project, we'll see what happens next," said Sarah. "I need more time to think through your offer while I decide whether to pursue my career, change direction or commit to the gallery."

The three women spent the rest of the day checking Internet sites, making phone calls and talking to agents. Megan watched and listened as the two young women made plans and negotiated deals, set up appointments and created timetables. She wished she'd had their sense of worth and self-assurance in her younger years, but better late than never.

As they drove to their first appointments, Megan delighted in Trina's enthusiasm. On their third visit, they found what they were looking for. A stand-alone villa just off the main shopping area near Ponsonby, currently being used as an office, was perfect. Negotiations didn't take long and, as an early settlement date suited the vacating tenant, Megan quickly became the owner of her new art gallery.

With the Christmas holiday period approaching fast, Nick wanted everything ready to submit to council beforehand to avoid any delays in getting the necessary consents. With many ideas of what was needed, Megan and Trina spent hours with Nick as they pored over plans and sketched concepts on paper. Meanwhile Sarah had discovered a new skill as a designer and set up the new websites for both the gallery and Nick's practice, and started a blog page. The two girls then began work on the colours, fittings, and layout and, once those were exhausted, got down to the invitation lists.

"There has to be a grand gala opening," insisted Trina.

Next was a name.

"I had a lot of trouble coming up with the company name in the first place and no amount of alliterations, family names or Cornish references feel right. I need help," said Megan.

"It can't be that hard," said Sarah. "What were you thinking of?"

"I'd like something that would acknowledge how the whole thing started. Without Isabel's journal – and the money from Constance – none of this would have happened. Isabel's love of art gave me the idea of a gallery."

"What's wrong with calling it 'Isabel's' or 'Constance' or maybe 'Isabel's Legacy'?"

"I think we need something more modern, something to move forward with the times. Names only mean anything to us."

"I agree with Megan," said Trina. "If the gallery is to become international, it has to have a professional-sounding name. Something with impact but easy to remember."

Different ideas were tossed back and forth over the next few days. Some caused mirth, others derision. Megan was glad the task proved more difficult than they'd expected, and at least it wasn't her decision only, any longer. Finally, Nick came up with the one word needed. Jaws dropped, eyes lit up, surprise and approval written on everyone's face.

"Brilliant," said Megan, clapping her hands. "Let's keep it a secret until the opening."

* * * * *

Christmas Day was fantastic. Nick's family joined the picnic barbecue on the beach, with food to rival the feast Trina's family had put on for her in Florence a little over six months earlier. Paul had couriered a parcel, heavily packaged, with instructions it only be opened on Christmas Day. 'Hope you like it. I'll be back in April', he wrote in the card.

The package almost created a gala event of its own when Megan showed the family.

Later that evening back at home, Megan held the sepia image of Isabel and child in her hand. The same image Paul had seen in Cornwall. It was only a copy, he'd written, printed onto canvas, aged, and framed to the best of his ability. Megan didn't care if it was a copy or not, it was stunning. Paul had been right. Whoever drew this was highly skilled and very much in love with the subject. Megan was even more convinced the art gallery was the right choice to honour Isabel. She hung the portrait in pride of place in her apartment. This one was private.

A week later, a walk on the beach in the misty rain at midnight on New Year's Eve washed away the last regrets for things Megan couldn't change. Her year of discovery, heartache, failure and success came to a close, and her new year couldn't have started better.

Francesca Antonia Marsh was born at 2.01 pm on 2 January 2012 – an auspicious date to Megan's mind – and she had been there to witness it! As Trina held the tiny babe in her arms, freshly swaddled by the midwife, Jason announced, "We wanted to honour Trina's mum, but also to remember Dad. But we'll call her Shesca."

Overcome with joy, Megan hugged everyone in the room twice, babbling she knew not what nonsense.

"I gather you're pleased," said Jason.

Pleased was an understatement.

While Jason and Trina learnt about being parents and enjoyed their new baby, Nick hired Steve as project manager and lined up the tradesmen who would be needed as soon as the consents came through.

The waiting game was tense. Restless, Megan often didn't know what to do to fill in her time. She couldn't do anything to help Nick, Sarah was at work and Bella usually went to school holiday programmes. With Jason at home, she couldn't spend as much time with Trina and Francesca as she would have liked, either. She was grateful for any small chance to be useful.

Instead of the organised holiday activities, some days she and Bella spent the day together and got into the habit of making afternoon teas. Megan came to relish these special moments with her granddaughter. Flour covered the bench as Bella waved the measuring cup around before she dumped the contents into the bowl. Bella insisted her job was to stir the mixture and drop spoonfuls into the patty cases, obstinately refusing any help until they were ready for the oven.

At other times, Megan's new interest in genealogy would keep her enthralled and tied to the computer for hours on end. She joined several research sites and scanned many of the free sites, learning a lot about what lists were available, where she could find records and the best sources to turn to for advice. As her skills improved, so did her determination to find Isabel's lover.

January turned into February. Jason's schedule kept him away for much of the time, a nanny was hired to help Trina, Bella went back to school and Sarah announced her decision.

"Mum, I've given your offer a great deal of thought."

Something about the tone of voice told Megan she wouldn't take up the business manager's role.

"Nick and I have talked about this a lot, especially since Trina and I have been working together. We think you should be the one to take on the job of business-cum-public relations manager. An ambassador for the gallery. You would be brilliant at it. You could do the networking, both here and overseas, to establish the brand identity and do the promotional work. Leave the finance side to the experts if you want to."

Sarah's confidence in her to undertake the one role not yet filled was the last push Megan needed to prove her judgement had been right after all. She said nothing, letting Sarah talk, but now her cup was full.

"Um. So what I'd really like to do is retrain as an interior designer. That way we can build Nick's architectural firm into a total package that's a bit different to other firms." Sarah hurried on before her mother could answer or find reasons why it wouldn't work. "I know we're putting all our eggs in one basket, Mum, but with the mortgage paid off now, thanks to you, and Nick's picked up several new clients already, we feel it's the right time. I hope you don't mind."

"Of course not," answered Megan enthusiastically. "I knew it was a long shot, but I wanted to give you first opportunity. And thanks for your vote of support, too. I believe you're right. I'm sure I could do that job myself, the more I think about it, but I'm so pleased for you. You've made a great choice. You'll make an excellent interior designer."

"Thanks, Mum. That's a relief, but I promise I'll help you and Trina with all the arrangements for the gallery opening. I don't start till next semester."

A few days later, she got the long-awaited call from Nick. "I've got the council consents."

At last! They could begin the alterations.

"It should take about six to eight weeks, if everything goes according to plan."

It didn't.

The rain was driving everyone to distraction. With one of the wettest summers Auckland had known, general grumpiness over a summer ruined was the norm, but those who relied on fine weather to get their work done were downright frustrated.

March literally flowed in and was almost washed out, and the weather didn't improve.

The building site turned into a quagmire and mud was traipsed everywhere whenever another tradesman arrived. Nerves were stretched and tension crackled. Somehow – helped by some home baking – Megan managed to keep everyone calm and on track. But their plans for a mid-April opening were looking shaky.

Fortunately, the internal refit had been going ahead. To Megan's eyes, the place looked wonderful.

Nick explained how all the ideas had come together. "See how well widening the central steps leading to the verandah running the width of the front has worked. It'll give people a bit of shelter before they move through the French double doors. It took a bit of work to get them restored but I think it's worth it."

"So do I," said Megan. "They look great. And I like the way you restored the bay windows on either side, too."

"They had to go back in. It would have been unbalanced otherwise. What was once the two front rooms and entranceway is now an open-plan gallery and I had the original wooden floor matched and repolished."

"I love it all," said Megan. "Thank you, Nick."

"Happy to have had a hand it in. At the back, there's a set of double, frosted-glass doors leading to the private customer viewing lounge, with another door to the office area."

"Is that where the storeroom, kitchen and bathroom are?"

"Yes, which you'll be able to access from the side entrance and back courtyard when it's all finished."

Outside, Steve had removed the front fence and garden to provide off-street parking.

"We haven't been able to do any of the paving, concreting and garden work yet," said Steve, "and the painters are struggling to finish the external painting, but don't worry too much. I reckon we'll still get it done in time."

Megan couldn't see how.

The rains suddenly eased, and Steve was proved right. Workmen appeared in their droves and completed the work in the space of two weeks. Megan was amazed.

Now they could formally announce the grand opening date.

CHAPTER 38

Suddenly, it was action stations.

"That's settled then. We'll go for the Tuesday in the last week of April, with drinks and canapés from five-thirty to catch people before they head home," confirmed Megan.

They had three weeks.

Megan stood back and watched in admiration as Trina and Sarah took control of the operation. Phone calls and emails quickly put plans into motion.

Trina supervised the installation of the artwork she'd acquired, while she talked on the phone. "And can we get the scheduled advertising promotion started tomorrow?" she asked Sarah.

"Yes, and the invitations need to go out."

They double-checked the delivery of orders, the caterer, the party planner, and numerous other details Megan hadn't considered.

"I can help too, Mum," said Jason, who proved the greatest surprise. "I'll do the social networking stuff," which, Megan discovered, meant blogging, tweeting, and posting on Facebook, Pinterest, and other sites she'd never heard of.

"I could do the cleaning," offered Megan one day amongst the chaos, but her comment simply caused a burst of laughter.

"No way!" said Sarah. "We'll all be had up for elder abuse if we let you do that."

"How about you personalise the printed invitations instead?" suggested Trina.

"And it's time you took Muriel out to lunch," added Sarah. "So, shoo."

To add to Megan's sense of anticipation, Jessica, and the boyfriend she had heard such a lot about were coming to the grand opening. Happily ensconced back in her father's law firm, Jessica no longer felt adrift, and one of the best decisions she made was to take that cooking class where she met Max. Megan couldn't wait to catch up with the latest news. Paul was also due home soon. So much was happening at once.

* * * * *

The day of the opening came. In contrast to the previous two months, the vastly improved April weather was perfect – clear, warm, and sunny – and promised a balmy evening. Strings of lights appeared, draped along the verandah and around the marquee erected in the forecourt, chandeliers lit the gallery and huge flower arrangements stood on tall stands. Megan could not fault its understated glamour.

"It's simply beautiful, girls. I couldn't have done it without you," she said with a hug and kiss for each one.

By half-past three, Sarah and Trina judged everything in place to their satisfaction. With the caterers due in an hour, they retreated to the private lounge to do the last-minute check and get changed.

"Shesca's asleep. You must be quiet," an excited Bella told them in a stage whisper, putting her finger to her lips. She had been allowed to come along after school to see the gallery all decorated and what the women were wearing, before being whisked back home by their nanny, well ahead of the guests' arrival. Sarah swept the child into her arms and cuddled her so tightly the girl's high-pitched squeal brought relieved laughter to the place for the first time that day. Francesca slept on regardless.

"I'll just phone Jessica and make sure she's OK. Poor girl was thoroughly jet-lagged yesterday," said Megan. She met Jessica and Max at the airport two days earlier. The young woman bubbled with enthusiasm and didn't stop talking. She tried to include Max as best as she could but often failed when she chatted about the things she and Megan had done together. They talked late into the night.

Max, Megan discovered, was a professional photographer.

"I'll be your official photographer for the night," he insisted, resisting her efforts to say no. He was her guest. Unfazed, he showed her his photos on the laptop to convince her.

"These are beautiful, Max. Thank you. I will accept, after all. I think you have a great future ahead of you. Good luck."

Megan had no doubts that Jessica had found her soul mate. She had also fulfilled many of her Paris dreams, from the cut of her clothes, which screamed class, to her love of art finding a new field of expression in Max's photos. And he loved to cook. What more could a girl ask? Max reminded Megan a little of Nick – calm, caring and devoted, and willing to fit around his livelier partner – even if he did tend to disappear for hours while he took and developed his photos.

As she dialled the number, she hoped he was back by now.

"Yes, he's back," laughed Jessica. "With some great photos, he says. He loves the light here. And I feel wonderful after my lazy day and all that pampering. Thanks for organising it for me."

"You're welcome."

Confirming the taxi would pick them up at four-thirty, she said goodbye and let her thoughts turn to Paul. She looked forward to him being at the function tonight. The past few days had been so busy they hadn't found time to catch up, not since Jessica and Max had arrived. The last time she saw him, he convinced her he should be the least of her worries. She had taken him at his word, grateful for his understanding. At least he'd accepted the invitation to dine with them all after the event.

Over a week had passed since they'd managed a wonderful couple of evenings together and had talked for hours over dinner and then back in her apartment. Sitting on the sofa together, they admired the charcoal sketch of Isabel on the wall.

"Do you think we'll ever find out who drew it?"

Paul shook his head. "Unlikely, unless we find that unique mark on another painting one day. One that's signed."

"One day, then. Anything is possible if you look for it hard enough."

"I tried my best to get the museum to let me buy it, or at least acquire it, for the Auckland Art Gallery."

"Could you do that?" Megan asked, hardly able to take her eyes off the sketch. "Are you that well in with the gallery?" She turned to look at him to gauge his response.

Paul laughed. "I bluffed. Hoping they might concede that point. If they had, I'd have been making some rather rapid enquiries amongst the Auckland people about who could make the decision to purchase a lost New Zealand artwork. But our friends in Cornwall didn't go along with the idea."

The best Paul had come up with was the digital image. "I managed to have it reproduced to look as close to the original as possible. I'm glad you like it."

"To say I like it is not enough. I love it." She took his hand briefly. "I haven't had a chance to thank you properly since it arrived. I can't begin to tell you how much it means to me."

Paul squeezed her hand in return. "It's a measure of how I feel about you."

Flustered, Megan wasn't sure what to say in response, but Paul didn't belabour his point, nor did he expect an answer.

"I have some other news, too," he continued carelessly. Megan raised her eyebrows. "I've secured an Emeritus Professorship. I'm back in Auckland permanently. I take up the role next semester."

At last! Megan's response had been spontaneous. She flung her arms around his neck, then, in an exaggerated fashion, cheek-kissed him on both sides – as she'd seen him do in Florence. They cracked up and broke into uncontrolled laughter.

For a moment she wondered what his return might mean for their relationship. Tony would always be a part of her inner core; she could never replace him, but ... she missed that special someone to talk to about her deeper thoughts. Some things you just couldn't talk to your children about – especially your doubts and fears. Paul, against all logic, had become a confidant in a way she thought she would never have again. She enjoyed his company and they were usually on the same wavelength about most topics. Having Paul living in Auckland would be marvellous.

She decided to be bold. "Paul, I'd like you to consider taking on the role of the art purchasing advisor for the gallery. Please? You'd be responsible for sourcing suitable paintings. And, no arguments, the position comes with a commission on each of the procured works."

It was his turn to look astonished.

CHAPTER 39

With little more than an hour to get ready, the three women managed the revolving door use of the bathroom very smoothly. Megan chose to wear the replica 1920s gown she'd had made in Cornwall for the grand opening, hoping it wasn't too much. As she emerged, the girls stood ready and waiting. The midnight blue satin shimmered in the light, and the silver beading sparkled.

Bella squealed in delight. "Nana, you look so pretty."

Sarah and Trina echoed Bella's thoughts.

"What a beautiful dress."

"Where did you find it?"

"I had it made," Megan said. "Constance wore the original for her twenty-first birthday portrait."

"How perfect for tonight! Simply stunning, Mum."

Megan's doubts evaporated and her spirits soared. "You girls look stunning, too," she said, carefully eyeing Trina, who sometimes looked as tired and strained as any mother of a four-month-old baby, even with a nanny's help, but not tonight. Trina was bursting with energy that only the young can exhibit, and her expertly cut deep-red gown and heels made her appear slender and taller.

Sarah, dressed in dazzling emerald green, poured them each a glass of bubbles in early celebration. "To the women of this family."

The clink of glasses and laughter met Nick and Jason, who had been banished to the hotel to change, as they walked through the door.

"Save some of that for us," teased Jason, taking a glass from Sarah as he crossed the room to stand with Trina.

"Ve-ry nice," he whispered, as his eyes said a lot more.

Nick put his arm around Sarah, kissed her gently on the top of her head and murmured, "You look beautiful."

Megan watched her two children and their partners, thinking how fortunate she was. They had both found their soul mates. What more could a mother ask? With her propensity for sentimentality, she wisely kept her thoughts to herself. Life had, after all, turned out better than she could ever have hoped after Tony passed away. His abiding strength had carried her through whenever things got shaky, and Megan knew he would have thought tonight a perfect outcome.

What had started out as an escape from her bleakness had turned into something she could never have imagined in a million years. By following in Isabel's footsteps, Megan had discovered a life so distant to the one she'd had she could hardly believe it possible. Somewhere along the line Isabel's journey had become of secondary importance. What was more important by far was what she had learnt from it.

This evening was hers and hers alone.

* * * * *

334

With a sense of déjà vu, Megan took her place to welcome people, pleased at how many of the guest list had accepted. Amid the convivial hum of conversation, the wait staff efficiently wove their way around the crowd. People wandered through the gallery, glasses in hand, stopping to study one or another of the paintings on display, or gathered in groups to catch up and share opinions. Jessica and Max had been one of the first couples to arrive. As soon as she could, Megan took Jessica by the hand and led her to a display at one end. On the wall, discreetly hidden by a screen and flanked by two grand floral displays, hung Megan's pride and joy – the painting of Isabel and Constance in the garden in Cornwall.

Jessica's reaction was just as she'd hoped. "That is beautiful." She hadn't seen the painting for some time, and not since Megan had had it professionally cleaned. The colours appeared clearer, softer, defining the fine details. Certain it was now worth far more than the Trevallyan Trust Board had thought when they gave it to her, Megan almost felt guilty. Almost. Later, as the pièce de resistance, the painting would be revealed.

"While we're by ourselves, I have something for you." Jessica handed Megan a white envelope. "From Dad. He said I was to give it to you tonight and not before."

"What now? Do you know what's in it?" Megan exclaimed, peeking in the envelope to see another one, aged and yellow, inside.

"It's the final part of Constance's will," answered Jessica.

Megan's interest was piqued. "When will that woman stop surprising me?"

"I won't spoil it any further. It's good news, and I've got some other news to tell you ..."

Just then Paul arrived with Muriel on his arm. Delighted at being included, the old lady had dressed specially for the occasion. Although somewhat dated, Muriel looked elegant in her best lace dress, long pearl necklace and crystal earrings.

"My dear, I'm so excited for you. The gallery looks wonderful, although I don't understand some of that modern stuff I see over there."

Megan laughed. When she had said something similar back in Florence, Trina had told her she didn't have to like it, only recognise its potential. And here she was, with that potential all around her.

Megan could see all four of her family working the room, making introductions and moving people into new groups. She called Sarah and Trina over to meet Jessica, whom they had spoken to on the phone but not met.

"What's this news you have for me?" asked Megan, wishing she could find a moment to read the letter Jessica had given her. She needed to settle her nerves about what it might say.

Jessica looked around for Max, who had been busy snapping candid images of the gallery and the gathering crowd. He quickly appeared by her side.

"I hope you don't mind me stealing some of your thunder, but I'm bursting to tell you all. Max and I got engaged today."

She showed them her new ring and was immediately swamped with hugs and kisses.

"Congratulations!"

"How exciting."

"I'm so pleased for you," said Megan.

"This place is the perfect choice to make it official," Max added, shaking hands with everyone.

Almost bouncing with excitement Jessica butted in. "And I want you, Megan, to be my special guest at the wedding. We'll have it at Trevennick Hall, of course. All the folk there are dying for you to come back. Say yes, please, say you'll come."

"Yes, yes, of course I'll come. Just try and stop me," said Megan, delighted to have the opportunity to return to Cornwall.

Before any further details could be discussed, Jason called Trina away to answer questions, and Sarah took Jessica, Max, and Muriel to meet Nick.

"You look wonderful," said Paul, stepping closer to Megan as he offered his arm. His eyes sparkled. "And I love that perfume you're wearing."

"Thank you, kind sir," she answered teasingly. "I'm glad you're here," admitting how much she had wanted him by her side tonight. "Let's get something to drink."

Taking his arm, she led him back into the marquee where people were now thronging. Wine and finger foods quietly appeared on trays before them, the delicate bite-size pieces as tasty as they were attractive. The couple moved around the room stopping to chat now and then to introduce themselves. An air of expectation filtered through the crowd. Compliments flew and business cards were exchanged. So far, the evening couldn't be better.

Paul glanced at his watch – six-twenty. "What time did you say the speeches were?"

"Seven. Have I got a few minutes to spare?"

"Depends. What do you want to do?"

"Jessica gave me a letter. I'm anxious to read it before I get caught up in the celebrations."

"Be quick."

They made their way through the private lounge to the office. Megan pulled the neatly folded envelope out of her bag and withdrew the brief letter from James. He formally advised her she had met all the conditions of Constance's will and he could now release her final letter, which he hoped would complete the cycle.

"James has been a cunning old devil, keeping this from me all this time," said Megan.

Once Paul had shut the door behind them and Megan was seated at the desk, she opened the letter from Constance.

Trevennick House
October 1983

My dear great-grandniece. I still don't know your name.

If you are reading this, then you have met all the conditions I stipulated. I am pleased. It shows you are made of the same marrow. You have spirit. I admire that.

My sister Isabel and I never did quite understand each other. I valued belongings more than people. Belongings can't hurt you. She valued people, especially those who created something with their hearts and minds. She loved beauty but was far too hysterical and got hurt dreadfully as a result. I used to think my way was best, but now I am alone and belongings no longer give me the joy they once did, I wish we had been closer.

I am sure you noticed the torn edges of pages missing from her diary. I am equally sure you sought to find what was missing. I will tell you what was in those pages.

She wrote of love, gushingly and indecently. Her words were far too embarrassing for me to repeat verbatim. I destroyed those pages, but I couldn't eradicate what was in them from my mind. Many of her letters are hidden in the library if you would care to look. I left the key with the Boscowans. I only kept the ones that were suitably decorous. I couldn't abide her brazenness.

She was passionate about art reflecting life. It was her abiding love and led to her downfall. She fell in love with an artist of little renown, giving up her name and completely turning her back on her Trevallyan heritage.

Her lover's name was Carlos Luciano Della Rossa. He was a tutor at the Florence School, I believe. Your grandmother Julia was their child. Isabel said there had been a civil marriage, but it may not have been officially recognised. What else would one expect from those foreign countries? And he was Catholic, to boot. He died during the First World War.

She took another lover, later. Not at all surprising, given her nonconformist ways. He was part of that art studio she worked at. He drew a frightful sketch of her and the child. I gave it away to my friend, whose aunt had been Jane de Glehn. His name I forget, but he was a native, born there at least, rather than being an English gentleman as befitted her birth.

Julia was sent away to school, thank goodness, and retained not only the Trevallyan name but also its principles, thanks to my intervention. I'm glad something of my values endured.

Now you know. I have given you all I have to give: my money and your history. Think what you may.

Constance Trevallyan

Her hand shook, but her eyes sparkled with elation as she handed the letter to Paul. A few seconds later Paul raised his head, his eyes agleam. "This is wonderful! And explains so many things."

"Isn't it? I'm not sure I would have liked Constance. She held some odd notions and was obviously very rude and abrupt when it suited her. You certainly couldn't say things like that these days, but I'm excited. It's exactly what I've been looking for – a starting point at last."

"You have several, my dear," declared Paul. "The real name for Luciano Rossi, a clue about the artist of the sketch, a definite link to Jane Emmett de Glehn and the family who held the sketch – she probably painted the scene where it was found – and confirmation Isabel worked for an art studio."

Paul was keen to tell the Cornish gallery about the find. "It would be a great coup if I could identify the artist of the house. If you don't mind?"

Megan caught his enthusiasm. "I can't believe it. There's so much to talk about and plans to make." She put the letter safely away in her bag. "How much time have we got?"

Paul glanced at this watch. "It's five-to."

"Goodness. We'd better hurry then. I need to be there for the auction."

The charity auction had been Trina's idea. "People like being nosy," she'd said. "You wait, they'll turn up to our gala opening to see what the competition looks like, but without a reason to open their wallets, they'll also go away again without buying anything."

"So what do you intend?" Megan had asked.

"We'll give them a golden opportunity to be seen by

their peers as generous and philanthropic. It's a game of one-upmanship. They'll look mean otherwise. And all proceeds go to the charity of their choice. Then you watch. The sales will follow one another."

As Paul and Megan re-entered the gallery and walked past the artworks, looking for small coloured dots, they discovered Trina's assessment accurate. Impressed, they found five paintings had been pre-purchased.

"At this rate, I might be successful in my own time," she joked.

"I think that's highly likely," he agreed. "And I'd like to be part of it."

Megan turned with a questioning look. "Are you saying what I think you're saying?"

Paul smiled and nodded. "I am, yes. If the offer's still open."

Trying hard not to skip like an excited child, Megan squeezed his arm a little tighter. "I'm glad."

With him finding the hidden gems of the art world and tracking down lost artists, her dreams were more likely to come true. Her legacy, she hoped, would be the discovery of a great new artist, or a great piece of lost art restored to the world. Fantastic as it sounded.

Maybe she wished for too much, but she couldn't help herself. Would Constance and Isabel approve? After reading Constance's letter, she believed they would. Thanks to Constance's passion to own things and the romantic Isabel's love of art – as well as the artists – Megan had found the perfect way of honouring her ancestors' memories.

Now maybe Paul would help her trace her great-grandfather's family tree, too, if she asked. They could travel, visit the art galleries of the world together, discover ...

"Mum," Sarah's voice commanded her attention. "It's time."

Butterflies immediately started fluttering in her stomach, and the adrenaline began pumping. It was her first official task as public relations manager.

Moving to one end of the room near the hidden portrait, Megan stepped onto a small podium and adjusted the height of the microphone. People had been ushered into the gallery and stood crowded, shoulder-to-shoulder, in front of her. Her stomach did another flip.

"Thank you, everyone, for attending the gala opening of our new gallery. I and my family appreciate your interest and for giving up your time to be here tonight." Megan briefly explained about her legacy and introduced the key people and their roles. "I want to thank my special guests, Jessica and Max, for travelling halfway around the world to be here tonight. According to Jessica, I come from a line of strong women. I believe strength comes in two ways – through necessity, or through strong foundations, as I learnt from my forebears. Without the foundation my family gives me, I would achieve nothing. With them, anything is possible, as this gallery proves."

Given the murmurs and applause that followed, she had struck the right chord.

"Behind this screen is the painting that started me on my journey. It's of Isabel with Constance in the background. We believe it is by Wilfred de Glehn."

Megan heard the gasps as the experts in the room recognised the name and its significance. Her stakes in the art world had edged up a notch. "It is with great pleasure I now reveal this painting and share it with the wider world. It is our family treasure ..." Applause followed as the curtain opened on the image she had carried with her from Cornwall. "And not for sale," she added, to the amusement of the crowd. "Now to the moment you've been waiting for – the charity auction."

At that point, Trina replaced Megan on the podium. Jason and Nick put the selected painting on an easel for everyone to see and Trina immediately impressed them by going into auctioneer patter and rattling off the call for bids. Sarah worked the room, nudging those whose expressions of interest she'd taken earlier. Trina's judgement had been correct. Competition was hot. The chosen charity would benefit well, indeed.

Just as Megan thought it was her turn again, Sarah jumped up to the microphone. "Before we finish, there's one more item. My mother knows nothing about this, so it will be as big a surprise for her as it is for you. I now invite Professor Paul Rosse to speak."

Megan was indeed surprised – mostly that Sarah would invite Paul to do or say anything at this event. While Sarah had accepted his presence, thanks to Trina, this was a family affair, and Sarah had made it very plain, more than once, that Paul was not family. What had happened to change her mind?

"Good evening, everyone. I am an art historian and part of my job is to identify works of art. I became aware of the possibility of a lost painting through a reference in the journal Megan has spoken of tonight. After extensive investigations, it is now my undoubted privilege to present Megan with the results of that research."

A buzz intensified among the gathered crowd as Jason and Sarah emerged from behind the curtain with a painting they placed on the easel. The portrait was exquisite and depicted a girl glowing in the bloom of youth, pregnant, sensuous and voluptuous. Megan's astonished expression turned to disbelief as she recognised the face. Isabel looked beautiful. The pose, semi-reclining, carefree yet bold, tantalised. The composition cried out skill and passion.

"This portrait," continued Paul, "is of Isabel and was painted in Florence about 1912. I believe the artist is one Luciano Rossi, a once-popular art tutor, although a somewhat renegade figure, whose work is generally unknown. It is with immense satisfaction I pass this heirloom to its rightful owner."

The noise greeting his announcement drowned out any further possibility of speech. Once the applause had died down, the volume of conversation rose. People clamoured to see the painting close-up.

Megan pulled Paul to the back of the room where it was slightly quieter. "Why didn't you tell me?" Even to her ear, she sounded critical and ungracious. She softened her voice. "The painting is superb. Thank you. But is this why you left Florence so suddenly, to search for it?"

"Yes. And it's taken me months. I had to keep it hidden from you, in case nothing came of the rumours I'd heard," Paul admitted. "But first I had to return to the States in order to complete a whole year's programme in advance. I wanted to get out of my contract early. And," he added, "so I could return to Auckland, and you, sooner."

He smiled as he took her hand. "I'm sorry I was tight-lipped. I'll make it up to you, I promise."

Jason promised the same thing – with some success. Now Paul was making promises. Life was on the up.

344

"I'm looking forward to telling you all about it. Where my search led me and what I found out about our elusive Luciano – even before your amazing letter from Constance."

Before Megan had a chance to respond, Sarah announced her return to the dais to close the evening.

Eager to wind everything up, now there was so much to talk about, Megan hurried through the last announcements. "I can't thank you all enough for your attendance tonight and for your generosity at the charity auction. Please put your hands together to acknowledge the young artist.

"I also wish to thank my family and friends for their support, and especially Paul Rosse for this extraordinary gift."

Their eyes met across the heads of the crowd. A look of great possibilities passed between them.

"For the final act of the evening, I would now like to officially name our new gallery – partly based on a name, partly on a concept, but mostly because of an inscription.

"To art, love, and family, in perpetuity. I hereby name this gallery, Continuum."

"There is **no end**. There is **no beginning**. There is only the passion of life."

– Federico Fellini 1920–93
(Italian film director and scriptwriter)

THANK YOU

If you enjoyed this book, discover more unforgettable family heritage stories inspired by immigrants seeking a better life in a foreign land.

THE NEW ZEALAND IMMIGRANT COLLECTION
suspenseful family saga fiction about overcoming the odds.

The Cornish Knot
Portrait of a Man

Brigid The Girl from County Clare
Gwenna The Welsh Confectioner
The Costumier's Gift

The Disenchanted Soldier

* * *

Available at
Amazon.com/vickyadin
www.vickyadin.co.nz

Please consider leaving a customer review.
I'd be delighted if you would sign up for my newsletter on my website.

* * *

Look out for the upcoming series
THE ART OF SECRETS –
dual-timeline stories about discovering your roots.
First book *The Art of Secrets* available now.

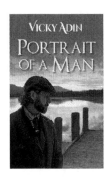

Portrait of a Man

The gripping multigenerational tale of lies, lost chances and misplaced love.

Will the secrets of the past destroy an artist's legacy?

The soul-searching conclusion to *The Cornish Knot*

An Italian artist, a Cornish knot and a Māori koru lead to a shocking exposé. As World War One escalates, can he keep his secrets safe?

In 1863, Matteo Borgoni is a desperate man. If he is to free his beloved wife held captive by her father in Melbourne, his picture framing business must succeed. Haunted by the memory of failure, he has many obstacles to overcome before he can establish himself with the artists of Dunedin, New Zealand and be reunited with his love.

Fifty years on, Luciano, a rakish Italian portrait artist fleeing from a life of lies, turns up at Borgoni Picture Framers seeking refuge. As the ravages of World War One escalate, an unusual friendship and newfound rapport brings unforeseen repercussions. A terrifying pandemic is the last thing they need.

Over a century later, a man recognises a portrait in an Auckland gallery, and demands it back. Amid another global pandemic, a marriage on the brink of failure, and a life-and -death struggle, the portrait exposes generations of family secrets and deceptions with life-changing results.

Portrait of a Man is told over three timelines through the eyes of different generations.

THE NEW ZEALAND IMMIGRANT COLLECTION

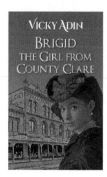

VICKY ADIN
BRIGID
THE GIRL FROM
COUNTY CLARE

Brigid
The Girl from County Clare

The heart-rending tale of Irish immigration in the 1880s

Like making lace – she pieced together a new life from a single thread of hope

Counterpart to *Gwenna The Welsh Confectioner*
Prequel to *The Costumier's Gift*

Eighteen-year-old Brigid faces an unimaginable choice. If she stays in her beloved Ireland, she is another mouth to feed in a land plagued by starvation and poverty. If she leaves, she will never see her family again. But leave she must.

Heartbroken, she travels by ship with her cousin Jamie to a new life in Australia. On the journey, Brigid meets a rough-and-ready Scots girl who becomes her best friend, a man who beguiles her, and a fellow Irishwoman who causes no end of trouble.

Brigid's skill as a lacemaker soon attracts attention, but it is her selfless nature that draws people to her. When the burden of choice is forced upon her once again, Brigid must find an inner strength if she is to fulfil her dream.

A new start in New Zealand offers hope – until the day she encounters the man who seeks her downfall.

The historical aspects of the story are so accurate and described so perfectly that the reader will frequently need to remind herself/ himself that the story is fiction ... This is a thoroughly satisfying read. It is the kind of story that passes the test as a work of history, and is equally satisfying as a novel that will have your attention from first to last. **** 4 stars – Frank O'Shea, *The Irish Echo*, Sydney

THE NEW ZEALAND IMMIGRANT COLLECTION

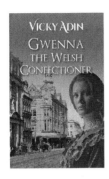

Gwenna
The Welsh Confectioner

A powerful tale of family life amid Auckland's bustling Karangahape Road at the turn of the 20th century

Against overwhelming odds, can she save her legacy?

Counterpart to *Brigid The Girl from County Clare*
Prequel to *The Costumier's Gift*

Gwenna's life is about to change. Her father is dead, and the family business is on the brink of collapse. Thwarted by society, the plucky sweet maker refuses to accept defeat.

Gwenna promised her father she would fulfil his dreams and save her legacy. But thanks to her overbearing stepbrother, that legacy is at risk. Gwenna must fight for her rights if she is to keep her vow.

She falls in love with the cheeky and charming Johnno, but just when things are beginning to look up, disaster strikes. Throughout the twists and turns of love and tragedy, Gwenna is irrepressible. She refuses to relinquish her goal and lets nothing and no one stand in her way.

But blind to anything that could distract her, Gwenna overlooks the most important person in her life, putting her dreams, her family, and her chance at happiness in jeopardy. *Utter brilliance. Vicky really brings the characters to life and you can really engage with what it must have been like to be a young girl like Gwenna going into business at the turn of the century in a male dominated society. Every character contributed to make this a truly wonderful story; my only disappointment was when it ended.* ***** 5-star Amazon review

THE NEW ZEALAND IMMIGRANT COLLECTION

The Costumier's Gift

An absorbing multigenerational dual-timeline family saga

Why does a stranger hold the key to untangling Katie's family secrets?

Continues the lives of *Brigid The Girl from County Clare* and *Gwenna The Welsh Confectioner*

Jane thrives in the one place where she can hide her pain and keep her skeletons to herself. As principal costumier at Auckland's Opera House in its Edwardian heyday, she is content – until the past comes back to haunt her.

Her beloved foster mother Brigid and her best friend Gwenna are anchors in her solitary yet rewarding life. When the burden of carrying secrets becomes too great, Jane surrenders her role as keeper of the untold.

Generations later Katie seeks refuge from her crumbling life with her Granna, who lives in the past with the people in her cherished photographs. Katie discovers she must identify the people behind the gentle smiles and reveal generations of secrets before she can claim her inheritance.

Through Jared, an intriguing new client, Katie revives her stalled career until she learns he holds the key to uncovering her past. Despite an increasing attraction, she shies away from any deeper involvement ... but without him she will never know the truth.

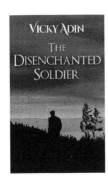

The Disenchanted Soldier

A heart-breaking dual-timeline family saga

From soldier to pacifist

In 1863, young Daniel Adin, a trained British soldier, embarks on an adventure of a lifetime. In pursuit of a new life and land to farm, he travels to New Zealand to fight an unknown enemy – the fearless Māori.

A hundred and thirty years later, Libby is fascinated by the stories of Daniel as he looks down at her from the aged black-and-white photos on the wall. Surrounded by four generations of his large family, she wants to know more, to know what he was really like.

As she researches his past, Daniel's story becomes so much more than she expected.

I loved this book and so will you if you like historical fiction and family sagas set somewhere you likely know little about. This is beautifully and sensitively written. The characters are terrific. The fascinating part to me was how Vicky was able to take us on the family's journey in a thoughtful and non-judgmental way.

***** 5-star Amazon review

THE NEW ZEALAND IMMIGRANT COLLECTION

The Art of Secrets

An uplifting tale of friendship, grief and lies.

Emma wants to forget; Charlotte never can. Together they remember.

First in the upcoming series THE ART OF SECRETS

A young journalist and an ageing author have little in common, until their secrets tear them apart.

Emma is an enterprising young journalist with a bright future, but her life and career are falling apart. In a last-ditch attempt to save her position, she accepts the assignment to interview the bestselling author, Charlotte Day.

The ageing Charlotte has a reputation for being cantankerous and is highly secretive about her past, one she considers too painful to relive and too shameful to share. Preferring her roses to people, she grudgingly agrees to meet this girl who gets through her defences, forcing her to confront her past.

As Charlotte and Emma's relationship deepens, they become enmeshed in a tangle of secrets that changes their lives.

The art of great writing! ... Adin keeps a tight rein on her leading characters, their actions and reactions credibly grounded in genuine emotions. The change of tone from Emma to Charlotte, from young to old, works, helps the reader see behind the lies and half-truths they tell each other. Their progress from antagonists to friends is seamless, as the layers of the story peel back like petals, exposing the truth at the flower's heart. Bev Robitai, author of *Sunstrike*

Book 1 of THE ART OF SECRETS series

ABOUT THE AUTHOR

Vicky Adin is a family historian in love with the past. Like the characters in her stories, she too is an immigrant to New Zealand, arriving a century after her first protagonists, and ready to start a new life.

Born in Wales, she grew up in Cornwall until aged 12. Her family emigrated to New Zealand, a country she would call home. Vicky draws on her affinity for these places, in her writing. Fast forward a few years, and she marries a fourth-generation Kiwi bloke with Irish, Scottish and English ancestors and her passion for genealogy flourishes.

The further she digs into the past, the more she wants to record the lives of the people who were the foundations of her new country. Not just her own ancestors, but all those who braved the oceans and became pioneers in a raw new land. Her research into life as it was for those immigrants in the mid-to-late 1800s and early 1900s gave her enough material to write for many years about the land left behind and the birth of a new nation.

Her first book, *The Disenchanted Soldier*, is the most biographical of all her books, inspired by her husband's great-grandfather. For the rest, while the history of the time is accurate, the characters are fictionalised to fit with the events and happenings as they occurred.

Vicky holds an MA(Hons) in English, is a lover of art, antiques, gardens, good food and red wine. She and her husband travel throughout New Zealand in their caravan and travel the world when they can. She hopes younger generations get as much enjoyment learning about the past through her stories, as she did when writing about it.

Author's Notes

In today's world, we often speak about degrees of separation. How many degrees depends on where in the world we live, or the community or social group we associate with. In many ways, it came as no great surprise to find those degrees of separation were as few in days gone by.

This novel was sparked by a newspaper article about a painting discovered in the attic of a Cornish cottage, which hid another beneath its layers of paint – a not uncommon event. That second painting was then attributed to Wilfrid de Glehn, a British artist of Baltic origin, whose art was well known. I've never found that article since so now put it down as a dream, except I know I read it – somewhere. However it began life, that mystery painting, Wilfrid de Glehn, his association with Cornwall, fellow artist John Singer Sargent and many other such artists of the time, became the foundation of this story.

The fact it emerged in Cornwall added to the appeal, as I hold fond memories of my early childhood home, but the resulting unlikely connection with New Zealand, my home of choice, sealed its fate. The more research I undertook, the more it became apparent how well connected the art world of the age truly was. Masters of their trade taught apprentices from across the globe, who became masters in their own right. The Italian artist Girolamo Nerli exhibited internationally, first at The New Zealand Exhibition in Dunedin in 1865, as a young man of only 21. He became one of the founding members of New Zealand's Otago and Auckland art societies. He knew artists in Florence, who knew others in France, England and America, including de Glehn and Sargent. Fellow New Zealand artist John Louis Steele was married to the daughter of a Florentine artist who worked with Nerli, and so the circle tightened and the degrees of separation became fewer.

What I found amazing about this circle was that it took place in the late 1800s and early 1900s without the aid of the Internet, cell phones, and fast, easy and comfortable travel. Ships of the time took many difficult weeks and months to journey from one land to another. Letters were few, as literacy was still generally low, and transport unreliable.

Neither was it unusual for the sons and daughters of the wealthy and elite to travel to Europe to further their education, or spend the summer in idle occupation.

With every new discovery, Isobel's story unfolded and, as a genealogist, it was easy to turn Megan's journey into reality. That is what I love about historical research the most – the surprising and unsurprising similarities to life as it was and life as it is, with all its foibles. We love, we laugh, we cry, the same now as then.

Nothing has changed about the human heart.

Acknowledgements

The last words written are the most important. Without the assistance of many people, this book could not happen. I am certain that in naming individuals I will miss some I should have included, so please take it as given – if you have assisted me in any way, I am deeply grateful.

I thank the members of the Mairangi Writers' Group who listened, critiqued and helped improve the storyline and language, but especially Jenny Harrison, Bev Robitai and Erin McKechnie, great authors in their own right, who as my beta readers gave me valuable feedback.

I am indebted to Adrienne Charlton, publisher, proofreader and editor extraordinaire, for her skill in ensuring this book is as flawless as humanly possible. Any remaining errors are mine and mine alone.

I pay tribute to families everywhere and their life stories. For a genealogist, research uncovers many family histories that deserve to be put into print. *The Cornish Knot* is an amalgam of those stories – stories of love and loss, of conflict and resolution, and of personal renewal.

I hope aspects of these themes will echo in the hearts of my readers but mostly it is my memories of Cornwall, where I spent many years as a child, my love of the Romantic and impressionist eras in art, and my home in New Zealand, that have driven the settings and themes for this novel.

Lastly, to my own wonderful family – my husband, children and grandchildren – thank you. Your belief in me keeps me going.